THE AMARNA AGE:BOOK 4

GATES OF ANUBIS

KYLIE QUILLINAN

First published in Australia in 2021.

ABN 34 112 708 734

kyliequillinan.com

A catalogue record for this book is available from the National Library of Australia.

Ebook ISBN: 9780648249139

Paperback ISBN: 9780648903970

Large print ISBN: 9780648903987

Hardback ISBN: 9780648903994

Audiobook ISBN: 9780645377125

This is a work of fiction. Any similarity between the characters and situations within its pages and places or persons, living or dead, is unintentional and coincidental.

Cover art by Deranged Doctor Design.

Edited by MS Novak.

ONE

"**H**arder," Intef said. "You're not trying."

He stood behind me with his arm hooked around my neck. I was supposed to stomp on his foot as I tried to escape his grip.

"I don't want to hurt you," I said.

I felt, rather than heard, his laugh.

"You won't."

"You think I cannot?"

I twisted around to glare at him. He released my neck and dropped his hand to my waist. Even with one arm, he could keep me pinned against him if he wanted.

His eyes were amused and he grinned. "Maybe you could hurt me if you actually tried, but you won't."

I looked away, not wanting him to read the truth in my eyes. I could hurt him, if I really had to. If I thought there was no other choice and I had reason enough to do so. But Intef would never hurt me. I sighed.

"This is pointless," I said. "I couldn't get away from you if you really wanted to restrain me."

"You can learn to defend yourself against other men. Not everyone is trained the way Renni and I are."

"When am I likely to need such a thing? I am never without at least one of you."

"We have a long way to travel yet and no idea who we might encounter. I need to know you can protect yourself if you must. And our babe."

He placed his hand against my belly, which wasn't even protruding yet.

"You know?"

"You have been vomiting every morning for two weeks."

The first time I had woken feeling nauseous, I barely had time to get out from under my blanket before I threw up. The others were concerned, but I waved away their questions. When we left Babylon four weeks ago, I had suspected I was with child, but it wasn't until the daily vomiting started that I was sure. Each morning I woke feeling unbearably ill, but it passed by the time the sun was at its peak.

"I was going to tell you, but I wanted to be certain first." I hadn't wanted to disappoint him. We would never know whether Setau, the child who had been born too early and who Intef had named for his father, was really his, but this babe definitely was. "It is a daughter."

I regretted the words as soon as they were out of my mouth.

"Did you…" His voice trailed away, no doubt realising that if I had taken any tests to determine whether the child was a girl or a boy — such as peeing over unsprouted barley and emmer — he would know. There was little scope for secrets when one travelled as we did. If I had brought trays of seeds with me, they would all know.

"I dreamed of a girl child. Once, a long time ago."

"Tell me. If you think it was our babe you dreamed of, tell me everything."

I suddenly realised my mistake. How could I tell him that I had seen myself on my knees before Osiris, offering the child up to him? I had no knowledge of the child's fate past that moment, although it hardly seemed likely she would live. In the other future, I had seen myself imprisoned, heavy with child, and knowing that death approached for both of us. I couldn't tell Intef about either dream.

"Does this child, too, have a sad fate?" he asked, when I didn't answer.

I dearly wished I could give him the assurances he needed. He had lost so much already — our son, his father, his arm. It was cruel to dangle the promise of a daughter in front of him, knowing that she too would be ripped away.

"I have seen only a glimpse of her future, and I have no idea what will push her towards one fate or the other." It wasn't quite a lie, but it wasn't really the truth either. "You know it never goes well when I try to choose the future that seems most desirable."

But was either future really desirable? If I reached that moment where I offered her up to Osiris, at least both the babe and I survived her birth. Perhaps we both survived the other future. Or perhaps neither of us did.

Intef looked into my eyes for a long moment, maybe searching for some sign of what I hid from him. Eventually he moved his hand to my shoulder and spun me around so that my back was to his chest. He looped his arm around my neck.

"Again," he said. "And try this time."

I stomped on his foot as hard as I could.

I was breathing heavily by the time Intef decided I had trained enough for today. Nearby where we had stacked our supplies, someone had built a fire pit and lit the kindling, although the afternoon was still warm. Sweating from our training, I pulled my blanket further back from the fire. Istnofret sat with her arms clasped around her knees as she stared into the flames. Mau snored beside her.

"Did you have fun?" Istnofret asked as I sat down.

"I don't think Intef intends these sessions to be fun."

"He wants to prepare you. You cannot be mad at him for that."

"I am not mad. Just exhausted."

She returned her gaze to the fire. "The babe probably fatigues you. You will build strength the more you train."

"You, too? Does everyone know?"

"Renni has said nothing, but Behenu suspects."

"I should have told you but…"

She glanced over at me when I stopped. "But what?"

"It is nothing. Just a superstition."

"Tell me."

"I thought maybe I could protect the babe if I pretended not to notice. I know it is silly."

"After what you went through last time, nobody could blame you for being protective."

"Where are the others?" I changed the subject before I was tempted to say too much.

"Hunting."

We lapsed into silence and Istnofret continued to stare into the flames. I lay back on my blanket. The sky was a brilliant shade of blue with just a few puffy clouds. Renni and Behenu returned soon after, carrying a young deer between them.

"He is going to want to smoke the extra meat." Istnofret was already on her feet. "I'll go find some sticks."

"I'll help you."

I started to get up, but she waved at me to stay.

"No, you rest. You've been training while I sat on my behind. It is my turn to do something."

"I don't mind helping." Even after all these months, I was still careful to do my fair share of the work. I didn't want to give them reason to leave me. At some point in our journey together, we had become friends. I would never be able to complete my quest alone, but more than that, I *wanted* to contribute.

"You can start sharpening the sticks," she said.

Istnofret's dagger was already in her hand as she headed to the nearby bushes to slice off some thin branches. I, too, carried a dagger now, although mine was usually in my bag, which was little more than a sturdy sheath on a rope I could drape over my neck or shoulder. Istnofret and Behenu had both taken to wearing belts around their waists with their daggers stuck through. They had encouraged me to do the same, but I felt uncomfortably conspicuous at being visibly armed. As a compromise, I tried to make sure the little bag I carried my dagger in was always close at hand, although I had left it in my pack while I trained with Intef. I retrieved it now while I waited.

Renni and Behenu set the deer down some distance away. Behenu came to collect some bowls from one of our packs while Renni began butchering the beast.

"I got a deer." She beamed at me. "Renni says if we smoke the extra meat, we won't need to hunt for at least a couple of days."

"You killed it yourself?"

"We kind of stumbled over it. We were tracking a hare and we came around a bush and the deer was just standing there. I grabbed it and slit its throat before I even thought about what I was doing."

"You must have been very fast."

"Renni said I moved like a deer myself."

She took the bowls back to Renni, who had slit open the deer's belly and begun removing its organs.

Istnofret dropped a bundle of green branches beside me. "Think that's enough? It is only a small deer."

"I'll trim them and let's see."

She sat beside me and we quickly stripped the twigs from the branches and sharpened the ends. We would thread strips of meat onto them and smoke them over the coals when the fire died down.

Intef came to pour himself a mug of beer. He downed it quickly, then left to tend to the horses. They were not far away, hobbled so that they couldn't wander, but close enough that we would hear if somebody thought to sneak up and steal them. There were eight horses, one for each of us to ride, plus three for our supplies. I was reasonably confident in my ability to stay on a horse by now, although I was still sore by the time we stopped each day. The only other beast I had ever ridden was the donkey that carried me away when the Medjay rescued me from Ay's men as they escorted me to the Nubian slave mines.

My horse was quiet with an agreeable temperament, and I had named her Nedjem, which meant sweet. Having never named a beast before, I had been at a loss as to what to call her. I would have simply called her Heter, which was our word for horse, if Istnofret hadn't already named hers that.

So I called mine Nedjem and it suited her as well as anything.

We passed a companionable evening around the fire. Renni roasted chunks of deer in the flames. They were charred and flavourful, and a welcome substitute for the hares and field mice we had been eating since we left Babylon. We carried plenty of supplies and there had been few nights when Renni had failed to catch something to supplement them with.

The night air was refreshingly cool and carried on it the quiet nickers from the horses and the chirping of bugs. The smoke from the fire mostly kept the mosquitos at bay, although we had taken to sleeping with our blankets pulled up over our heads to avoid being bitten. Intef lay against my back, his arm draped companionably over me.

"You have been very quiet this evening," he said. "Are you well?"

"Just tired. I wish we could afford to rest for a couple of days in the next town."

"We can. There is no deadline for us to reach Crete. In fact, maybe we should find somewhere to stay for a few months. Pick up our journey again after the babe is born."

We travelled in search of the Eye of Horus, an artefact that initially we weren't even sure existed outside of legend. The Eye was believed to bestow great power on the one who possessed it, but it could only be used once and never for ill intent. If I could find it, I could use it to take the throne back from Ay. If I was queen again, I could resolve the simmering tension between Egypt and Hattusa. We had heard numerous stories of skirmishes between the two countries over the last few months. There had been minor battles, and it seemed there would be no reconciliation until Egypt and Hattusa faced each other in outright war.

The Hittites had not forgiven us for the death of their prince, Zannanza, who was murdered as he travelled to meet me in Memphis. Although Ay was the one who ordered his death, I felt responsible. After all, if I hadn't asked his father to send me a husband, Zannanza would have had no reason to come to Egypt and our two countries wouldn't be on the brink of war.

I feared that war with the Hittites would be something Egypt would never recover from. Too many would die — on both sides — and if Hattusa was victorious, we might well lose control of our own country. If I had borne an heir back when the advisors first told me to, things would be different. If I had been stronger when my brother Tutankhamen was young, we might have fended off the advisors together. If I had been wiser when I chose a man with whom to have my first affair, I might have made a strategic alliance that could have helped me fend off Ay. But I wasn't yet out of hope.

We had tracked the Eye to a man named Djediufankh, who had lived in Babylon. Shortly before his death, he gave the Eye to his friend, a Greek priest named Antinous. Djediufankh had urged him to hide the Eye where it would never be found. We knew Antinous had intended to take it to Crete and it was his trail we followed now.

Although I prayed the Eye was still in Crete, my dream of handing a newborn babe to Osiris told me we would be back in Egypt before she was born. Maybe the Eye was indeed in Crete and we found it in time to return home before her birth, or maybe we found only another clue and Egypt became the next stage of our journey. But the dream of myself imprisoned, feeling the babe within me move, suggested other things might yet delay us. If the babe was to be born in Egypt, I had to move forward while I could.

"I think we should keep going," I said, at length. "We have no idea what is ahead of us yet."

I felt, rather than heard, his sigh.

"I just want what is best for you and the babe."

"Me too," I said, very quietly. "Me too.

TWO

Nedjem was a quiet and steady mount, which left me free to admire the changing landscape instead of spending all my time focusing on clinging to her back. I grew up surrounded by desert, wide open sky, and rocky cliffs. Babylonia was a flat land, lush and green, and entirely alien from my homeland.

We had initially travelled north east from Babylon until we encountered the series of roads that would lead us all the way to the Mediterranean coast. Some days later, we had reached a land of flat grasslands and stumpy bushes, which had none of the thick lushness of Babylonia. Over the last day or two, the landscape had become rolling hills, barely noticeable at first but now a mountainous region lay ahead of us. We didn't know whether this was still Babylonia or whether we had reached Anatolia, the land of the Hittites, which we would have to pass through on our way to the coast.

"Will the horses cope with that mountain?" I asked Intef, who rode beside me.

"Many travellers come this way so it cannot be impassable.

If it is too steep, we will walk so that the horses can make their way up more easily." He shot a glance towards my belly. "Can you manage? We will go slowly."

"What other option is there? I either cope, or we turn around and go back to Babylon."

"It is not too late to turn back if we must. We are only a few weeks from Babylon. It will be hard for you, travelling like this while carrying a babe."

"It is no more than I have done before."

I regretted my sharpness as soon as the words were out of my mouth. After all, last time our journey had mostly consisted of sitting in the bowels of ships. Other than when we had walked from Qift to Leucus Limen, which had only taken five days, the travelling had not been physically demanding, for us women at any rate. Intef and Renni had worked with the ship's crew, which kept them both fit and exhausted.

"But you were not ill with it last time."

Intef's tone was as easy going as always, which made me feel even worse.

"I am sorry. I didn't mean to snap at you. I am feeling unreasonably irritated today."

He shot me a smile but said nothing. He knew me well enough to know that anything he said now would only irritate me more.

"There is no choice but to continue," I said. "The babe will not be born for seven months. We cannot go back to Babylon and wait that long. Surely we are at least a third of the way to Sardis by now. We will be there before travelling becomes too uncomfortable."

Intef brought his horse a little closer to mine and reached for me. I took his hand, albeit a little uneasily since that left him with no way of holding onto his horse other than with his legs.

"I just want to be certain you can manage," he said. "We all want to find the Eye, but it is more important that you and our babe are safe. If that means we need to go back, or wait somewhere for a few months, that's fine with me, and I know it will be for the others as well."

"I want to keep moving forward while we can."

The hills ahead of us grew larger as we drew closer. By midafternoon we reached a narrow valley that seemed to cut right through the mountains, although it was a winding path and we couldn't see far ahead. We stopped to give the horses some water.

"Perhaps we should camp here tonight?" Renni suggested. "There's no way of knowing how long that valley is. I don't fancy the idea of spending the night in there."

"At least it will give us cover from the breeze overnight." Intef studied the path ahead with a frown. "Since we don't know how long it is, I cannot see the point of losing the rest of the light. It might take us days to pass through."

"Let's get moving then," Renni said. "If the gods are gracious, it will only be a couple of hours."

As we followed the road, the peaks on either side of us rose up so high that I could barely see the sky. The further we went, the more uncomfortable I became. I was used to deserts and wide skies, not mountains and narrow valleys. I could hardly breathe in such a place. My palms began to sweat and my heart beat far too fast.

The path was wide enough for two horses side-by-side but no more. Nedjem walked beside Intef's horse, and both seemed unusually skittish. Ahead of us was Behenu, with

Istnofret and Renni in front of her. I shot a glance at Intef and caught him looking back behind us.

"Something wrong?" I asked quietly. I didn't want to alarm the others if it was nothing.

He shook his head but didn't look at me.

"Intef?"

"Be quiet."

I looked ahead to where Renni was. He had twisted around to signal at Intef. Both men's faces were grim.

"Intef," I whispered. "You're scaring me."

Renni drew his horse to a stop and we all halted behind him.

"Intef?" I rested my fingertips against the little bottle I wore on a cord around my neck, taking reassurance from its coolness. Cold meant there was no danger.

"It is nothing. I was just…"

"Thinking this was a good place for an ambush," Renni finished.

"An ambush?" Istnofret's tone rose in alarm. "But nobody even knows we're here. Who would want to ambush us?"

"I didn't say we were *being* ambushed," Renni said. "Just that it would be a good place for it."

"I don't like this," Intef said. "We should turn back. Find another path. This cannot be the only way through the mountains."

But before we could move, a noise from up ahead reached us.

"What is that?" Istnofret whispered. "It sounds like…"

"Soldiers." Intef's mouth was a thin line. "Marching towards us."

"A lot of them," Renni said.

"Turn back." Intef tugged on his horse's reins. "Get the

horses turned around and get out. Better that we encounter whoever it is out in the open."

But the horses had picked up on our unease and were unwilling to be turned in such tight quarters. Then from behind us came the sound of more soldiers.

"What do we do?" Behenu whispered.

"Now we can only wait." Intef gave up on turning his horse. "The main force is ahead of us. Those coming from behind are likely a patrol group. There's few enough of them that we wouldn't hear them unless they wanted us to."

"There was nobody around when we came in here," Istnofret said.

"There are probably plenty of places a few men could hide and watch," Intef said. "We made a grave mistake in coming in here."

Mau yowled and Behenu reached down to the basket strapped across her horse's rump. But the cat was as uneasy as the horses and wouldn't be calmed.

"Please Mau," Behenu whispered. "Just a little longer. I will give you a tasty treat as soon as we are done."

The place where we waited was no more than a hundred cubits long. We could see nothing past that, for the road twisted and turned through the rocky outcrops, its builder having followed the natural path between the mountains rather than making any attempt at a straight road. We waited for what seemed like a very long time, considering how loud the sounds of marching men were.

"How close are they?" I whispered to Intef.

"Cannot tell. The acoustics in here are strange. They could be some distance off or just around the next bend. Samun, you must do whatever they tell you. No matter what the cost. Our priority must be to keep you and the babe safe."

"What are you talking about?"

He grabbed my hand. "I love you."

"Intef-"

I got no further before the men behind us — the ones Intef thought might be a patrol — rounded the bend and stopped. There were ten of them, short and well-muscled, with full beards and dark hair. They didn't look surprised to see us. One stepped forward, his sword already in his hand. He spoke, his tone belligerent, then waited.

I could feel my friends looking at me. After all, they were accustomed to me translating for them. We had been fortunate so far that wherever we went, we could usually find someone who spoke Akkadian, the language of diplomats, which I had learned as a child. I didn't know the language this man used. However, my spell bottle was still cold so despite his posturing, he didn't intend us any harm.

He spoke again, more aggressively this time, and pointed his sword towards us.

"I think we should get down," Intef said, quietly. "We could be seen as hostile if we stay on the horses. Move slowly."

We dismounted. I clutched Nedjem's reins and prayed that Isis would spread her wings of protection over us.

"I think they are Hittites," I whispered.

"I agree," Renni said. "They look much like Arnuwanda."

"The man who came to speak with Samun when she asked for a husband from the Hittites?" Istnofret asked. "Oh, that is not good."

As soon as we had all dismounted, the Hittite troop moved forward. A man grabbed me by the shoulder and pushed me away from Nedjem.

"Wait-" But the man glared so fiercely that I said nothing further.

They herded us into a group and shuffled us away from the horses.

"They don't know Mau is there," Behenu whispered. "Should I go get her?"

"No," Intef said. "If you move, they might not wait to see why."

I wanted to ask what he thought they would do, but just then the larger force — the one which approached from the direction in which we were headed — came into view. The path was only wide enough for them to march four abreast. One of the men in front called out to the ones who surrounded us.

"Be still," Intef whispered.

In moments the entire space in which we stood filled with men. From the movement and chatter beyond our sight, it was clear there were more. Many more.

"Is it an army?" Istnofret whispered.

"Perhaps," Renni said. "Hard to say when we cannot see how many there are, but they are armed and they look fit."

The men who appeared to be the captains of each force had reached each other by now and they looked us up and down. A few comments passed between them and I got the feeling they were trying to decide what to do with us. From the corner of my eye, I caught movement within the larger force. I turned in time to see a familiar person push his way between the men.

"Arnuwanda." I breathed his name, my legs wobbling with relief. Here was someone I could communicate with, for he spoke both Akkadian and Egyptian. Also, he knew that my intentions had been good. However the situation had been twisted afterwards, he knew I had meant for Zannanza to be pharaoh.

Arnuwanda went straight to the two captains. He didn't look pleased and he spoke with vigour, pointing towards us. Towards me.

"I don't think he remembers you fondly," Intef muttered to me.

"I was nothing but pleasant to him," I said, a little indignantly.

Arnuwanda had apparently finished his conversation with the captains and now he approached us.

"Arnuwanda," I said in Akkadian. "You may not recognise me. I am sure I look very different from when we last met."

He gave me a cold stare. "I recognise you well and your name will long be remembered in Hattusa."

I doubted he intended that as a compliment.

"I am terribly sorry about what happened. There was a misunderstanding and nobody would listen to me."

"My king trusted you. He believed you. He sent you one of his sons as you asked."

"Ay used the situation to his own advantage. He knew your men posed no threat. There were too few of them to be any danger to us."

"Too few to be a threat and yet not too many to slaughter."

"They were all killed?"

I had never even asked after the men who had travelled with Zannanza. But of course Ay would not have wanted anyone left alive to tell tales back to their king.

"Our prince and all of his men," Arnuwanda said. "Our king was devastated when the news reached him. He swore he would never again trust Egypt, and he would never again trust the word of a woman."

"I had no part in killing your men. I swear it. I was waiting for Zannanza to arrive. He was to be my husband. Why would I have him killed?"

"Because you are Egyptian and all Egyptians are liars. Because Egyptian women are liars. My king has learned the error of his ways. Never again will Hattusa and Egypt be friends."

"Arnuwanda, please believe me. I had no part in this. I would have done anything to stop it."

Arnuwanda gave me a measured look, then turned and walked back to the men he had arrived with. He said something in his own language and two men stepped forward, their swords drawn.

"Please, Arnuwanda." My hands were clammy and a cold sweat raced over my skin.

"You will come with us," Arnuwanda said. "We travel elsewhere first, but when we return to Hattusa, our king will decide whether you may have the opportunity to explain yourself to him. Or he may simply choose to punish you for your treachery. The life of one woman for that of his son and the fifty men who died with him cannot compensate, but it may give our king some small measure of comfort in his grief."

I felt Intef bristling, although neither he nor Renni reached for their daggers.

"They will kill us all if we resist," Intef said to me, very softly. He took my hand and squeezed it. "They have a whole army. We cannot stand against that. You must let them take you and then you, at least, will have the chance to survive. You will win Suppiluliumas over. I know you will. When our daughter is born, you should name her for your sister."

I wanted to tell him that he was wrong. My spell bottle was

still cold; we weren't in any immediate danger. Then the men reached us. They shoved my friends out of the way and grabbed my shoulders. The smaller scouting troop turned and headed back in the direction from which we had entered the pass. The larger group followed.

As they dragged me away, Intef continued to hold my hand until the last moment. Then he released me and I was alone, surrounded by Hittites.

THREE

As the soldiers started to march, I tried to peer between them to see my friends. To see Intef. But all I could see was Hittites. Then I caught a glimpse of Arnuwanda, only two or three men away.

"Arnuwanda!" I called over the sound of marching men. "Please. You don't know what you are doing. Let me explain."

He was close enough that he must have heard, but he didn't acknowledge me.

"Please," I called. "Don't separate me from my friends. One of them is the father of my babe."

He turned then, but the look he gave me was cold and I knew he wouldn't aid me even if I got down on my belly and begged.

"Every man should have the opportunity for his son to grow up beside him," he called to me. "But when that son's mother is a harlot and a liar, the son is not entitled to the same."

"Arnuwanda, please. What will happen to my friends?"

He didn't turn back towards me again, but I could still hear him clearly over the marching men.

"They will be killed."

My head swam and there was a buzzing in my ears. My legs wobbled and I almost fell. Then somebody grabbed my arm and barked a command. I was dragged along with the marching men, as much by the force of the bodies surrounding me as by the man who clutched my arm.

"Wait." I tried to pull away, but he barely seemed to notice my struggle.

I tried to stop walking, but the men behind me merely pushed me forward. I had no choice but to walk or be trampled by them. A cry came from behind me, Istnofret's voice raised in a shout.

"Let me go with her," she called. "I am her lady. I attend to her. Please, take me too."

But if anyone understood her, they made no reply.

"Where are you taking me?" I asked. "I demand answers."

But of course there was no response.

"Arnuwanda! Please let me explain."

I caught a glimpse of him not far ahead. I surged forward, but the men in front of me were a solid wall and the soldier who held my arm merely yanked me back by his side.

"Please let me go," I beseeched him. "Don't take me from my friends. It was a misunderstanding."

If he even heard me, he steadfastly ignored me.

We marched back out of the narrow valley and continued on, following the road. They were going to Babylon perhaps, or even Persia maybe. Having already travelled this path, I knew what lay ahead: the mountains would turn into rolling hills and eventually be replaced by flat grasslands.

Another hour or so passed before the army stopped to rest.

Around me, men set down their weapons in the stubbly grass beside the road. Some retrieved food or drink from their packs. Others stepped off to the side to relieve themselves. More than one shot sideways glances at me but their faces were more curious than hostile.

I looked around for Arnuwanda, but as soon as I started to step away, the man who had been holding my arm cleared his throat. I glanced at him and he shook his head, then pointed to the ground. He said something and his tone was kinder than I might have expected. Maybe he told me to rest while I could.

I sat. The grass was prickly beneath me and there was no shade anywhere. I was a little too hot, for the days were warm yet, although the nights were cool. Tears filled my eyes and I quickly blinked them away. These men needed to see me as strong. A queen. I could find a way out of this yet. Would Arnuwanda really be so heartless as to kill Intef, Istnofret, Behenu and Renni? It seemed an unthinkable act, but I supposed it was no more than had been done to their men as they escorted their prince to Memphis.

A shadow fell over me and I shielded my eyes against the sky's brightness to see who it was. A woman wearing a long dress and a headscarf offered me a mug. I started to get to my feet, but she waved me back down. She pressed the mug into my hand, then offered me something that looked like a strip of dried meat. She spoke, but I could make no sense of her words.

The mug contained beer. Somewhat stale and more bitter than I was accustomed to, but it wet my throat well enough. The meat was tough and just short of being rank, not dried with Renni's skill. I watched for Arnuwanda as I ate but didn't see him anywhere. As soon as I had drained my mug, the woman took it from me and disappeared back into the army before I could thank her.

All too soon, the men were getting to their feet. I rose quickly before anyone took notice of me. As they stowed away rations in their packs, I realised that once again I was entirely dependent on others. I had nothing but the sturdy travelling gown I wore. There were, of course, jewels stitched into its hem, but they would do me no good here. I had no food, no blanket. Nothing useful other than my dagger. At least it seemed my captors intended to feed me. My eyes filled again and I blinked the tears away. I would not stand in the middle of a hostile army and cry. Whether my friends were safe or not, I could do nothing to help them now.

Nobody was coming to save me this time. Even if — and it was a big if — my friends were still alive, they wouldn't be able to reach me in the middle of the Hittite army. But I was no longer as helpless as I had been when I first left Memphis. Intef had been teaching me to defend myself, and I knew enough about foraging to feed myself if I escaped. I would stay alert and watch for an opportunity. I only needed one chance to get away.

The army walked until the sun started to set. Once they stopped, men worked quickly to build fire pits. They retrieved food and blankets from their packs and gathered around their fires. The aroma of cooking food wafted through the air. Nobody even looked at me and I had never felt more alone as I sat by myself. They surrounded me with laughter and boisterous talk, none of which I could understand. I couldn't see Arnuwanda anywhere.

What was I supposed to do? I was too intimidated to join any of the groups at their fires, but it would be a long, cold night without even a blanket. I was sharply reminded of our journey from Qift to Leucus Limen, when Intef and I had shared our blankets. That was before we reconciled and I had allowed him near me with reluctance. But his warmth had gotten me through the nights even if I hated him in those moments. The nights here weren't yet as cold, but I would have nothing other than memories to keep me warm.

Panic welled within me. Everything had gone wrong so quickly. One moment we had all been together, travelling in the way people who are well accustomed to each other do, and hopeful that our long quest was drawing to an end. I had food and companionship, love and hope. Once again, the tears came and I wiped my eyes before they could spill over. I had to trust that the others could look after themselves. If anyone could get out of a situation like that, it would be Intef and Renni. Even Istnofret and Behenu had some ability to defend themselves now, for Renni had been training both of them. They would save themselves and hopefully Mau too and maybe even Nedjem. I could do nothing to help them, but I might yet save myself.

I had no information about where the army was going except that it wasn't to Hattusa, which now lay behind us. From everything I had heard about Suppiluliumas, he was a reasonable man. Surely he would allow me to explain what had happened. He would understand it had been a terrible mistake and he wouldn't punish me for something I had no control over. He would undoubtedly release me.

But even as I told myself such things, the image from my dream danced in my memory. The alternative future, in which I was bound in a dark room and felt the babe within me move. I still had a few months yet before my belly would be that big, but surely this was what now lay ahead of me. When we reached Hattusa, I would be bound and locked away. It was possible — perhaps even probable — that my daughter and I would die. I would never reach Crete. I wouldn't find the Eye.

Nobody would prevent the coming war between Egypt and Hattusa.

My stomach growled and I was suddenly aware of the dryness of my mouth. Movement nearby jolted me from my thoughts and the woman who had given me food earlier appeared. She held something out to me, but in the flickering flames I couldn't see what it was. When I hesitated, she spoke sharply, clearly a command, and I quickly reached for whatever she offered.

I found myself with a bowl and a mug. The contents of the bowl were bland, a barley stew perhaps. Nonetheless, it was warm and filling, and I ate until the bowl was empty. As I drained the mug, I felt a little more hopeful. At least they didn't intend me to starve. With nothing else to do, I lay down and curled myself into as tight a ball as possible.

"At least you are warm," I whispered to the babe in my belly. There was no response, but of course it was too soon to feel her moving.

Then the woman returned. She offered me a blanket and I took it eagerly. She collected my bowl and mug, then turned to leave.

"Wait," I said. "Can you understand me?"

She looked at me blankly. I repeated my words in Akkadian, but she still didn't respond. Frustration welled. This was the only person who had shown me any kindness and I had no way of communicating with her. I hadn't realised before how fortunate we had been to always find someone who spoke one of the two languages I knew. The woman never even glanced back at me as she walked away. Who was she? The wife of a soldier? A servant or slave? A prostitute who followed the army? I would probably never know.

Around me, the men began to quieten. Someone nearby

already snored. A log shifted in one of the fires, sending up a wave of sparks. Soon it seemed I was the only one awake. Was this my moment to escape? I had promised myself I would take the first chance I had, but now I hesitated. There might be a better moment if I waited a little longer. But we were less than a day's walk from the valley and if I left now, I could be there by dawn. I only had to follow the road. If I didn't go now, while I still knew how to get back, I might never find them again. If they were dead, then at least I would know. I wouldn't spend the rest of my life wondering if they had somehow gotten away. I wouldn't always wonder whether my daughter might yet meet her father.

I rolled over onto my back, trying surreptitiously to see if anyone was watching. As far as I could tell, they were all asleep. Surely there must be men standing guard. Even when we were leagues away from anyone else, Intef always insisted someone had to be awake through the night. As I tried to gather my courage, I looked up into the sky. The stars were shrouded tonight and it was like looking up into nothingness. But then the clouds parted and two stars peeked through. They shone so brightly that I wondered I hadn't seen them even through the clouds. Was this my father and my brother, still watching over me? The thought gave me the courage to escape while I could.

I started to sit up, but someone nearby groaned and rolled over. I froze, hardly daring to breathe. But he didn't move again.

I sat up and waited a little longer. Nobody stirred. I eased myself to my feet and waited. My knees trembled and I couldn't get a full breath of air.

If those stars were my father and brother, I wanted them to

see me acting bravely, not cowering in the middle of a foreign army.

I took a single step. The fires gave enough light to make out a path between the men. I could see where a man had his arm flung out or where a leg stuck out just where I might trip over it. If I moved slowly and carefully, I could get past them. I would learn soon enough whether anyone kept watch.

I took a second step, but no sooner had I done so than one of the men nearby sat up. He looked right at me and said something in a low growl. I froze, barely breathing, praying to Isis that he would let me go. After all, who was I to him? Just an unknown woman. I didn't even look Egyptian, dressed as I was in my Babylonian travelling clothes and without any kohl around my eyes.

I took another step and the man started to get up. Then the woman was at my side, clutching my arm and pulling me back down onto the grass.

"No," I whispered to her. "You don't understand. Let me go."

She murmured something, her tone soothing as if calming a frightened child. I tried to shake her off, but then the man stood over us. He hissed down at me and the menace in his voice shook me, even though I understood nothing of what he said. Perhaps he did know who I was after all.

"I need to relieve myself," I said to the woman. It wasn't a lie, even if it wasn't the reason I was trying to leave.

She shook her head. I didn't know how to convey my intent and my vague waving of hands obviously meant nothing to her. She spoke to the man towering over us. Her tone was conciliatory and he replied gruffly. She smiled and he grunted before returning to his blanket.

"Please," I said to her. "You could help me if you wanted to. They trust you."

She shook her head and patted me on the arm, encouraging me to lie down again. She pulled the blanket up over me. I gave up. There was no point. It had been unrealistic to think I could escape from the middle of an army anyway. I lay down and closed my eyes and tried to ignore my full bladder. Eventually the woman left.

I let myself cry then, no longer caring if anyone noticed. I sobbed until I had no tears left and my eyes were so swollen I could barely see. I looked back up at the sky, seeking the comfort of the two stars, but they were gone. I was more alone than I had ever been in my life.

FOUR

I woke as the army stirred around me. The sun was barely risen, but the men already gathered their belongings and stomped out the last lingering fires. Nausea rushed through me, sudden and vicious. There was no time to seek privacy and I vomited onto the grass. The men nearest me stepped away with noises of disgust.

As we set off, I tucked my folded blanket under my arm. Better to carry it all day than to risk not being given another tonight. The men ate as we walked. I watched for the woman who had fed me yesterday but didn't see her. Waves of nausea flooded my belly and I was almost thankful that nobody had offered me any food.

Eventually I couldn't ignore my full bladder any longer. With no other options available to me, I simply stopped walking and squatted. Nobody seemed to pay any attention although from the corner of my eye, I saw a nearby man pause. I didn't look at him and when I resumed walking, he did too.

We walked until the sun was high. It was only then that the woman found me and pressed a chunk of bread and a mug of beer into my hands. The nausea had settled by now and I ate gratefully. As soon as I had finished, she took my mug and disappeared back into the crowd. I quickly lost sight of her, for there were too many men and she was much smaller than they. I was tempted to follow, but the man who seemed appointed as my guardian was already giving me suspicious looks.

Each day followed the same pattern. We rose at dawn and walked all day. When we stopped at night, I found myself a quiet spot that wasn't too close to any of the groups of men. The woman would bring food and stay with me while I ate. Then she would take my bowl and mug, and leave. We communicated only with glances and nods and a quiet thank you from me. She made no attempt to reply.

My appointed guardian was much more obvious about watching me after that first night. He glowered at me all evening and even after he went to sleep, he woke every time I so much as sniffled. I caught others watching me from time to time but was never sure whether they too were charged with guarding me or if I was merely a curiosity in their midst.

For a week, each day passed much like the one before it until the day when the men seemed more boisterous than usual. Maybe we were almost at our destination, wherever that was. It was only the middle of the day when we stopped at a wide, scrubby plain bordered on one side by a river. Mountains towered in the distance but here the land was flat and the vegetation sparse. There was nothing special about it, so far as I could see, but it seemed to have some significance for the men by the way they clapped each other on the back and smiled and shouted.

I was fed up with not knowing where we were going and what was happening. Arnuwanda was somewhere in the midst of all these men and he seemed to be the only one who spoke a language I knew. I would go find him and the gods could damn the man who growled every time he thought I might leave.

I waited until he was occupied in talking with a small group of men, then slipped away into the crowd. I had only gone a couple of steps before he grabbed my arm and yanked me backwards. He snarled at me, but his words were unintelligible. I glared up at him.

"I want to talk to Arnuwanda," I said.

"Arnuwanda?" Despite his thick accent, I could make out the name well enough.

"Yes, Arnuwanda." I gestured at the men around me. "Where is he?"

The man said something I couldn't understand.

"Arnuwanda," I said, more forcefully. "Take me to Arnuwanda."

He cocked his head, studying me. I couldn't tell whether I intrigued or repulsed him.

"I demand to be taken to Arnuwanda."

He laughed and said something, then pointed at the men around us.

"If you won't take me to him, I will find him myself."

I shot the man a defiant look and stepped away into the crowd. I waited for him to grab me again, but this time he let me go. I could have gone in search of Arnuwanda days ago if I had been brave enough to confront my guard.

I quickly realised my task was hopeless. I hadn't understood just how big this army was — several hundred, at least

— and I would never find Arnuwanda in the midst of so many stocky, black-bearded men. Still, I searched for some time. I called his name, but quickly found myself the target of mocking calls by men who clearly impersonated me. Someone grabbed my buttocks and squeezed hard. My cheeks flamed and I stopped calling out, not wanting to draw extra attention to myself.

I was almost ready to give up when my spell bottle suddenly heated. Only now did I realise how precarious my situation was. I was in the middle of a large group of strange men, none of whom had any responsibility for my safety, and a number of which leered at me. Even as I stood there, somebody's fingers snaked around my ankle, caressing it. I quickly stepped away.

I had been stupid to leave my guard. I hadn't realised he wasn't just preventing me from leaving but was also protecting me. And how would the woman who fed me find me now?

Searching for my guardian was as hopeless as looking for Arnuwanda. Every time I stopped walking I found myself the subject of unwanted attention, sometimes mere comments and catcalls, but twice I was physically grabbed. The attention was half-hearted, though, and I easily broke away each time.

My heart pounded in my ears and I was trying not to hyperventilate when someone grabbed my arm and swung me around. My knees buckled when I saw that it was my guardian. He growled something, but I was so relieved to see him that I smiled. His eyebrows shot up and his lips twitched. He almost looked like he wanted to smile back.

"I am sorry." He wouldn't understand my words, but maybe he could infer some meaning from my tone or my face. "I was stupid to leave you."

"Arnuwanda," the man said, followed by a string of words in his own language.

I shrugged and he tugged my arm, clearly telling me to follow him. My spell bottle was cold again. This man, whoever he was, meant me no harm. I let him lead me back to his campsite, relieved to see my blanket still folded neatly where I had left it. He pointed at it, a stern look on his face. I sat. I had learnt my lesson about wandering off. I would still watch for Arnuwanda, but I wouldn't leave my guardian again.

When the woman came to bring me food that evening, I asked her about Arnuwanda. If she recognised his name, though, she gave no indication of it. As always, she waited while I ate, then left with my bowl and mug.

I lay on the grass, my blanket wrapped around me. I wasn't close enough to any of the fires to feel their warmth, but the many bodies around me seemed to warm the air and, if nothing else, they shielded me somewhat from the breeze.

I slept late the next morning and woke realising dawn was long past. I vomited, as usual, and it was only when I had finished that I finally realised the army showed no sign of moving on. Some men sat by their fires while others stood in small groups. Almost everyone had a weapon in his hands and was busy sharpening or polishing or doing whatever it was that men did with their weapons. Perhaps they were resting for a day after more than a week of marching. I was thankful for any chance to rest but surprised to discover that a trained army needed it after doing nothing more than walking.

The morning crept on and eventually the woman brought bread and beer. After what I had experienced yesterday when I tried to look for Arnuwanda, it was only now that I appreciated what she must endure every time she came looking for me.

"Thank you," I said.

She acknowledged my words with a nod, as if she understood them, and crouched down to wait while I ate.

"I wish I knew what was happening." I tore off a chunk of the bread. It was so stale as to be nearly inedible, but when softened in the beer, I could force it down. "What are we waiting for?"

She obviously understood the question in my voice even if she couldn't comprehend my words. She said something, then gripped my shoulder and looked into my eyes. It seemed that whatever she was telling me was of great importance and I desperately wished I could understand.

I finished my meal in silence, then handed the mug back to her. She reached out to touch my cheek, a gentle caress that took me by surprise. Why would she offer me any affection? She looked into my eyes for a long moment, shook her head sadly, and left.

A short while later, a great shout arose. A trumpet sounded and the men quickly stowed their belongings away in their packs. Daggers were slipped through belts, swords grasped firmly. They shouted to each other and clapped their fellows on the back. I didn't need to understand their language to know what happened. The army was going into battle. They surged forward and amassed in orderly rows at the end of the field.

Suddenly, the woman appeared, speaking urgently and tugging my arm. I grabbed my blanket and let her lead me towards the far end of the field where several tables were set up. They were nothing more than rough planks balanced on crates. Here gathered the men who were too old to fight, along with several dozen women. So, there were other women after all. There were children, too, mostly babes in arms but a few toddlers as well. Why would anyone bring children to follow an army?

There were a number of small wagons lined up in an orderly row. Presumably they carried supplies although perhaps this was also how the children and old men travelled. The horses that must pull the wagons were nowhere in sight. I couldn't quite imagine how they had managed to take the wagons through the narrow valley they had captured me in.

The woman pointed to a spot on the grass, clearly indicating that I should sit there and keep myself out of trouble. What if Arnuwanda was killed in the battle? These final few moments before it started might be my last chance to speak with him.

"You know Arnuwanda, don't you?" Who else would have told her to make sure I had food and a blanket? If not Arnuwanda himself, he had sent someone to tell her. "Where is Arnuwanda?"

But no matter how many times I said his name, she pretended not to understand and only continued to point to the place she wanted me to wait. I gave up and stood where she indicated, although I scowled at her.

She gave me a pleased smile, then went to one of the tables where baskets of bandages were arranged in a long row. She began retrieving an assortment of jars and bottles from a crate. This must be a makeshift medical centre to care for injured soldiers.

The trumpets sounded again, louder than before, and a great cry rose from the men. Then came the clash of swords and, shortly afterwards, the screams of dying men.

For a few moments I was frozen. This place seemed dangerously close to the battle. Most of the women had their backs steadfastly turned and busied themselves with preparing for the aftermath. A few had gathered the children into a group and tried to occupy them with games and songs. The old men avidly watched the battle and made commentary on it.

I had never seen a battle before. I heard the fight on the ship, of course, when we were attacked by pirates as we sailed from Leucus Limen to Suakin. The fight in which Intef's arm had been so badly damaged that I decided to remove it in order to save his life. But I had never seen a battle with my own eyes, and the death and destruction left me numb.

I saw men fall. Men who were mortally wounded lay down on the bloodied grass and waited to die. A few lucky ones made their way back to where the women and old men waited to patch them up as best they could. Some went straight back into the fight as soon as their bleeding was staunched. I supposed I had known that this was what battle was like, but knowing was a different thing from seeing it with my own eyes. Surely no argument needed such a resolution. This was exactly what I was trying to prevent by finding the Eye.

I couldn't watch anymore and looked away into the bushes ringing the plain. I suddenly realised: this was my moment to escape, if I dared. For the first time since I had been taken, nobody watched me. I should go now. I could follow the road back to the valley. If the others were still alive, I would encounter them on the way, for surely they would come in search of me. They might even be close behind us. My heart lifted.

But I had waited too long and as I turned to run, the woman glanced over to check on me. She came rushing over, shaking her head and saying something.

"I have to go." I hoped she would understand. "Now, while the men are engaged. This is my only chance."

I took a step back, but she grasped my wrist in a surprisingly strong grip. I tried to shake her off.

"Please, you don't understand. You have to let me go. I have to find my friends."

She held my wrist even tighter as she replied. With a heavy heart, I reached into the little bag hanging from my neck and withdrew my dagger. She glanced at it, but clearly thought me no threat, for she didn't release me.

"Please. I don't want to hurt you, but I will if I must. Let me go."

Still she hung on.

I half-heartedly waved the dagger towards her. Her eyes widened a little, but she wasn't alarmed enough to let go.

I could hear Intef as he trained me. Never draw your dagger unless you intend to use it, he had said. But never use it unless you have no other choice.

I steeled my heart. I knew what he would want me to do. I slashed at the woman and drew my dagger across her forearm. She hissed and released me, stumbling back as she stared down at the blood welling from her arm.

It was little more than a shallow cut. I hadn't wanted to kill her, only to make her let go.

"I am sorry. I had no choice."

As I turned to run, one of the old men rushed up. I had taken no more than a single step before he hooked his arm around my neck.

I froze and for a moment my mind was blank. Then Intef's training came back to me. Don't hesitate. Act immediately. They won't expect it.

I stomped on his foot as hard as I could, then dug my elbow back into his stomach. We had practised this move so many times, Intef and I. The old man grunted and his hold on my neck loosened. I easily broke away from him. Then I ran.

As I raced past the wagons that stood in a row at the very edge of the field, I spotted a basket of bread. I had a week's walk ahead of me. With ready supplies, I could save the time I would otherwise spend foraging. The thoughts went through my head at lightning speed as I veered over to the wagon, shoving my dagger back into my bag as I ran. I snatched up the basket, revealing a woven sack behind it. I grabbed that, too. A couple of loaves spilled from the basket. I left them where they fell.

I ran until I was out of breath, which probably wasn't all that far considering how unaccustomed I was to running. I could walk all day if I had to, but I hadn't run since I was a child. I dropped my stolen goods on the grass and faced the way I had come while I caught my breath. If anyone followed, they probably weren't far behind.

There was no sign of pursuit by the time I caught my breath. Perhaps they had decided that one woman was not worth chasing after. I checked my stolen goods. The sack contained strips of smoked meat. I couldn't have gotten luckier. Between that and the bread, I would have enough food to get me back to the valley.

I briefly tried to find a way to combine the contents of both receptacles into one, but they didn't fit. I didn't want to leave anything behind, so I resigned myself to carrying both. I would be thankful for the inconvenience when I had food whenever I wanted it. The road I followed lay alongside a river for most of the way so I would have water enough too.

I ran a little further, then walked until the sun had set and it was too dark to go any further without risking injury. The moon was only a sliver tonight and didn't give enough light for me to make my way safely. I found a place where a couple of spiky bushes mostly shielded me from view of the road. I had no flint to start a fire and I had lost my blanket. I had only my dagger and the food I had stolen. It would be a long, cold night, but at least my belly would be full.

FIVE

It took five days to reach the valley where I had last seen my friends. Every day the mountains grew closer. Every day I prayed to Isis that I would encounter them along the way. Surely they would come for me if they could. But every sunset, I found myself a lonely bed and shivered through the night.

I listened constantly for any sound of pursuit. Surely, someone — Arnuwanda, or the man who had guarded me — would realise I was gone. The woman and the old man had seen me flee. They would tell someone once it was all over, if there was anyone left to tell. They would come after me. But although every now and then I heard something like the crunch of sandals on rocky path, nobody came. Were they all dead? Or did my capture mean so little that it wasn't worth the effort to search for me?

On the last night, I couldn't bear to stop and sleep. I was so close to the valley. I knew by now that they were probably dead, but I refused to think about it. Surely the gods would not take Intef from me before he could meet his daughter. I had to believe they would let me have more than the few months of happiness we had shared.

I walked through the night to reach the valley. The moon was a little larger and brighter by then, so there was enough light to make my way by, if not enough to hurry. But when I finally arrived, I found myself reluctant to enter the pass in anything less than full daylight. I listened carefully but could hear nothing from its depths. I was struck with the ridiculous thought that maybe they were waiting there. Since this was the last place we had seen each other, wouldn't it make sense for them to wait here until I found my way back?

"Hello?" I called. "Intef? Istnofret?"

The only reply was my own voice echoing through the pass and a startled crow that squawked at me from a nearby bush.

"Behenu? Renni?"

Still no reply.

"Mau? Nedjem?"

I waited. Maybe they had heard me but couldn't reply for some reason. Maybe they were already hurrying out to meet me. I had only to wait. But it felt like time was running out as I stood there, shifting from foot to foot. I would have to enter the pass.

Yet I couldn't make myself move. It is easy, I told myself. Just take a step and then another. One foot in front of the other. That is all you have to do. But then my stomach cramped and the morning sickness began. I vomited until there was nothing left in my belly. Perhaps I should wait until the sun was fully risen. I would rest in the meantime and try to eat. I would have more strength once I was rested.

So I sat and ate from the meagre remains of my stolen supplies. I had enough to last me one more day. The sun was well above the horizon by the time I stirred myself. At the entrance to the pass, I listened, hoping and praying I might hear them. Perhaps if I waited long enough, they would come out and meet me. But of course, there was no sound from within. I took a deep breath. It was time to go.

I crept along the path, trying to make as little noise as possible. I hadn't feared this place the first time we entered it. The high rocky walls and narrow path made me uneasy, but it wasn't until Intef said it was a good place for an ambush that I had even thought of danger. Now I wasn't sure what I feared more: the possibility of once again being trapped between hostile forces, or the increasing likelihood that I would find the bodies of my friends.

Had we gone this far in last time? Perhaps I had missed the place where we stopped before realising we were trapped. I walked a little further and recognised a narrow section. This was where Intef and Renni had begun talking to each other in their silent language. This was where we had dismounted. There, some horse droppings. Evidence that someone had been here. But there were no bodies, no blood, no signs of disturbance, just smooth rock, a hard-packed road. If my friends had died here, there was no evidence left of it.

I let myself lean against the rocky wall and sob. I had known it was unlikely I would find them alive and it was only now I realised just how hard I had held onto the hope that they would be here. Or that they would have left some sign to show me where they had gone. Even finding their bodies would have been easier. At least then, I would know. Now, I would probably never know whether they had left this place alive.

The day was half over by the time my tears stopped. I had no idea how much of the narrow pass remained ahead of me. This point where I stood now was as far as I had seen the first time. Should I go back while I still could and wait until morning before attempting to make my way through? Or should I keep going?

I wasted more time debating with myself and even longer sitting numbly. Eventually I pulled myself together. I had to focus long enough to make a decision. I had only a day's worth of food left. I could stretch it for two days but no more. I would have to forage, and without flint, I couldn't start a fire to cook anything. Herbs or fruits would keep me alive but wouldn't give me the strength I needed to walk all day. But if I kept moving forward, perhaps I could be out of the pass before I ran out of food. And maybe there would be a village not all that much further along. Maybe not, but at least if I continued on, there was hope. If I turned back, there was nothing but the possibility I might encounter the army again.

I got to my feet, surprised to find my legs were a little wobbly. But of course, I had had no water since I came in here and my tears had probably dehydrated me even more. I wouldn't let myself cry again, at least not until I found a stream. I picked up the sack with the last of my food and walked on.

I tiptoed along the pass, stopping every few minutes to listen for any sound of someone approaching. I watched for places I might hide in, but if I had thought to find some cave or crevice in the rocky walls, I was sadly mistaken. At one point, I thought I heard the crunching of sandals and I cowered against the rocks, so terrified that I wet myself and didn't even realise until later. But nobody came and eventually I convinced myself that I must have imagined it, although I spent the rest of the afternoon checking that nobody was sneaking up behind me.

Long before I expected it, the light began to fade. I walked a little further, but the path ahead was unchanging. Just more of the hard-packed road bordered on either side by tall, rocky walls, with just a narrow stretch of darkening sky visible between them. The path wove in and out, seemingly following a natural divide, so I could see little either ahead or behind me.

At length I reached a longer straight stretch and it was here that I decided to spend the night. I sat with my back against the rocks and ate just enough to ease my grumbling stomach, leaving as much as I could for tomorrow. The stale bread stuck in my throat and I could barely force it down. It made me ever more conscious of my thirst. I prayed I would reach the end of the pass tomorrow.

As the last of the light slipped away, my fear returned tenfold. Every sound seemed magnified now and the twisty pass which had been devoid of life during the day suddenly seemed filled with a variety of creatures that skittered and scuttled, although how much was real and how much merely my imagination, I didn't know.

The narrow patch of night sky above me was totally dark. I had hoped to see the moon or even a few stars. It was as if I was suddenly the only living thing left in the world, except for the scuttling creatures that I couldn't see and which maybe didn't really exist.

I was too scared to sleep, or even to close my eyes. At least the rock behind me was still warm enough to keep me from being too cold. I must have eventually drifted off, for I found myself surrounded by my friends, or at least a paler version of them. They hovered in front of me and stared at me with beseeching eyes.

Then they changed. Intef lost his remaining arm, leaving him with two stumps which he held pleadingly out to me. Renni held his hands over his heart. Blood dripped between his fingers. Behenu's head hung to the side, her neck broken.

Only Istnofret seemed the same, although her face was skinnier than it should be and darkened with bruises.

It is my imagination, I told myself firmly. I know they are dead and I am dreaming about the ways they might have died. But I could still feel the fading warmth of the rock behind me, the hard path beneath me, the breeze that somehow seemed to find its way down the winding pass, and I wasn't entirely certain I was asleep. Perhaps I was wide awake and these were the *ka* of my friends, come to haunt me for leaving them to die.

Eventually I fell asleep, although I could still feel them watching. I dreamed of the day I would return to Egypt. I saw myself confronting Ay. He sat on his throne, looking older and more haggard than I remembered. I stood in front of him, my head held high. My dream didn't reveal what I said, but it did show Ay's face become ashen. He pointed to me and shouted. Guards came running. I tilted back my head and laughed, clutching my fist tighter around something small and hard.

Then the dream shifted and I was no longer in the throne room at Memphis. Now I stood on the edge of a battlefield. Two armies fought and my heart was heavy as I watched them. Some of the men were clearly Egyptian, in their knee-length *shendyts*, their shaved heads shining with sweat. They fought their enemy with spears where they could, and daggers in closer quarters. The other army consisted of men with dark hair and dark beards, who methodically cut down the Egyptians in front of them. Someone beside me spoke and I turned to face him. It was another of the dark-haired men. His eyes glittered coldly.

"Now I will lay waste to your entire country," he said. "Never again will Egypt dare to kill a son of the Hittites."

I woke with tears running down my cheeks and only just managed to turn my head to the side to avoid vomiting on myself. The sun had risen and my friends were gone, if they had ever really been there.

For the first time, my dreams had shown what would happen if I failed in my quest. I had never seen Suppiluliumas in life, but it was undoubtedly he who stood beside me in the second dream. His army would invade Egypt. We had faced invaders before, many times, but this would bring death and destruction on a scale we had never before seen. I had to find the Eye.

Not all my dreams contained truth, but this one did. It showed me not only two possible fates, but it also revealed a hidden truth: my friends were dead. I would face Ay alone, which was something they would never allow so long as any of them lived. So it was up to me now. I had to find my way to Crete and locate the Eye. For Egypt's sake.

SIX

I had no idea how much time passed as I sat there, alternating between vomiting and crying. At length both subsided, leaving me exhausted and trembling. At least I was no longer thirsty. That was a good thing. Thirst was uncomfortable.

I nibbled at the last of my bread and dried meat. What remained wasn't enough for even one meal. I must have dozed off, for I woke with a start, my heart pounding. But I was still alone. Even the *ka* of my friends were gone. I hoped that meant they had gone on to the Field of Reeds, but the Hittites wouldn't have bothered to preserve their bodies. I should have felt sorrow, but I was numb.

The day was passing and still I sat there. I had to follow the path. Get to the end of the pass. Get out of this gods-forsaken place. It took a long time to get to my feet. My head spun so badly that I couldn't tell which way was up until I landed on my face. I tried again but my legs wobbled and this time I landed on my behind. Eventually I managed to stand.

I had to lean against the rocky walls as I stumbled along

the pass. I breathed too hard and my heart beat much too fast. I had no sense of time. At some point I realised it was dark again and I let myself slide down along the rocks until my bottom reached the path. I sat there for a while before it occurred to me that I should eat. There was hardly anything left in the sack so I ate it all, then immediately vomited it back up. It seemed my stomach would take nothing so it hardly mattered that I had no supplies left.

It was Sadeh who came to haunt me tonight. Sadeh silently asking why I had sent her to die in my place. I tried not to look at the gaping wound in her neck. Intef had cut her throat himself, to save her from a worse death, he had said. It had taken me a long time to forgive him, and even longer to forgive myself. I wrapped my arms around my legs and rested my face on my knees. Perhaps if I couldn't see her, she would go away. But she stayed until I slept. When I woke, the sun had risen and Sadeh was gone.

As always, morning brought nausea and vomiting. I was too slow this time and vomited all over myself. I had no spare clothes and no way of cleaning myself up. I would probably die in this wretched pass. It hardly seemed to matter if I did so covered in my own vomit.

Somehow I got to my feet and staggered on, using the same method of sliding along the rocky walls as I had the day before. Then I rounded one last twist in the path and emerged into dazzling light.

I could see nothing but whiteness. It was too bright. Tears streamed down my cheeks as I squinted into the light.

I stepped forward, but the rocky wall suddenly ended and I landed face down in the grass. I couldn't move my arms, couldn't turn my face to the side to breathe more easily. I closed my eyes and waited to die.

When I next woke, it was night and Behenu's face hovered in front of me. I closed my eyes with a sigh. Another *ka*.

Behenu spoke and something was pressed to my lips. I opened my mouth without thinking and warm soup trickled down my throat. It was only then that I realised it was the first time any of the *ka* had spoken.

Soup spilled over my chest as I tried to sit up. Behenu made a startled noise. When I looked at her more carefully, I realised it wasn't her, but rather a young woman of around the same age of thirteen years. Her hair hung in little braids to her shoulders and her skin was several shades darker than mine.

I tried to speak, but all that came out of my mouth was groans.

"Am I in Syria?" I managed at last. Why else would I be in the home of a Syrian woman? "How did I get here?"

She made soothing noises and pushed at my shoulders until I lay back down. She offered me a bowl and I took it with shaking hands. I probably spilled more than I managed to get into my mouth, but she seemed unperturbed at the mess. When I had finished, she removed the thin blanket that covered me and it was only then that I realised I was naked beneath it. She quickly drew a clean blanket over me.

"Thank you." I had vague memories of having vomited all over myself. "I must have been a terrible mess."

She patted my shoulder and took the soup-covered blanket away. I lay on a low bed in a hut that seemed to comprise a single chamber. A bench along the far wall held an assortment of bowls and cooking utensils. Other items were stacked haphazardly on a shelf above the bench. Bunches of herbs hung from the ceiling, infusing the smoke from the hearth with a pleasant scent.

"Where are we?" I tried to sit up, but it seemed like too

much effort and I sank back down into the bed. "Who are you?"

I repeated my question in Akkadian, but she gave no indication of having understood. Perhaps she only spoke Syrian, which I had never bothered to learn despite travelling with Behenu for so long. We had expected to pass Syria on our way to the coast, but not for at least another week or more, and that was on horseback. My time in the valley was hazy, but I couldn't possibly have walked all the way to Syria.

Two days passed before I had enough strength to get out of bed. The woman held my arm firmly until she was satisfied I could stand on my own. I wrapped the blanket around myself and staggered to the door. I had expected to be in a village, but outside was an endless vista of plainlands.

"Where are we?" I asked, even though I knew by now that she couldn't understand me.

The woman came to stand beside me and gave a contented sigh. She liked this place, it seemed.

The sunlight on my skin was like a balm. My father had believed his god could see him whenever the sun's rays touched him. I no longer worshipped Aten, but it seemed appropriate that I give thanks to someone.

"Thank you," I whispered. "For guiding me out of the pass. For leading this woman to find me. For giving me a safe place to recover."

My thoughts strayed to my friends and I quickly pushed them away. Their loss was too fresh and I wasn't ready to grieve them yet. Once I had regained my strength, I would mourn them properly. I placed my hands on my belly.

"I wish I knew whether my babe was well."

The woman seemed to understand my comment and came to place her own hands on my belly. Her confident fingers

probed firmly. She gave me a small smile, seemingly unconcerned about whatever she had discovered.

I spent a week recovering, mostly lying in the bed or sitting
outside in the sun. My host slept on a blanket in front of the
hearth and if she was bothered by my use of her bed, she never
showed it. She had washed my gown and although it was
stained, at least it was clean. When she wasn't looking, I
quickly felt along the hem, but the gems hidden there seemed
untouched. She must surely have noticed them and I
wondered what she had thought. I drank the soups she gave
me and after several days I was able to eat a small piece of
bread. By the end of the week, I had recovered enough
strength to think about continuing my journey.

I had spent the last two days grieving. For Intef. For my
daughter who would never know her father. For Istnofret, who
would never have her little house by the sea, and Renni who
wanted only to be by her side. For Behenu, who would never
get to go home. I even grieved for Mau. Perhaps she had
escaped, but she had no experience in hunting. She must have
either starved to death or become prey for some other creature
by now.

It was only after I had been there for a full week that I saw
someone other than my host. I jumped when a knock came,
but she didn't seem surprised. She opened the door and
ushered in a woman who looked as if she had not slept for
days. Her face was lined and haggard, and she walked
hunched over as if her belly hurt. My host pointed her to a
stool, then indicated that I go outside. She closed the door
firmly behind me.

At first I was confused until I realised she probably wanted
to speak privately with her guest. Surely it must be clear that I
understood not a word of her language. I sat on the grass to

wait. The day was chilly and the sky grey. The air was thick and heavy, much the way the air felt in Babylon before the rains came. Despite the sun, I shivered a little, wishing I had brought a blanket out with me.

Eventually the door opened. My host's visitor didn't look at me as she hurried away. I caught only a glimpse of her face, but it was enough to see that she had been crying. My host waved at me to come back inside, but I waited a little longer, watching the woman walk away. Where was her home? In the direction in which she headed, I finally saw smoke, presumably from fireplaces. Why hadn't I seen it before? I had sat out here several times wondering where the nearest village was. Perhaps there had been no fires at the particular times I had looked, or perhaps the wind had swept the smoke away before I could see it. Or maybe I had simply looked in the wrong direction.

"Who was that?" I gestured after the departing woman.

My host looked at me for a long moment, seemingly undecided. She touched her eyes, and then her heart, before gesturing in the direction the woman had gone. I had no idea what she was trying to say.

We spent a quiet evening together. She fed me more soup, made with wild onions and herbs picked from behind her little hut. She baked the occasional loaf of bread, although I had no idea where she obtained the flour for it. I had seen no evidence that she ate meat or cheese or anything else. She drank water from a nearby stream, so she had no need to brew beer. It was a simple existence and I was torn between wanting to try such a life for myself and knowing that I could never live like this.

SEVEN

L ate the following morning there came a knock at the
door and my host gestured for me to answer. I found
there an old man whose eyes crinkled as he smiled. I couldn't
help smiling back. When he spoke, it took a few moments to
realise that his words were in halting Egyptian.

"You are Egyptian?" I studied his face.

He did indeed have the look of one of my countrymen, but
his skin was not as dark or as sun-weathered as I would have
expected of someone his age.

He laughed with delight. "It has been many years since I
have spoken this language. Not since I was a child. I was born
in Egypt, in a small village on the banks of the Great River. I
have forgotten what it was called. I was taken from there when
I was barely seven years old."

"Taken? What do you mean?"

"I was playing by the river. A man came and took me. He
sold me to another man who made me work as a ship's boy.
One day, while the ship was docked in Sardis, I left. Eventually

I made my way here, where I found a community of people like me."

"People stolen from their homes?"

"Outsiders. Those who do not fit in anywhere else. Somehow we have all made our way here and have found a home with people who do not judge us. Who accept us for the outsiders that we are."

Behind me, my host spoke.

"She says you should invite me to sit," he said.

"You can understand her? Who is she? Where are we? How did I get here?"

"Aah. You have many questions and I am afraid they will be too much for me to answer, not while I still stand and have not even been offered refreshments. I have walked a long way to speak with you."

"Me?"

"I must sit."

"Of course."

I waved him in, thankful to close the door, for the breeze was cold today. There was nowhere to sit other than the bed and the floor and a single stool on which currently rested a basket of onions. I led him to the bed and he sat with a sigh. My host offered him a mug and he thanked her politely before draining it.

"That is better," he said, at length. "Now I can answer your questions."

"How did you know I was here?"

"The woman who came here yesterday. She returned to the village with news of an Egyptian who had been taken in by the *ka*-seer."

"*Ka*-seer? I have never heard such a thing."

"The people here call her something else. I do not know the

Egyptian word for it. *Ka*-seer is as good as anything."

I studied the woman carefully. If she understood our words, she gave no indication of it. I was no longer sure whether what I had seen in the pass was the *ka* of my friends or merely hallucinations brought on by dehydration. Was there some connection between those events and this woman? Had my friends led her to me? The mountains were some distance from her cottage, at least an hour's walk by the look of it. It seemed unlikely that she would have been wandering that far from her home at the exact time I was lying there.

"Why does she live here all alone? Why does she not live in the village?"

"Aah, there are some people who are considered outsiders even amongst outsiders. She is one such."

"Because she is a *ka*-seer?"

He looked hopefully towards the woman and tipped his mug in her direction. She quickly refilled it.

"It scares people. They do not like to think that someone knows them better than they know themselves. That someone knows the secrets they hide."

I lowered myself to the floor and sat cross-legged, facing him. I avoided looking at the woman. What did she know about me that I didn't?

"See," he said. "You know what she is and already you are uncomfortable."

I stared down at my hands while I tried to find a response.

"Are you not?"

"I am too old for such nonsense. I have no secrets. Besides, what secrets can a boy who is taken from his home so young have anyway? There is no time for such a thing when you labour all day to please your master."

"But surely it has been many years since you laboured like that. You must have bought your freedom?"

"I could never have saved enough. I ran away. I kept on running until I reached a place where nobody would ever come looking for me."

His words brought Thrax sharply to mind, the Thracian slave I had taken as my lover without knowing who he really was. He too had run from the fate destined for him. At the time I had been appalled, but I was no longer the woman I was then. Behenu had been a slave when I purchased her. Even when she first travelled with me, she was a slave.

"I had a friend who was a slave once," I said. "Like you, she was taken from her home. But she bought her freedom."

"And what did she do with her freedom once she bought it?"

"She didn't have much time to do anything with it. She went to the West soon after."

She had bought her freedom with a ring I gave to Istnofret, but she had chosen to stay with me. She should have gone home instead of dying in that gods-forsaken pass. The man looked at me blankly.

"She died. I am sorry, I thought you would understand."

"Aah. If I ever heard such an expression before, I have long forgotten it. How did your friend die?"

I looked away. My chin wobbled and I wasn't sure I could talk about it yet.

"I don't know. We were… separated."

"Then how do you know she is dead? Might she not be somewhere else, perhaps searching for you?"

I shook my head, letting my hair fall down to shield my face. It was shoulder length now and I was just starting to discover how useful that could be.

"So you are here alone?" he asked.

"My friends all died."

"You should come back to the village with me. There is a hut which is empty at present. All outsiders are welcome, provided they mind their own business."

"What makes you think I am an outsider?" My tone was a little sharper than I intended, but he didn't look offended.

"You are here alone, and a long way from home. Why else would an Egyptian woman, and a noble one if I am not mistaken, be in Armenia and alone if she were not an outsider?"

"Armenia?" I tried to picture the map we had studied before leaving Babylon. We had intended to pass through Armenia on our way to Sardis. Syria was, if I remembered correctly, to our west. "We are not in Syria?"

He laughed a little. "Why would you think that? Syria is a long way from here."

I nodded towards my host.

"She is Syrian and she was the only person I had seen here, until the woman yesterday. I have no memory of how I got here, so it didn't seem unreasonable that I might have somehow found my way to Syria."

My host had moved the basket of onions and sat on the stool. She waited patiently and seemed unconcerned that she didn't understand our conversation. He spoke to her in a language that was not Egyptian. She answered and he gave a satisfied nod.

"She was searching for a particular herb which grows in the cracks of the rocks at the base of the mountain. She found you, unconscious on the ground. She says you were fortunate she was looking for that herb on that very day. She says you would not have survived another day without help.

She does not know how long you lay there before she found you."

"How did she get me here? Surely she couldn't have carried me so far."

"She had a blanket with her, in which to wrap the herb, for it doesn't like to be exposed to the sunlight. She rolled you onto the blanket and dragged you here."

"Please thank her for me. I am most appreciative."

He relayed my words and the woman gave me a brief nod.

"What is her name?"

"Khannah," he said. "But most people just call her the *ka-seer*."

"Khannah, thank you," I said to her, then turned back to the man. "You must think me terribly rude. I didn't even ask your name. I was so surprised to encounter someone who spoke my language."

"My father called me Seni."

"I am Samun. Or at least that's what my friends call me. The name my father gave me is much longer."

"Here you may use whatever name you wish and nobody will judge you for it. Many of those who live in our community do not use the name they were given by their fathers."

I was tempted to tell him who I really was but clamped my mouth shut before the words could escape. Perhaps Ay's power couldn't reach this far, but I had no wish to endanger anyone who had been kind to me.

"It is odd that you should arrive when you did." Seni's words jarred me from my thoughts. "We do not normally see so many Egyptians here."

The hope that blossomed within me was so immediate and fierce that I realised I hadn't believed they were dead after all. Not truly. Not in the depths of my heart.

"What other Egyptians? Quickly, tell me."

"I have not seen them myself, but I heard they arrived at a village about a half day's walk past our community. Three of them."

My hope was fractured. Only three.

"And a dog," he added, as an afterthought.

"A dog? Are you sure?"

"A wretched, skinny thing from what I heard. So I suppose you could say there were four of them."

It couldn't be them. Not with only three and a dog. I dipped my head, once again letting my hair fall down to shield my tears.

Seni stood with a groan. "I shall take my leave of you. It is a long walk back and I have no wish to walk so far in the dark."

"Thank you for coming. I have enjoyed having someone to speak with, and I am pleased to know Khannah's name."

He studied me for a long moment.

"Should you decide to join us, Khannah can point you in the right direction. You need only keep walking and you will find us, or we will find you."

"I thank you, but I cannot stay. I will only be here another day or two while I regain my strength and then I must leave."

It was only after Seni had gone that I realised I should have had him tell Khannah I would soon leave and ask if she might have any suitable supplies I could take. I could hardly carry bowls of soup with me, and the herbs and wild onions she ate wouldn't sustain me for long as I walked.

I tried to convey my intentions to Khannah, but she seemed to think I was hungry and kept offering bowls of soup. At length, I gave up. I would walk to Seni's village and perhaps there I could trade for supplies, although I had nothing but my gems and they might have little value in such a place.

After we had broken our fast the next morning, I asked Khannah where Seni's village was. I didn't know the name of the village, but she seemed to understand. She took me to the door and pointed. I tried to convey my thanks and she dipped her head in acknowledgement, then gestured for me to wait.

She rustled through a basket on a shelf and when she returned, she pressed something into my hand. It was an acacia seed pod strung on a thin piece of hide. She motioned towards my neck and I understood it was intended as a neck-lace. I had a vague notion that acacia seeds were used for protection. I hung it around my neck and tucked it beneath my gown, where it hung beside the little spell bottle. Then I left, taking nothing with me but her gift.

The walk to Seni's village was longer than I had antici-pated, or perhaps I was not yet as strong as I had thought. I could barely make my feet move another step by the time the village came into sight. A young man driving a flock of sheep between the huts started when I called a greeting to him. When he turned to face me, I saw he had only one eye and the other side of his face was terribly disfigured.

"I am looking for Seni."

I hoped that, like Khannah, he would understand Seni's name if nothing else. He gave me a suspicious look.

"Seni?" I repeated. "Please?"

He pointed, then quickly drove his flock away.

The huts were solid, if not made with any notion of art or beauty, and most had tidy gardens planted beside them. I knocked on the door of the one the young man had pointed to.

"You came," Seni said. "I thought you would."

"I am not staying, but I need supplies and Khannah does not have such as what will travel well."

"Of course. Tell me what you need."

"Bread, dried meat. Perhaps a little cheese if you have any to spare. A blanket. I can pay."

"Not necessary. I will be glad to help a traveller and a fellow Egyptian. You should stay the night, though. Rest under a roof while you can. It may take some time to gather supplies for you."

We passed a pleasant evening in his hut. He fed me stew with chunks of lamb, and although the bread was at least a day old, I welcomed the change after a week of Khannah's onion soups.

Early the next morning Seni went out. When he returned he presented me with a large sack of supplies. I tried again to offer payment, but he would take nothing. Apparently each of the villagers had offered up a little something, a small amount they could easily spare. This was what they did when travellers came through. Everybody gave what they could so that nobody went hungry, including the traveller.

He pointed me in the direction of the road to Sardis. The road was only an hour or so to the west, he told me. If I followed it, I would encounter a village around a half day's walk away. It was only after I left that I realised I should have asked if this was the village he had mentioned yesterday, the one where the other Egyptians were. The ones who were not my friends.

The day was bitterly cold. Someone had provided the blanket I asked for and I wrapped it around my shoulders as I walked. The sack was heavy over my shoulder, but I was thankful for the provisions it contained.

The village was much further than a half day, at least at the pace I could manage, and it was not until late afternoon that the huts came into sight. Lamp light shone around the cracks in the window shutters and smoke poured from the chimneys. After the bitter cold of my walk, the village looked like a haven of warmth. What was I to do, though? Walk up to someone's home and knock on the door? It had been one thing to go to Seni's village, for I knew he would welcome me. But here I was a stranger, and not all villages are welcoming of strangers.

I hesitated for too long. The light already faded from the sky and as bitterly cold as the day had been, the night would be worse. I would have to start knocking on doors and hope I could find somewhere to spend the night, or risk freezing to death outside.

While I mustered my courage, I spotted a man returning from across the plainlands, carrying a pair of hares. His silhouette was so familiar that for a moment, I thought my eyes misled me.

"Renni? Renni!"

He stood stock still for a moment, as if wondering whether he had seen a *ka*, before he ran towards me. I dropped my sack to throw my arms around him.

"I thought I would never see you again," I said.

"We were waiting for you. We figured the army would pass back this way eventually and we were going to try to extricate you when they came."

"Tell me quickly, who isn't here?"

"What do you mean?"

"I heard there were three Egyptians. Who is missing?"

"We are all here."

"All four of you?" I wanted to be very certain that I understood correctly before I let myself feel any relief.

"Intef, Istnofret, Behenu and Mau are in one of the huts."

"Mau even?"

"Of course. You do not think we would leave her behind?"

"But what about the dog?"

"What dog?"

"Three Egyptians and a dog was what I heard."

"Perhaps you heard about someone else? We don't have a dog."

"A wretched, skinny thing," I said. "Are you sure?"

"I think I would know if we had a dog. But come, let's get you inside. It is freezing out here."

Maybe Renni had been off hunting when they had been seen by whoever had passed on the news of three Egyptians and a dog. Maybe someone had seen Mau in dim light and mistook her for a dog. It seemed unlikely, but I didn't know how else to make sense of such confusion.

Our reunion was a tearful, excited jumble of people talking over each other and laughing. Intef came straight to me and wrapped his arm around me. I leaned against his chest and sobbed. I tried to tell him I had feared our babe would never meet her father, but I cried too hard for him to understand.

"Ssh, Samun," he whispered in my ear. "Whatever it is, it is all right."

"They led us out into the desert," Renni said. "More than a day's walk. Then they left us there. We managed to skirt the mountain as we crossed the desert and ended up on the other side."

"Arnuwanda told them to," Behenu added. "I saw him speaking to the men who took us out there."

I could only stare at them, speechless with rage.

"He wasn't trying to kill us," Intef said. "He was being merciful. Perhaps it was the only way he could."

"You call that mercy? Leaving you in the desert with no

supplies and no idea of where you were? If I ever see him again, I will kill him myself."

"Remember Arnuwanda travelled with Tuta from Hattusa to Egypt," Intef said. "He would have learnt much about our training. Not that Tuta would have told him anything he shouldn't have, but a man who knows what he is looking for can learn much by merely watching."

"You have a strange idea of mercy," I muttered, but even so, I saw the sense of his words.

Arnuwanda may have found himself in a situation where his king's army had captured people considered enemies. Perhaps he knew more of the truth than he had let on, and had done what he could to save them. I suppose he figured the rest was up to them.

EIGHT

I woke the next morning with Intef pressed against my back and his arm draped over me. The cottage we occupied had until very recently been owned by an elderly pair of Armenian sisters. They had died not long ago and within days of each other. Or at least that was what my friends understood from the villagers with no more than a few words in common.

Mau was skinnier than I remembered, with her ribs and hip bones far too prominent. Behenu had been trying to coax her to eat with little success. Perhaps we had been wrong to bring the cat with us. Shala would have gladly looked after her if we had left her in Babylon.

Intef insisted we stay in the village another day or two while I regained my strength. Renni and Behenu had found most of our horses, who had made their way out of the pass and were gathered not far from the place where Khannah must have found me. I was pleased to hear that Nedjem was among them. Two horses were still missing and despite searching for several days, they had found no sign of them.

We were limited in our ability to trade for travelling

supplies, as the villagers had little more than what they needed to survive. But portions of a wild boar Renni shot with an arrow were exchanged for flour and Behenu set to work baking loaves of bread. Renni caught a few hares and some plump, speckled birds of a sort we weren't familiar with. Istnofret and I spent a full day drying the meat over a smoky fire. Intef made his way through the village, trading for what he could. A few extra blankets, for the nights here were even colder than on our walk to Leucus Limen. Some boots for Behenu as one of her sandals had broken while they were out in the desert. Bowls, baskets and a cooking pot, for most of those sorts of items had been carried by the two horses that were never recovered.

When we finally left, we quickly fell into our usual travelling patterns. Renni would go hunting as soon as we stopped to make camp. Sometimes Behenu would go with him; other times she helped Intef build a fire pit and collect wood. Istnofret and I would forage for herbs or wild vegetables to supplement our supplies.

As we made our way through Armenia and towards Hattusa, I became increasingly uneasy. What if we encountered the Hittite army again? I wasn't sure whether Arnuwanda was actually our ally, but surely he was the only one who might try to help us, even if covertly. But someone else might have sent a message to Suppiluliumas and even now, there could be squads out looking for us.

"Intef, I need to tell you something," I said one evening as we lay tangled together beneath our blankets. I kept my voice low so that Renni, who was keeping watch, wouldn't hear.

"Mm," he murmured, already half asleep.

"Wake up." I elbowed him in the stomach and he jerked awake.

"What is it?" he whispered. "Did you hear something?"

"No, I am trying to tell you something very foolish, but you were too busy sleeping to listen to me."

"I am listening, my love." He tucked himself closer against my side and hooked one foot over my ankle. "Tell me."

Knowing that I had his attention, I was suddenly embarrassed.

"Never mind. Go back to sleep. I am sorry I woke you."

"Oh no you don't. You have already woken me, so now you have to tell me."

"I cannot, Intef. It is too silly and you will think me the most incredible fool."

"Tell me, my love." His voice was gentler now. "I promise I won't think you a fool."

"I am afraid."

"Of what?"

"Of… everything. Trying to pass by Hattusa without being captured again. The rest of this journey. Reaching Crete. Not finding the Eye."

"We take this journey one step at a time. Don't worry about what the days ahead may bring. Worry only about today."

"That's easy for you to say," I said. "You're not the one…"

"The one what?"

"The one who might fail. Might let everyone down."

"You won't." His voice held nothing but certainty. "The gods have shown us where the Eye is. They will hardly keep it from you now. We just need to get you to Crete."

"But Maia said there will be a price to pay. What if I cannot?"

"What price would you not be willing to pay after all we have endured to get this far?"

"I would give anything."

"Then why are you worrying? We don't know whether Maia is correct or not. The price could well be the journey. Maybe when you find the Eye, you will discover you have already paid the price."

"What if I haven't? What else could the gods possibly ask for?"

I was starting to suspect I knew, but I couldn't tell Intef. He shrugged against me.

"I don't know, my love, and I cannot see the sense in worrying about it. We will deal with it when we get there. For now, all you need to worry about is getting some sleep. Tomorrow will be another long day."

He seemed to fall asleep almost immediately. I was still awake when Behenu came to tell me it was my turn to keep watch. I sat up and wrapped a blanket around my shoulders. The air was so cold that my lungs hurt when I breathed. The fire had died down to mere coals and everyone else seemed to be sound asleep. Off to my left, one of the horses huffed.

I looked out into the dark, trying to stay focussed on my task and forget about my worries for a time. The horse huffed again and shifted restlessly. I sharpened my attention in their direction. Uneasiness from the horses could mean someone — or something — was nearby. Perhaps I should wake Intef? But no, I had kept him awake long enough tonight. I would wait until I was certain there was a problem.

The bag with my dagger was right beside me and I eased my weapon out, just in case. The horse huffed again and one of them nickered. Then suddenly my spell bottle was burning hot. I shook Intef gently and he was instantly awake. He looked up at me, a question in his eyes. I marvelled that even in this first moment of waking from sleep he had enough presence of mind to keep quiet. I leaned down and whispered into his ear.

"The horses are restless."

Beneath the blanket, I felt him moving, no doubt reaching for his dagger. He began to slowly sit up. On the other side of the fire, Renni did the same, although how he had known to wake, I didn't know.

Then there was a shout and dark shadows ran towards us. Istnofret screamed once, then abruptly stopped. Intef and Renni were on their feet, daggers slashing. Behenu snatched up Mau and darted off into the darkness.

I barely had time to get to my feet before the fight was over. Three men lay dead, with Intef and Renni panting over them. Blood ran down Renni's arm and my heart stuttered as I remembered the wound that had led to us removing Intef's arm. But Renni wiped the blood away with a blanket and seemed unconcerned. Intef had blood splattered all over his chest, too much for him to still be on his feet if it was his own.

"Any more?" Intef asked.

"At least one." Renni's tone was curt.

"Best we go after him. Where is Behenu? Istnofret?"

"I am here." Behenu emerged from where she had hidden behind a shrub, clutching Mau. She bundled the cat back into her basket. "She is most disturbed. I think it better if she cannot see what is happening."

"Ist?" Renni called.

She didn't reply. Terror welled within me and from the look on Renni's face, he barely controlled his own fear.

"Istnofret?" I called.

"Do you have your dagger?" Intef asked me.

I retrieved it from the dirt. In all the confusion, I had somehow dropped it.

"Go stand beside the fire, you and Behenu. Stay in the light and keep your daggers ready. Call if you hear anything. Anything at all. You understand?"

I tried to blink away my tears before he saw them and realised I was a coward.

"Please find her," I whispered.

"We will." His tone was grim.

Meanwhile Renni had stirred up the fire and took a burning branch from it. He inspected the ground around us.

"She went this way." He pointed at something in the dirt. "Small feet, barefoot. Running."

"Hold your dagger up where it can be seen," Intef said. He squeezed my hand briefly, then hurried after Renni.

"Behenu, are you all right?" I asked.

"I am unharmed, as is Mau, although I might have squashed her. She bit my arm."

I wanted to say something reassuring, but Behenu was here and I could see she was safe. It was Istnofret I worried about. I stared out into the darkness and eventually enough time had passed that I figured she wasn't expecting a reply anyway.

The night air was chill and the fire at our backs seemed to barely warm me. My heart pounded so hard that I probably wouldn't hear anyone sneaking up on us. I barely even noticed that my spell bottle had cooled.

It was a very long time before we heard movement in the dark. Someone who made no effort to be quiet.

"It is just us," Intef called.

"Do you have her?" My voice trembled more than I would have liked.

They reached us before he could reply. Istnofret was on her feet although she walked a little stiffly. Renni was at her side and the way he kept reaching for her told me he desperately wanted to help her, but Istnofret had her arms wrapped around herself and her face was full of fury. Blood soaked the front of her gown.

"Ist, are you hurt?"

Tears already welled in my eyes. If she died, it would be all my fault. I was the one who had insisted on going to Crete. I should have made her stay in Babylon where she was safe.

"I am well." Her tone was curt and I flinched a little.

"She is uninjured." Intef wrapped his arm around me and I leaned into him. "You're trembling."

"There is so much blood," I whispered.

"She killed him. It was over before we found her."

"Istnofret killed someone?"

"She can take care of herself."

I found myself unsurprised. Istnofret had shown herself to be more than capable on the occasions she had cause to defend herself. Of course she would have killed him.

"What did they want?" Intef knew no more than I did, but I needed to make sense of the attack.

He shrugged. "Our supplies, I presume. Maybe the horses. We have warm clothes, food, weapons. There's plenty to attract men who would rather take what belongs to someone else than work for their own."

All this time I had thought Intef was overreacting when he insisted someone keep watch through the night. I had thought we were safe if we were alone and that even if someone stumbled across us, they would have no reason to attack strangers. It seemed obvious that someone might want our supplies, but I hadn't thought they might try to kill us for them. Even after travelling for so long, I still knew so little.

NINE

I didn't have a chance to speak privately with Istnofret the night she killed a man. Renni hovered over her, trying to help her change into her spare gown and wash the blood from her skin, but she rebuffed his aid.

Then she wrapped her blanket around herself and lay with her back to the fire. I watched her for a while and thought I saw her shoulders shaking a little. She might have been crying. Or maybe she was shaking with fury.

Intef dragged the bodies away. I didn't ask what he did with them, whether he buried them or left them for the beasts of prey. They had intended to kill us, so why should I care? Still, I felt a little odd that I didn't feel some glimmer of regret for their deaths, although I couldn't have said why. I slept restlessly, waiting for any warming of my spell bottle, and when dawn came, I was wide awake.

Istnofret's fury hadn't abated. Renni tried again to comfort her, although she hardly seemed to need it and she certainly didn't want it. She pushed him away and stalked off by herself.

I wasn't able to speak with her until we stopped to rest in the middle of the day. The day was once again bitterly cold and we built a small fire to warm ourselves by. Behenu handed around strips of dried bird.

Mau stood close by the fire. She liked the cold the least of any of us. Behenu had padded her basket with a soft blanket to try to keep her warm as we travelled, but she never missed a chance to be as close as possible to a fire.

Istnofret sat and stared into the fire, maybe thinking, maybe trying not to think. She didn't touch her food and didn't look up as I sat beside her.

"Ist?" I ventured eventually. "Are you all right?"

If she heard me, she made no response.

"Ist?" I put my hand on her arm and she jumped as if I had attacked her.

"Don't sneak up on me," she snapped.

"I didn't. I've been sitting here for a while."

"Well, I didn't hear you." Her tone was irritable and she sounded not at all like herself.

"Do you want to tell me about what happened?"

"No."

"It might do you good to talk about it."

"I killed him. What more is there to say?"

"I thought talking might help. I, too, have killed a man."

She didn't reply for some time, but when she finally spoke, her voice was small.

"You told me once that it changes a person to kill a man. What did you mean?"

It took me a while to find a reply. I only vaguely remembered the conversation she referred to, and if there had been some particular purpose to my comment at the time, I had long forgotten it.

"I don't really know."

"So it didn't change you?"

I floundered. Had I been changed by Thrax's death? I had stabbed him with Intef's dagger. He died in my bed with his blood running over my legs.

"I don't know." It was a weak response. Cowardly, perhaps.

"Maybe when you figure out how it changed you, we can talk. Until then, don't presume to lecture me."

It was as if she had slapped me in the face. Istnofret had never spoken to me like that before. Tears sprang to my eyes. Not wanting her to see how her words stung, I went to stand some distance from our fire where I could pretend I merely looked out at the landscape. The flat plainlands had ended and we once again approached a mountainous region.

"My love?"

I hadn't noticed Intef until he spoke. I couldn't stop the tears from spilling down my cheeks. He wrapped his arm around my shoulders and I leaned against him.

"She doesn't mean what she says," he said. "She is hurting. Give her time."

"I know." My words ended in a hiccup. "She just sounded so... I don't know. Like she hates me."

"She doesn't hate you. She is confused and wondering whether she did the right thing in killing him."

"He probably would have killed her if she hadn't."

"He tried to rape her."

"Oh, Isis. He didn't, did he?"

"She didn't say and I didn't think it right to ask. He had taken off his trousers and I can think of no other reason why a man would do so in such a situation. Renni will try to find out later once she is calmer."

"It is a terrible thing to carry a babe and not know whether its father is the man you love or…"

"Ssh." He pulled me closer. "Now do you see why I insisted you learn to defend yourself? You used your skills when you were taken from us, and Istnofret used hers while Renni and I were right here. We will resume your training when we stop tonight."

"Do you think that's a good idea? Maybe we should wait until Istnofret feels better. It might upset her to see us training."

"She doesn't look upset. She is furious. If anything, she will want to learn even more now."

"Why is she so angry? Why isn't she sad? Or scared?"

"It is a big thing to kill a man. You know that. This is her way of processing what happened. Give her time. Remember, she acted out of necessity and had no time to think about what she would do. It was different for you."

"I acted out of necessity too." My tone was more defensive than I liked.

"I didn't say you didn't. I only meant you had a choice. You could have chosen differently. That doesn't mean the decision rests easier with you."

"She asked how I had been changed."

"What did you tell her?"

"I am not sure I was changed. Does that make me a horrible person, Intef? To be the sort of person who can kill a man and be unchanged?"

"You think you were unchanged?" He rested his hand on the side of my face. "My love, that moment was the first time you ever made a decision to give up something you wanted."

"Ay had already made the decision."

"No, he decided to send Thrax away. This decision was all your own."

"Do you think me selfish?"

"Quite the opposite, in fact. It was the most generous thing you could have done for him."

I didn't kill Thrax out of generosity. I killed him because I knew he would prefer death to the slave mines. And because he had said he would fight when they came for him. That he would take as many of them with him as he could, and that might have included some of my own men. It might have included Intef, although I didn't know at that point that I loved him.

"But what do I tell Istnofret?"

"Tell her whatever is in your heart. You will know the right thing to say when the moment comes."

Istnofret's fury subsided and after a few days, it seemed like nothing untoward had happened. Renni managed to ascertain that she had killed the man before he did any more than remove his trousers.

As we made our way through the mountains, at least once a week we passed a village where we could replenish our supplies. Occasionally we were able to spend a night under a roof, even if it meant sharing space with a farmer's livestock. My morning sickness finally passed and my belly suddenly began to poke out.

"Do I finally look like I am carrying a babe?" I asked as Intef and I lay together under our blankets one night. He stroked my belly gently, as if he thought the babe inside could feel him.

"It is certainly obvious now, and you look less unwell. I was worried."

"Many women get sick like that for the first few weeks, or so I hear."

"But you weren't sick last time."

"Apparently sometimes it happens and sometimes it doesn't. The last few weeks have been miserable."

"Would you be so unhappy if the gods blessed us yet again?"

My dreams had never shown me any babe other than the daughter I now carried. They hadn't even shown me Setau, the baby boy who was born too early.

There had been two fates in my dreams. When I was with the Hittite army, I thought I was on the path to the future in which I was a captive. Had I evaded that fate? Was the future in which I offered up my newborn babe to Osiris the one that now lay ahead? If only I knew which would be worst.

In the dream in which I was a captive, I had been certain that death approached for both me and the babe, but was there some possibility I survived? That we both survived? If only I knew what came after that moment, I would know whether it had been a mistake to escape from the Hittites.

It was some time before I realised I hadn't replied to Intef, but he had fallen asleep by then. I lay awake for a long time before I too finally slept.

TEN

We kept the Tigris on our left as we travelled. We crossed other rivers, although we didn't know their names. Some we traversed on stone bridges, others were barely more than streams which the horses splashed their way across. We passed over a series of hills, which gradually built into yet another mountain range. The road traced a clever path through the mountains and there were few places that were too steep to ride the horses.

I lost track of the days. The weather grew ever more bitter and we amassed so many blankets that we had to trade for an extra horse to carry them. We even managed to secure a small shelter comprising of large pieces of hide skilfully stitched together and propped up with poles. There was only enough room inside for two people, or three if we lay close together, so Intef and Renni insisted we women sleep in there. On the very coldest nights, we all huddled inside together, although it left no room for anyone to lie down. Still, it kept us from freezing to death and if we were tired the next day, I supposed we should be grateful to be alive.

The road skirted the occasional city, but we were reluctant to enter any further than the very outskirts in order to trade for supplies. Who could know how far Suppiluliumas's reach might stretch?

My belly grew ever larger and I started to wonder if I had misjudged how far along I was. Surely my belly had not been this big so early when I carried Setau. Late one night as we all huddled in the tent, I felt a flutter. It was gone almost before I noticed it.

"Are you well, my love?" Intef murmured.

"I think the babe moved."

"Really? Can I feel it?"

He placed his hand over my belly, but she was still now. He tried to keep the disappointment from showing on his face.

"It was very quick. I barely felt it."

The grass was frosty the next morning and crunched underfoot. We had long since packed away our sandals and started wearing boots like the people here did. It was a strange feeling to have my feet entirely encased and I didn't particularly care for it, although it was better than my toes freezing solid and snapping off, which was my secret fear. I had also stowed away my gown, replacing it with trousers made of hide and a thick fur coat, a furry hat and woven mittens. At first such clothing felt bulky and awkward, but I quickly grew used to it and was thankful for the warmth.

We emerged from the mountains to discover a landscape different to anything we had ever seen before. Large wedges of land were separated by deep crevices. Further in the distance, rocky outcrops littering the landscape looked as if they had been pushed up from the underworld. There was no sign of people or habitation.

"What is this place?" Istnofret asked, as we stared in amazement.

"We are somewhere in Asia Minor." Renni looked to Intef for confirmation. "But I am not sure where exactly."

"I thought we would reach the land of the Hatti after the mountains," Intef said. "But this place is so strange I cannot imagine anyone could live here. Look at the ground. There is no flat land on which to build houses."

"What do we do now?" I asked.

"We keep moving forward," he said. "Follow the road until we reach Sardis."

We urged the horses on, but before we went much further, Behenu drew hers to a halt.

"Do you see that?" she asked.

I peered ahead. Behenu had the sharpest eyes of any of us and I couldn't see anything unusual. Not yet anyway.

Renni shielded his eyes as he stared in the direction Behenu pointed. "A body?"

"I think so," Behenu said.

Intef's dagger was already in his hand. "Be alert. It could be a trap."

We approached slowly and halted some distance away. It was no wonder I hadn't seen her, for her brown hide clothes were almost the same colour as the ground on which she lay.

"I'll go." Renni slid off his horse. "Stay back."

He approached slowly, his dagger held ready. He dropped to his knees beside her and reached out to touch her face.

"She is alive, but barely. Her skin is very cold."

Intef nodded towards Behenu. "Go see if you can help but be careful. It could still be a trap."

Behenu slid off her horse and hurried to Renni. She

crouched beside him and they examined the woman. Behenu pointed at her hand and they both leaned closer to inspect it.

"She has been bitten by something," Behenu called to us. "A snake perhaps. She is very ill."

"She must live somewhere near here." Intef turned his horse around as he looked in every direction.

"They might have very low dwellings," I suggested. "Built close to the ground to avoid the wind. Her house could be tucked up against one of these rocky ledges."

"This is the strangest place I have ever seen," he said.

"I feel like we are completely unprepared for this," Istnofret said.

"Renni has taught you better than that." Intef's tone was faintly disapproving. "We are no less prepared here than anywhere else. We just need to stay alert while we gather information about this place. We will figure it out, and if we don't, we will pass through it soon enough. We cannot be more than a few weeks from Sardis."

Istnofret pulled out her dagger and turned her horse so she could watch behind us.

"That's better," Intef said. "Think like a soldier. Be prepared for anything." He glanced at me. "That goes for you, too. Where is your dagger?"

I fumbled for the little bag hanging from my neck.

"You and Renni already had your daggers out. I didn't think I would need mine."

"You must not assume you are safe. What if I am taken down and cannot protect you? How will you protect yourself if your dagger is still in your bag?"

I finally managed to retrieve my dagger, almost dropping it in my haste. The woollen gloves were excellent for keeping my hands warm, but they made me clumsy.

"I have it now."

"Good."

Renni jogged back to us. "She is conscious but barely. She pointed to the west, so maybe she lives in that direction. Behenu and I will carry her and see if we can find her home."

"We will wait here," Intef said. "Best that the rest of us keep our distance until we are certain it is safe."

Between Renni and Behenu, they managed to lift the woman. They had gone only as far as the first of the strange rocky protrusions when they stopped. They looked around, seeming confused, but the woman pointed at the rock. They carried her around behind it and disappeared.

Uneasiness rose within me as we waited. Where had they gone? Had they laid her down behind the rock? Had something happened to them?

"I don't like this," Istnofret muttered. "We have no idea what is happening."

"We don't need to see them," Intef said. "We need only wait. We should not assume the worst just because we cannot see them."

"I know. Renni has told me the same thing. He says a good soldier waits patiently."

"Renni is a good soldier. You should listen to him."

She glared at Intef who seemed to be trying not to laugh.

"Look." I interrupted their banter as Behenu appeared from behind the rock and waved at us. "What if it isn't safe?"

"She would not be waving us over if they weren't sure," Intef said.

We urged the horses on and as we came around behind the rock, I saw the most marvellous thing: the rock had low windows carved into it with shutters that stood open. It even had a wooden door, which was currently ajar.

"Is this her home?" Istnofret's voice was incredulous.

We looked towards the other rocks. From here, I could see other windows and doors.

"Are they all homes?" I asked. "Is this a village?"

We dismounted and hobbled the horses. I pushed the door open some more and stepped inside. Somewhere nearby, a baby cried.

Narrow steps carved into the rock led down. A lamp set on a shelf carved right out of the rock provided enough light to navigate them. Istnofret was right behind me as I descended. I reached a landing and then a passageway. More lamps set on rocky shelves led me along the hall, at the end of which was a roomy chamber. The woman lay on a bed which, like everything else here, seemed to be carved right out of the rock, albeit softened with a pile of blankets and furs. Behenu crouched beside her, inspecting the woman's hand. The baby stopped crying.

"Have you ever seen anything like this before?" I asked as I joined Renni at the window, which was only just above the ground. Was there more of her home further beneath us?

"I have never even dreamed of a place like this. If someone described this to me, I would think they were lying. Look at how many rocks there are just like this one. Is each one someone's home? Where do they grow their crops? Where are their livestock?"

I could see why Istnofret liked him so much. He had such a clever brain. It hadn't occurred to me to ask questions like that. I was still marvelling over the woman's home. Rocky shelves circled the room. A low rocky bench. Rocky stools covered with soft cushions. All the furniture she needed was carved out of the same rock as her home. Like Renni, I would never have dreamed of such a place. Behenu rushed back into the chamber. I had been so absorbed in examining our surroundings that I hadn't even realised she had left.

"I found these." She placed several small ceramic pots on the bed. "They have herbs of some sort in them."

Istnofret returned carrying a babe. "He was in the next chamber. It seems to be another sleeping area."

"How old is he?" I reached for the babe's hand and he wrapped his fingers around mine. An unexpected grin came to my face.

"Maybe a year or so," Istnofret said. "Young enough that he still needs his mother's milk."

Meanwhile, Behenu had tipped the herbs onto the bed to examine them. She sniffed them and even took a cautious nibble of a couple. At length she shrugged and pointed to one of the piles.

"This one tastes a little like coriander, which is used to relieve pain. I am pretty sure this stuff that looks like bark is cinnamon, although it is not very fresh. It is used to treat wounds. And I think this is fenugreek, which reduces inflammation. I could make a poultice from them to put on her hand."

"How do you know so much about herbs?" I asked.

She avoided my eyes as she gathered the herbs up again. "I learnt as a child. Studied with a healer for a time."

"You must have been very young." She couldn't have been more than seven or eight years old when Horemheb captured her.

Behenu didn't respond.

"Do whatever you think best," I said. "I know little about herbs, so I am not much help."

As Behenu left, the woman moaned and rolled her head from side to side. Her eyes fluttered open briefly.

"I will go help Behenu," Renni said. "She will probably want a fire for the poultice and we can heat some water to wash the woman's hand. You should be careful not to touch it in the meantime. There might be venom on her skin still."

The woman moaned again, louder this time.

"Try to soothe her," Renni said. "Don't let her get up."

He hurried out, leaving me standing by the bed, wondering exactly what he intended me to do. The woman was dark haired with skin that was somewhat lighter than mine and I had little sense of whether she was slight or stocky under her bulky clothes. She moaned.

"Ssh." I put my hand on her forehead. She felt far too warm, especially since this room was quite cool. How did she warm her home? There was no hearth in here and yet it was warmer than I would have expected, even if it wasn't as warm as I would like for myself.

The woman opened her eyes and looked right at me. She spoke, something brief and I sensed a question in it.

"The babe is fine, if that is what you're asking. Lie still. Behenu is making a poultice for your hand. It might help if we knew what had bitten you, though."

She stared up at me, frowning, and repeated her question. She struggled to sit up and I put my hand to her shoulder.

"Just a few more minutes." I pressed her back down onto the bed. "You need to lie still."

She raised the hand which had been bitten and said something. Her hand already looked more swollen and I was sure it was redder. Then it seemed she had decided to get out of bed. I stepped back, unsure what to do. I could hardly wrestle her down onto the blankets.

Then Intef was by my side, gently pushing her back down. She said something, her tone bitter, but he just smiled and shrugged at her. She glanced from him to me and seemed to resign herself to staying in the bed.

"We are trying to help you," I said. "I promise. Intef, where have you been?"

"I went back out to check on the horses and a man offered some space in his barn. It is cut into the rock just like this house is. The horses will be much warmer in there. Mau's basket is just by the door here. I didn't think she would appreciate staying with the horses, but I have not let her out yet."

"He didn't mind sharing his barn with a stranger?"

"He gave me an odd look, but I couldn't understand anything he said. He seemed happy enough to take the horses, though."

Renni returned with a steaming bowl and a linen towel. He set the bowl on the floor.

"Can you wash her hand?" he asked. "I will go see if Behenu needs help."

He left. Intef and I looked at each other.

"I suppose this is a job for someone with two hands," he said, with a shrug. He went to the window and looked out. "Someone needs to keep an eye on what is happening outside anyway. Make sure that fellow doesn't suddenly decide we are hostile and bring his friends to move us on."

I turned back to the woman.

"I am going to wash your hand. See?" I dipped the towel in the water and showed it to her, then motioned towards her injured hand. "May I?"

The woman must have understood something of my intent, for she didn't pull away when I took her hand. I gently bathed the wound.

"I don't know if this is useful, but what else can we do for her?" I asked Intef.

"Perhaps I should see if I can find a healer?" he suggested. "If all the rocks out there are homes, there must be many people living here. Surely they will have a healer amongst them."

"But how would you tell them what you seek?"

"I could bring someone here to speak to her." He motioned to the woman on the bed. "Surely she could tell them what she needs."

"We don't know whether these people are friendly. That one man you met might not be like the others."

Istnofret returned, carrying the babe who looked calmer now. She put her hand to the woman's forehead. "She has a fever."

"Should we bathe her with some cool water?" I asked.

"We can put a compress on her forehead," Istnofret said. "Try to bring down the fever. Here, take the babe and I will fetch some more water."

I hadn't held a babe since Setau and the sudden burst of longing took me by surprise. The babe's face was still red from his cries, but he was peaceful now. He looked up at me and seemed not at all alarmed to find himself in the arms of a stranger. Other than Setau, I hadn't held a babe since my youngest sister was born.

It was odd, this awkward feeling of not knowing what to do with him. I hadn't felt like that with Setau. Holding him had been as natural as breathing. I tried to remember exactly how I had held him — where I had put my hands — but those few hours I had with him were a haze of pain and sadness, and I couldn't quite remember.

"It is good to see you like that." Intef's voice was hesitant.

I glanced up, surprised, for I had forgotten there was anyone in the chamber other than the babe and I.

"With a babe in your arms," he said. "I know it has been hard. That you mourned our babe."

"I am afraid," I whispered.

He came to wrap his arm around my waist. "Of what, my love?"

I let my hair shield my tears from his view. I couldn't answer. The unvoiced sobs in my throat were waiting for a chance to burst out. If I said anything right now, I wouldn't be able to stop myself from saying too much.

"You are afraid of the babe being born too soon," he said.

I nodded and said nothing. Of course that was what he would think I meant.

"The timing was all wrong last time," he said. "You had been through a terrible shock. It must have been awful for you, listening to the battle up above and not knowing what was happening. Then there was my arm and you didn't know whether I would live. If we are still travelling as your time comes closer, we should find somewhere to stay. Give you time to rest. I want you off your feet well ahead of the babe being due. I am sure that will make things easier this time."

I stared down at the babe so that I could avoid meeting Intef's eyes. My feelings were conflicted. He was trying to look after me, to protect me, but my dream of the green-faced god told me the babe would be born in Egypt. Even once we got to Crete, it might take some time to locate the Eye, and then we still had to travel home. I couldn't afford to sit around for months. If the green-faced god was my fate — and my child's — I had to keep moving forward while I could.

ELEVEN

I stnofret and Behenu returned while I was still trying to think of a response. Behenu applied her poultice to the woman's hand, then bound it up with a cloth.

"There, I think that is all we can do," she said. "It is up to her now."

Istnofret nodded towards the babe in my arms. "Want me to take him? You look exhausted."

I handed the babe over, then sank down onto the floor to lean against the rocky wall. I hadn't even realised how tired I was until that moment.

"I think we should spend the night here," Istnofret said. "She and the babe live alone as far as I can tell. Somebody needs to look after him until she can."

"I would suggest that her neighbours could do it, but I am just as keen as you to have a night under a proper roof." Renni draped an arm across her shoulders. "Go lie down, my love. I can watch her while you all rest."

"Once the cloth on her head warms, rinse it in the bowl and

put it back on her forehead," Behenu said. "If her fever seems worse, come and wake me. I will be in the next chamber."

Seeing her yawn made me do the same.

"Go on," Renni said. "All of you."

Intef hauled me to my feet. My belly wasn't even that big yet and already I had trouble getting up off the ground by myself. I stumbled after Behenu and found her already asleep in the bed in the next chamber. There was plenty of room for two, so I climbed in beside her. The rocky ledge was surprisingly comfortable, padded as it was with a stack of furs that were at least a palm in height, and I quickly fell asleep.

The chamber was almost dark when I woke. I could just make out the shape of Istnofret lying on a pile of furs on the floor, the babe fast asleep beside her. Intef lay in front of the doorway. I got up slowly, trying not to wake any of them, and tiptoed across the room. Intef was awake before I reached him. He touched my ankle gently as I stepped over him, then closed his eyes again. I found Renni standing at the window in the next chamber.

"How is she?" I asked quietly.

He turned away from the window. "I thought her breathing had changed for a while, but it seems more steady now."

I removed the cloth from her forehead and touched her skin. "I think the fever has broken."

"It broke a while ago. I've been keeping the cloth cool in case it came back."

"Have you checked her hand?"

"I didn't want to touch it. Behenu seemed to know what she was doing. Best we leave that to her." He nodded towards the woman. "She woke up an hour or so ago. Tried to tell me something but went back to sleep."

Things would be so much easier if only we all spoke the same language.

Behenu woke soon after and came to check on our patient. When she unwrapped the woman's hand, we saw that the swelling had reduced and the skin was only a little too red.

"I think she is improving," Behenu said.

"Anyone hungry?" Istnofret asked from the doorway. "I feel like I haven't eaten for a week. Can you listen for the babe to wake while I go find some food?"

"I can go sit with him," Behenu said. "I am not needed here as long as she sleeps."

They both disappeared and it was just Renni and I again with the sleeping woman.

"You should go get some sleep," I said. "I can keep watch."

"Intef should be up soon." He was already halfway out of the chamber. "You sure you don't mind?"

"Go. Rest while you can."

Not that there was any hurry. With nobody else to care for the babe, we could hardly leave before the woman was back on her feet. I itched at yet another delay, but there was nothing else we could do short of leaving the babe to fend for himself. Besides, a night under a solid roof was a welcome luxury.

I laughed to myself at the thought of my previous life, where I had lived with the steadfast belief that every indulgence would be available to me. I had only to mention that I was hungry or thirsty or hot, and accommodations would immediately be made for my comfort. Actually, I would have been annoyed if I had even needed to say anything, for I had expected my ladies to anticipate my needs. The thought of Sadeh, and then Charis, erased the smile from my lips. How would they have coped with such a journey? Probably better than I could have ever expected.

Look at Istnofret, after all. She tolerated the long days of travelling, the bitter cold, the monotonous diet of half-stale bread and wild game, and sleeping on the ground with barely a grumble. The fierce cold meant we had to adjust to bathing infrequently and wearing the same clothes for days on end. She had saved us all at least once. The image of Istnofret tossing the warm contents of a chamber pot in a guard's face and then smacking him in the head with the pot itself never failed to bring a grin to my lips.

I took Renni's place at the window. The enormous rocks threw long shadows across the jagged landscape as the sun set. Lamp light flickered in other windows, evidence that the woman's neighbours were at home. I had thought that Babylon was the most alien place I would ever see, but this far exceeded anything there. Soon enough, Istnofret returned, bearing a tray with several bowls.

"I found some grains. I don't know what they are, but they did well enough for a soup. We will leave her some of our supplies in exchange."

"Thank you. I am ravenous." I took a bowl from her.

She set the tray down on the floor beside the bed. As if she had smelled the soup, the woman groaned and opened her eyes. She didn't seem concerned at finding Istnofret standing over her.

"How do you feel? Are you hungry?" Istnofret asked.

The woman tried to sit up and Istnofret propped a cushion behind her back before setting a bowl on her lap. The woman examined her bandaged hand.

"We don't know what bit you," Istnofret said. "But we washed the wound and put a poultice on it. I hope it feels better."

From the next chamber, the babe cried. The woman started and almost knocked over her soup.

"Ssh, the babe is well," Istnofret said. "Don't fret. Our friend is with him."

Behenu came into the chamber, bearing the sobbing babe. His mother reached for him and she handed him over with a sigh of relief.

"He is probably hungry," Behenu said. "I was about to suggest that someone should go look for a cow or sheep that can be milked."

Indeed, his mother had obviously come to the same conclusion, for she already had him on her breast. He settled quickly, happy to be feeding.

I ate my soup looking out the window, shivering as a chilly gust blew in. It had grown far too cold for an open window. I reached for the shutters but paused as something caught my eye. I peered into the darkness. Something moved, but all I could see was shadow.

"Put out the lamp," I said. "Quickly."

Istnofret had done so almost before I finished speaking. We waited in terse silence while I stared out into the darkness. Torches flared. They were some distance away, separated from us by many of the strange conical rocks that we guessed were houses.

"Men," I said. "Maybe a dozen."

Intef must have just woken, for he was suddenly at my side. "It could be local men doing… I don't know. A night hunt. But we should prepare to leave, just in case. Behenu, go wake Renni."

"I left most of our provisions in the kitchen." Istnofret hurried to the door. "I will go pack them up."

A torch held aloft shed light over a familiar profile.

"It is Arnuwanda," I said.

Renni and Behenu returned just in time to hear me. Intef's hand on my back was a welcome reminder that I wasn't alone. We watched as the men split into several groups and disappeared into various homes.

"We must assume he is searching for you," Intef said. "We need to leave."

"I will go help Istnofret pack up," Behenu said.

Mau already waited in her basket as if she knew we needed to leave quickly. Behenu slung the basket over her shoulder.

"Leave whatever she hasn't packed," Intef said. "We cannot afford to wait."

Behenu hurried away.

"But where will we go?" I asked. "They will see us if we take torches and we would fall and break our necks if we tried to travel across this land in the dark."

The woman rose from her bed and came to peer out of the window with us. She gave me a shrewd look and spoke, her tone urgent. With her babe in one arm, she reached for the shutters and swiftly latched them closed.

"I am sorry, we cannot understand you," I said. "But we need to leave."

The woman was busy fastening the babe to her chest with a long piece of cloth, although she struggled to tie the knot with her bandaged hand. As soon as the babe was secure, she motioned for us to follow.

"Do we go with her?" I asked.

"She seems to understand that we need to leave," Renni said. "I think she guesses they may be looking for us. Perhaps she can lead us away in another direction."

"If she is a Hittite, she might well lead us straight to them," I said.

"I think we have no choice. She knows we aided her today. Perhaps she intends to repay us by helping us to get away."

We grabbed our packs. Istnofret and Behenu rushed back in, laden with the sacks containing our supplies. I expected the woman to lead us out the front door, but instead she hurried along the passageway. She paused to gesture again for us to follow, then disappeared down some steps.

"I don't think she understood." We had lost the chance of an ally because of our language barrier. "We should go. Maybe we can get far enough ahead of them that they won't notice us."

Intef and Renni looked at each other for a moment, then both nodded.

"Hurry." Intef grabbed several packs from Behenu and set off in the direction the woman had gone.

"But we need to leave," I said. "She is going the wrong way."

"Have faith," Renni said to me. His own pack was already slung over his shoulder and he took the remaining sacks of supplies from Istnofret. "I think we can trust her."

"It is not about trust. She just doesn't understand. If we leave now-"

"Samun, come on." Intef's tone was sharper than I was accustomed to. He had stopped at the top of the stairs and motioned for us to follow. "She understands. Let's go."

"Maybe she intends to hide us," Behenu said and hurried after him.

I looked at Istnofret, expecting her to support me but she already followed Behenu.

"I think we're making a mistake."

If she realised we were Egyptian, she might turn on us. Surely all Hittites knew of the tension between our countries.

That Egypt had killed one of their sons. We couldn't afford to trust any of them.

Renni waited for me at the door. He didn't respond, only motioned for me to move. With a sigh, I shouldered my pack and hurried along the passage.

TWELVE

Intef, Behenu and Istnofret had already disappeared. I swallowed my misgivings and followed with Renni close behind me. A dozen stairs down, a long passageway, then more stairs. The woman waited at the bottom with the others, but as soon as Renni and I arrived, she set off again. The only light in these passages came from the lamp she carried.

We passed through a doorway. The woman motioned at Renni, who was the last through, and he closed and locked the door. She led us on a winding, twisty path carved through the rock. We went up and down stairs, along various passages, through numerous doorways. Other passages and stairs branched off from the path we followed. We would have been completely lost if we had been on our own, but the woman never hesitated.

We rounded a bend and reached yet another passageway. On our left, stairs led upwards. The woman indicated we should stay here, then hurried up the stairs.

"I don't like this," I whispered. "Why is she leaving us here? We will never find our way out without her."

"I think we can trust her," Intef said.

We didn't need to wait long before the woman reappeared, motioning for us to follow. She led us up and along a short passage, then into a chamber where a man and a woman waited. Was this their home?

She waved at us and seemed to indicate we should follow the man. Surely now Intef would be more cautious?

"Go," Intef said. "Quickly."

I kept my mouth shut and hurried after the man. He led us on another winding series of stairs and passageways. At times we passed through chambers that seemed to be part of someone's home and twice we encountered other people. But the man spoke softly to them and we hurried past without incident.

"Do you think we are beneath their city?" Istnofret asked me, quietly.

I didn't have breath enough to reply, for our guide moved at a brisk pace. He led us up yet another set of stairs and I sighed as I followed. Suddenly he held up his hand to stop us and put a finger to his lips. We crowded behind him on the stairs. He waved at us to go back down.

My heart pounded and my mouth was dry as we hurried back along several passages and into a chamber. He closed the door, slid the bar into place, and motioned again for us to be quiet.

This appeared to be a sleeping area. A wide shelf carved into the rock and covered with blankets provided a spacious bed. Narrower shelves supplied places for the inhabitant's possessions — a couple of changes of clothes, more blankets, a pair of boots. A rug kept the worst of the chill from the floor at bay.

We stood close together. I shivered a little, although I

wasn't really cold after our long walk. I wanted to go to Intef and have him put his arm around me, but the set of his shoulders told me he wouldn't appreciate being distracted. Istnofret sidled closer to me and slipped her cold hand into mine. I squeezed it gratefully. At least I wasn't the only one who needed comfort.

From the passageway came the slap of boots on rock. Several men. In a hurry and not bothering to try to be quiet. I held my breath until they had passed. Intef put his ear to the door and listened. He signalled to our guide and the man cracked open the door. He peered out, motioned for us to wait, then disappeared down the stairs. He was only gone for a moment before he rushed back in and closed the door.

We waited as the footsteps returned. Our guide slowly slid the bar into place, locking the door with just the faintest click. Footsteps came up the stairs and the door handle rattled. There was a brief comment and the footsteps retreated. We waited another few minutes but heard nothing further.

"I count six," Intef said to Renni, very quietly. "Do you agree?"

"At least six. No more than eight. Soldiers, by the way they walk."

"We could probably take six untrained men, but I wouldn't like to try our luck against that many soldiers. We will wait another few minutes to be sure they're gone. Once they have checked this passage, they're not likely to come back unless they have a reason to."

Not knowing whether the men who searched for us knew we were here made me want to scream. I wanted to run away as fast as I could. We should be fleeing, not waiting for them to find us.

From the way Istnofret shuffled from foot to foot, she was

as uneasy as I. Behenu spoke soothingly to Mau and seemed calm enough, but even so, she kept darting glances at Renni and Intef. Our men seemed at ease. Occasionally a comment passed between them in their language of hand signals, but they didn't speak out loud. Were they using the hand language to say things they didn't want us to hear or were they just being quiet?

We waited for a long time. Our guide kept shooting glances at Intef and seemed to be waiting for him to make the decision to move. Twice more Intef listened at the door before he opened it. Hand signals flashed between them before Renni slipped out. He returned shortly after.

"Looks clear," he said. "At least for the next couple of turns."

"That will have to be good enough," Intef said. "I don't want to be here all night."

"Would that be such a bad thing?" Istnofret asked. "We could spend the night here, where we know we are safe, and move on in the morning. Arnuwanda and his men will likely leave once they have satisfied themselves that we aren't here."

"I would rather not risk it," Intef said. "We don't know these people or their customs. That woman might seem willing to help us slip away, but how will she react if they question her? If they see something we left behind, how will she explain it? Best that we get as far away as we can."

"This place is like a warren," Renni said. "So many turns and branching passages. And solid rock, no dust. We're not leaving any tracks to be followed. If we can get far enough ahead of them, we have a good chance of slipping away."

My shame that I hadn't thought about whether we left any tracks must have shown on my face.

"I didn't think about leaving tracks either," Istnofret whispered as we hurried down the stairs.

I shot her a grateful smile, although I didn't believe her. Renni had taught her much and she had proved herself to be an able student. I doubted that she had followed as unthinkingly as I had.

We hurried along the passageways. Once again, our guide led us on a path that seemed utterly incomprehensible to one who wasn't familiar with the tunnels. Renni walked beside him and Intef followed behind us women. I still sometimes found it disconcerting to not have Intef walking ahead of me, as he always used to when I was queen and he was the captain of my guards.

I glanced back at Intef, just for a moment, but it was long enough that I missed whatever happened. There was a thud and someone groaned, then Istnofret, who was walking ahead of me, stopped so abruptly that I slammed into her. Knocked off balance, she careened into Behenu, who crashed into the wall.

"I am so sorry." Whatever else I had meant to say died on my lips as I saw the body on the floor. A pool of blood quickly spread around it.

Our guide stared down at the body, his face pale. Renni looked between our guard and the man on the floor, with dawning horror. Then Intef was beside him.

"I had no time to think," Renni said. "We came around the corner and he was coming towards us. I acted too fast. I didn't stop to consider that he might not be hostile."

"We are trained not to hesitate," Intef said. "Hesitation can kill you, or the ones you protect. You did what you were trained to do."

Our guide crouched beside the man and reached for him with a trembling hand.

"He knows him," Behenu whispered in my ear. "He would not react in such a way to a stranger."

"Dear Isis, I hope it is not one of his family."

"What happened?" Istnofret asked in a tiny voice. "Renni, did you stab him?"

"I did, and I very much regret it," Renni said with a heavy sigh.

Our guide finally stood up and looked Renni in the eyes.

"I am very sorry," Renni said.

Surely our guide understood, for Renni's voice was full of remorse. Still, the man's face was cold. He looked at Renni for a long moment and shook his head. He pointed in the direction we were headed and rattled off a stream of instructions. Then he pushed past us and went back the way we had come.

"Wait, please." Istnofret grabbed his arm as he passed, but he shook her off and walked away.

"We will never get out of here without him." My breath was ragged and I could see nothing other than the body on the floor.

"We will figure it out," Intef said. "We don't have any other choice."

"Can you make him show us out?" I asked. "Surely it cannot be much further."

"What do you want me to do, my love? Take the man hostage and torture him until he shows us the way out? He would likely go running straight to Arnuwanda the moment we let him go. In fact, he is probably doing that now anyway. We should leave."

"What do we do with him?" Istnofret motioned towards the dead man. "It feels wrong to leave him lying there."

"His family will come for him soon," Renni said. "Best that we leave the body for them to take care of. But Intef is right; we need to go. We don't know whether his people will seek revenge and I for one want to be well away from here before anyone comes for him."

So we stepped over the body, being careful not to walk in the growing pool of blood. Intef went in front this time and he set an even brisker pace than our guide. I glanced over my shoulder at Renni, who had replaced Intef at our rear. His face was schooled to blankness. Whatever he felt about killing a man who might not have posed any threat to us, he would not dwell on it until we were safe. I should do the same.

"We will take the next exit that leads into someone's home," Intef said quietly over his shoulder. "All homes will have a way of getting outside and we have been in here too long. We will start heading back up towards the surface. As best I can tell, we must be five or six stories below."

We had gone up and down so many flights of stairs that I hadn't realised how far below the surface we were. If the tunnels collapsed, we would be crushed. The earth must be so heavy that surely even the smallest of cracks could be dangerous. We should move faster. We had to get out before this whole place came tumbling down.

I caught my toe and would have fallen flat on my face if Renni, who was right behind me, hadn't moved so quickly to grab me around the waist. Ahead of us, Intef turned briefly to check what had happened, but seeing that I was apparently fine, he kept moving.

"What were you doing?" Renni asked. "You were looking at the ceiling."

"Checking for cracks."

Heat rose to my cheeks although I wasn't sure why I was

so embarrassed. It wasn't unreasonable to check whether the roof was about to collapse.

"Keep going. This place has probably been here for hundreds of years. We don't need to worry about it falling in on top of us."

We went up, along another passageway, then up again. Eventually we reached a door. Intef and Renni looked at each other.

"I will go first," Intef said. "If there's anyone inside, they might feel less threatened by a one-armed man."

The chamber was empty. A door on the far side led to another passageway, with several chambers branching off it. One of the doors was open and from within the chamber came the sounds of snoring.

We tiptoed along the passage and up the stairs at the end. Another passageway, more chambers, more stairs. Eventually a door led us outside.

THIRTEEN

Surely we had been in the tunnels for hours, but the sky was still dark with not even a hint of sunrise. I dropped my pack and took a deep breath of the cold night air. I felt like I had been holding my breath for hours.

"Oh, it is a relief to be out of there," Istnofret said. "I don't know how they can bear to live like that. Can we rest for a few minutes? My legs are so tired."

"No time, I am afraid." Intef's voice was terse. "We don't know where Arnuwanda and his men are. I want to be well away from here before they realise we are no longer in the tunnels."

He led us across the field. It was only as I looked back that I realised how far we had come. We had crossed right under the plain and perhaps even further.

"Do you think we're on the edge of the village?" Behenu asked.

"No way to tell," Intef said. "Those tunnels could go for leagues yet."

"So we head north," Renni said. "We will cross the road sooner or later."

"We will walk until sunrise," Intef said.

"What about the horses?" I asked.

Intef shook his head. "We cannot risk it. We will have to leave them."

I was sorry to leave Nedjem, although I knew he was right. We set off, but despite our brisk pace it wasn't long before I was shivering.

"We can stop for a moment if you need to get a blanket out of your pack," Intef said to me. "You could wrap it around your shoulders."

"I am f-f-fine." My teeth chattered so hard I could barely speak.

Intef stopped walking. "There's no point continuing if everyone is so cold. We get too cold, we won't think properly and that's when we'll make a mistake. Better that we stop and warm up."

"Could we have a fire?" Like me, Istnofret had her arms wrapped around her. Her face was red with the cold.

Intef and Renni looked at each other, considering. Renni was the first to shrug.

"It is not going to matter how far away we are if we freeze to death," he said. "If we were to stumble across Arnuwanda right now, we're too cold to defend ourselves properly."

"I have seen no sign of anyone following," Intef conceded. "Let's get a fire started and we'll rest until dawn."

Renni offered to take the first watch. I slept uneasily, waking every time the fire crackled. When Istnofret shook my shoulder, I jumped.

"Samun," she whispered. "It is time to leave."

"Why are you whispering?"

"Renni said we should be quiet. He says sound will carry easily in this place."

Behenu passed around the last of our bread and we ate as we walked. The foggy morning cleared into a crisp day with the kind of brilliant blue sky that reminded me of Egypt. I felt a pang of longing for hot sand beneath my toes, a warm breeze sweeping in over the desert, sunlight glinting off every surface until I had to squint to see. We kept careful watch for any sign of being followed but saw nothing. It seemed we had eluded Arnuwanda. For now, at least.

The landscape here was still jagged and sparse although devoid of the enormous rocks they carved out as homes. We found game enough to keep us fed once our supplies ran out. We saw no more of the Tigris, although whether it was because that river had reached its end or the road had merely deviated away from it, we didn't know. There were sufficient streams along our way that we didn't go thirsty for too long. At length a river crossed our path. Its water was a murky brown and even as thirsty as I was, I wasn't inclined to drink it.

"Intef, didn't you say the last river was supposed to be muddy?" Behenu asked as we walked along its banks, looking for a shallower place to cross. "We must be almost there."

Intef stared out at the brown water. "I suppose this could be it. It is certainly muddier than any other we have seen."

"Can you smell the sea yet?" Istnofret asked.

Behenu closed her eyes and took a deep breath. "Not yet. The air is changing, though."

Intef must have seen the disappointment on Istnofret's face.

"That doesn't mean we aren't almost there," he said. "We knew only that the last river would be muddy. We don't know how far from Sardis we are."

Istnofret gave him a small smile but didn't seem cheered by

his words. We were all thoroughly sick of travelling. We had obtained more horses at one of the towns we passed through, but my new horse was not as sweet as Nedjem and we took an instant dislike to each other.

We walked some way to the east before we found a place shallow enough to wade the horses through. The water was only knee deep here, but even so, I was drenched up to mid-thigh by the time we reached the other bank. My pants clung to my legs. I pulled off my boots to pour the water out of them, then set them on a rock to dry. I rubbed my lower back. It had ached all morning and my legs were tired, even though I had done no more than sit on my horse.

"Should we keep going?" Renni asked. "We might be able to reach Sardis by nightfall. I would kill for a night under a roof and a meal that isn't wild-caught game."

"Let's at least wait until our boots dry," Istnofret said.

"I'll make a fire," Intef said, already looking around for a suitable spot. "We need to dry out and warm up anyway. Let's plan to spend the night here. Hopefully we'll be at Sardis tomorrow."

We women agreed, possibly a little too enthusiastically, and I didn't miss the hurt that flashed across Renni's face. He said nothing, though, only that he would go hunt for our dinner.

"Is Renni well?" I asked Istnofret as we searched for firewood.

"He has been out of sorts for the last few days. Says he is a soldier, not some travelling tinker. He is longing to set down roots again. At least we don't have much further to go."

"When I find my Eye, we can all go back to Egypt."

I collected a bundle of dry sticks and it took some time to notice that Istnofret stared at me.

"What?"

"Your Eye?"

"What do you mean?"

"You just said that when you find *your* Eye, we can go home."

"Did I? I didn't notice. You know what I mean, though."

She didn't comment again and when we had collected as many sticks as we could find, we took them back to where Intef had built a fire pit.

Istnofret kept shooting me worried looks all afternoon, which annoyed me so much that I went to bed as soon as we had eaten. I wrapped myself in my blanket and lay where I couldn't see her. My belly was larger now and it was increasingly difficult to find a comfortable position on the ground. Intef came to crouch beside me.

"My love, are you well?" he asked softly.

"I am fine," I said, a little snappily, even though it wasn't him I was annoyed with.

"Is the babe unsettled?"

"The babe is fine. Why do you always assume there is something wrong with her?"

His steady inhalation told me I had irritated him and he was trying to calm himself. Why did he always need to be calm? Why couldn't he ever let go and say what he really thought? I wrapped the blanket tighter around me and shut my eyes. If I pretended he wasn't there long enough, he would go away.

"I have suggested before that we should find somewhere to stay until the babe is born," he said. "Perhaps it is time to consider that again. After such a long journey, three more months is nothing. I think we should stay in Sardis until the birth."

I squeezed my eyes shut tighter. If I stayed perfectly still, he would think I was already asleep and hadn't heard him. He was like a buzzing insect sometimes, always turning up at the moment I most wanted to be left alone. Eventually he went away.

We broke camp early the next morning and my mood was dark. Nobody asked how I felt, which rather surprised me. Surely they had noticed how irritable I was yesterday? Did not one of my companions care enough to ask?

Intef set a slower pace than usual, and the realisation that he likely thought I couldn't keep up had me fuming. It wasn't like I needed them anyway. I could find the Eye by myself. Besides, it was clear that I was the only one who would be able to wield it. The others were wasting their lives tagging around after me. Not that I supposed they had anything better to do. But I certainly didn't need them following me once I had found the Eye. I would take it back to Egypt myself and once I was pharaoh, things would change.

Eventually I realised that Behenu rode beside me. How long had she been there? Had I been muttering to myself? I probably looked like a crazy woman.

"We have made a decision," she said.

I shot her a sour look. "Go on."

"We will wait in Sardis until the babe is born."

"Intef's idea, I assume?"

"We all agreed."

"Do I have no say in this?"

She gave me a cautious look and seemed to weigh up her words before she spoke. "You are... not yourself at the moment, and we have made the decision we think is best for you."

"I cannot afford to sit around for three months."

"The Eye will still be there in a few months. Delivering the babe safely is more important."

"I will go on by myself."

"Intef thought you would say that. He says none of us will travel past Sardis until the babe is born."

"Intef has no right to decide for me. I will go by myself if you're all too afraid to go any further. Stay in Sardis. I don't need any of you."

"He only wants what is best for both you and the babe."

"Intef is a coward. You're all cowards. Why didn't Intef tell me this himself?"

"We knew you wouldn't be happy. I am sorry."

She clicked at her horse and rode on to catch up with the others.

Sometime later Istnofret dropped back to ride beside me. She said nothing for a long time and finally I snapped at her.

"Well, go on, then. You wouldn't be here if you didn't have something to say."

She gave me a measured look. "You promised once that if I told you something in particular, you would listen. I hold you to that promise now."

"Don't be obscure. Speak plainly and tell me what you want."

"Maia warned that as you got closer to the Eye, you might start to want it for yourself."

"That's ridiculous."

"Do you not remember Maia's warning?"

"Of course I do, but I never said anything about wanting the Eye for myself."

"Maybe you haven't explicitly said it, but I think that is what's happening."

"You're just like Maia, thinking I am looking for power."

"You promised you would listen if I told you."

"I am listening, aren't I?"

"No, I don't think you are. You hear my words, but you aren't really listening to them."

"You are being obscure again."

"Let me say this plainly then. We know the Eye is powerful. We don't know exactly how powerful or how far its reach stretches, but I believe it twists your mind. It makes you want its power for your own glory. Maia warned this would happen and you promised to listen when I told you."

"Are you in agreement with Intef that we should stay in Sardis?"

"Don't change the subject. I want to know that you've heard what I said."

"I heard you." I didn't even try to keep the irritation from my voice. "I don't know what you expect from me, though."

"You need to be careful. We have no idea what the Eye could make you do. You need to be on guard against it twisting your thoughts or affecting your actions."

She left before I could reply, guiding her horse over to walk beside Renni's. I wasn't sorry to be left to ride alone. Was this how my friends saw me? Craving power? Wanting the Eye for myself?

It wasn't until sometime later that I realised what I had been thinking before Behenu came to talk to me. I had been picturing myself on the throne — not as queen but as pharaoh.

FOURTEEN

We reached Sardis only to discover that it wasn't on the coast like we had expected. After much debate — and a fierce argument between Intef and I — we decided to spend the night here and leave the decision of whether to travel further until the morning. Intef insisted that we wouldn't be boarding any ship for Crete until the babe was born. I was equally insistent that I wouldn't wait.

At Sardis, we quickly found accommodation, thanks to the fact that we encountered several people who spoke Egyptian. In fact, there seemed to be people of all nationalities here, although the greatest proportion was Greeks. I had never learned any Greek, not expecting it to be a language I might have any use for.

I was up early the next morning, having slept little due to being too busy thinking about all the things I intended to say to Intef. Nobody else was awake and I suddenly realised this might be my chance to slip away. I would find my way to Smyrna, the coastal town from which the ships departed. Surely once I got that far, it would be an easy enough matter to convince a captain heading to Crete to take me with him. The voyage would only take a few days and I still had a whole handful of jewels with which to pay my way. It would be easier to go on alone than to spend the day arguing with Intef about it.

"Where are you going?" Intef asked as I slipped out the door.

"For a walk." My tone was curt. I wanted him to know I was still angry with him.

He started to get up from his mat. "Wait a moment while I dress. I will come with you."

"I don't need an escort and, in fact, if you intend to badger me, I would much prefer to go alone."

I expected him to put up more of a fight, but he merely gave me a dark look and lay back down again.

"Suit yourself."

My conscience was heavy as I closed the door quietly behind me. Intef would blame himself for not going with me when he realised I had left, but I couldn't afford to worry about it right now. I would make things right with him once I had the Eye. That was the only thing that was important.

There were plenty of people up and about already. I stopped a man who looked Egyptian and was pleased to find that we did indeed speak the same language. When I enquired as to which direction Smyrna lay, he looked down to my belly.

"Surely you don't intend to walk? It is fifteen leagues."

I tried to hide my dismay. "I have travelled a long way already. Another day or two is nothing."

He shook his head. "I could walk it in two days, but you won't. Not in your condition."

"I need to be there as soon as possible. Today, if I can."

"It can be done in a day, but only with fresh horses along the way."

I took a deep breath. Maia had said the gods would put obstacles in my path. This was just one more.

"How else can I get there?"

He considered me for a long moment.

"I know someone who will be heading that way later this morning. He is taking a load of grain and I cannot think that he would object to you riding in the cart with it if you can provide your own food along the way. He will be in Smyrna in about a week."

"Is there no faster option? A carriage perhaps? I have means to pay whatever the cost is."

He started to eye me suspiciously.

"Even the fastest carriage won't get you to Smyrna today."

"There must be a way."

"What are you running from? Your husband? Your master?"

"I have neither. I am travelling alone."

"Hmm." He didn't look like he believed me.

"Please, is there some other means of transport you can suggest?"

"You could try the courier. He will have fresh horses along the way. Probably get you there late tonight."

"Will you take me to him?"

The courier who transported mail and small packages between Sardis and Smyrna was a Greek who spoke no Egyptian. The man helping me knew only a smattering of Greek words himself, but between those and some vigorous sign language we managed to convey my request. The courier eyed me somewhat suspiciously and turned his face to spit on the road. He shook his head and started to walk away.

"Please."

I fished in the pouch where I had been keeping my jewels since swapping my travelling gown for hide pants. I retrieved a gem and offered it to the Greek. It was a pretty blue sapphire, one of six from a bracelet I had favoured, and I would be sorry to give it up. He barely glanced at it before making a peculiar motion with his hand.

"He says you must pay more," the Egyptian said.

"More? Does he realise how much this is worth?"

"Do you want to ride with him or not?"

With a sigh, I retrieved another sapphire.

"That is all I have."

I had been foolish to show I had such wealth and where I kept it.

The Greek held out his hand. I dropped the sapphires onto his palm.

The courier's cart was already hitched to two horses and it seemed I had caught him only just in time. There was barely room for a body amongst the various sacks and crates. He shifted things around to make a little space for me, although not without many grunts and groans at the extra work I caused him. I managed to haul myself up into the cart and settled in for a long ride.

The rhythmic jolting of the cart sent me into a light doze. The babe was restless today and constantly wriggled. I woke every now and then when she delivered a particularly strong kick.

"You don't like the jolting, do you?" I murmured to her, although I doubted she could hear me over the noise of the horses and cart. "Once we are on the ship, you'll be able to rest."

She kicked again, as if in disagreement, and I grinned a

little as I rubbed my belly. She was feisty, this babe. A fighter. She would need to be with what the gods had in store for her.

We stopped regularly to change the horses, but even so, the sun was well past set before the cart jolted to a stop and the courier came around the back.

"Smyrna," he muttered at me, or that was what I thought he said through his indecipherable accent.

He didn't offer to help me and I extricated myself from the cart with great difficulty. My legs were cramped, my back ached, and I was so hungry I could barely think. The courier waited only until my feet were on the ground before he set off again. I stared after him in surprise. Was the man not even going to help me find accommodation for the night? I supposed he figured he had done what I paid for. He had gotten me to Smyrna. The rest was up to me.

He had deposited me at the harbour, which was surprisingly busy for such an hour with several ships apparently preparing to depart in the morning. Men rushed everywhere, crates were being loaded, and a family that looked like they might be passengers waited to board. I looked for anyone who appeared to be Egyptian and spotted a nearby woman.

"Are any of these ships bound for Crete?" I asked.

She pointed. "That one. She will be leaving at dawn."

"Do you know where the captain is?"

"Haven't seen him all day. Probably won't do you much good anyway unless you speak Greek."

"Does he have any crew who are Egyptian?"

"They're all Greek. He doesn't trust anyone who isn't and I hear he has a particular dislike for Egyptians. Something to do with a battle years ago in which one of his ancestors was killed."

So there was little chance of convincing the captain to take me to Crete, even if I could communicate with him. I considered my options as I walked a little further along the harbour. A wave of dizziness made me stumble. It had been far too long since I had eaten. The babe kicked again.

"Ssh," I whispered to her. "Just a little longer."

Eventually the noise of the docks died down and suddenly there seemed to be nobody around. I supposed they had all gone for dinner and perhaps to enjoy one final night on land. I hadn't expected an opportunity like this.

I tried to walk as if I was meant to be there. The ramp connecting the ship to the dock was rickety and I was halfway across when it wobbled violently. I froze, my heart pounding. The babe kicked and I forced myself to walk on before I was caught. There seemed to be nobody on the boat as I crossed the main deck.

Moonlight through the hatch illuminated enough of the area below deck for me to see that it was filled with orderly rows of crates. They were only piled two or three high but would provide enough cover that I would be out of sight behind them. I needed a spot where I would be safe if the crates shifted. I made my way to the back, feeling a path between the crates since the moonlight didn't shed any light this far in, and eventually found a suitable place in the back corner.

I only needed to stay hidden for a day or two. Once we were that far out to sea, the captain wouldn't want to take me back to Smyrna, even if someone found me. He would have to allow me to stay until we landed, where I would no doubt be unceremoniously removed from the ship. That didn't matter, though. I would have achieved my goal: reaching Crete. I was so close to finding the Eye. Nothing could stop me now.

FIFTEEN

Time passed slowly as I waited in the dark. I was so hungry that food became all I could think of and I passed the time remembering my favourites. Roasted duck, dripping with fat. Soft, creamy cheese. Sweet melon juice, which I hadn't tasted since we left Egypt. Eventually it occurred to me that perhaps some of the crates contained food. After all, the supplies for the crew must be stored somewhere. But before I could haul myself to my feet, I heard footsteps on the deck above. I had missed my chance and would have to wait.

Still, it was another long time before the ship started creaking and shifting. I managed to doze a little, although it was hard to sleep while sitting with my back against the bulkhead and not so much as a blanket for comfort. My hunger had faded, but my mouth was sticky and my throat was so dry I could hardly swallow. I needed to wait until we were well out to sea before I made any sound, or they might be willing to turn back to Smyrna if they found me. The babe wriggled, making sitting increasingly uncomfortable.

"Just a little longer," I whispered to her. "We will be able to get up soon."

I waited and waited. My head was cloudy and the babe continued to kick. The sea seemed rougher than usual and I was queasy from the ship's movement and the lack of fresh air. My back spasmed from sitting on the wooden planks for so long and I couldn't take it a moment longer. I had to roll over onto my hands and knees in order to get up. Before I could get to my feet, the boat suddenly shifted and I was knocked onto my belly. The spell bottle around my neck was burning hot.

"Oh no, oh no. Are you all right?"

The babe responded with a hearty kick and my limbs went weak with relief.

"I am so sorry. I will be more careful."

I managed to get to my feet, but then the boat tilted and I was flung backwards against the crates. A corner dug into my hip. It would undoubtedly leave a bruise. A loud rumble cut through the creaking of the ship and the roar of the waves. Lightning crackled, bright enough for me to see even down here. We had been fortunate on our travels so far. Despite several lengthy ship voyages, we had mostly had fine weather. There had been one or two storms, but nothing severe enough to endanger the ship or throw us off course. So many ships departed port and were never seen again. It seemed my luck had run out this time.

The storm sounded like it was right on top of us. Panic seized me. Nobody knew I was here. If the boat sank, nobody would come to get me. I would drown and Intef would never know what had happened. Why hadn't I waited until I could convince him to come?

"Isis, protect me."

Lightning cracked, even louder this time. The ship groaned.

"Everything is well," I said to the babe. "The ship isn't breaking apart. We would have to hit something for that to happen."

Lightning cracked again, far too close this time. I smelled smoke.

"We need to get up there so they know we're here."

I was tossed from side to side as I made my way between the crates. Many had shifted, and the upper rows had largely toppled off, blocking the previously orderly aisles. At least the lightning gave enough light for me to see by, even if it was just for a moment at a time.

Eventually I managed to get as far as the hatch. I hadn't anticipated how difficult it would be to climb the ladder while being tossed around. Rain splattered against my face and made the ladder slippery. My belly left me off balance and at one point it was all I could do to cling to the ladder and pray that Isis would wrap her wings around me.

"We will be all right," I said to the babe. "You wait and see. We just need to get up there."

I finally managed to scramble the rest of the way up and out through the hatch. I was immediately drenched from the heavy rain. Lightning had struck the mast, splitting it and sending it crashing through the bulkhead so that it dangled in the water. The sea flooded in through the damaged section. Several sections of the deck were aflame, despite the rain.

The crew worked steadily to smother the flames and bail out the water, but even I could see they couldn't possibly succeed. There was nobody who looked like they were in charge. I grabbed the arm of a nearby man.

"What happened?" I asked.

He gave me a blank look and uttered something in a surprised voice. Then he shook off my hand, waved at me to get out of the way, and went back to bailing water.

The gravity of my situation hit me hard. I was on a sinking ship in the middle of the Mediterranean Sea. Nobody knew I was here, not my friends, not even the captain. Only the crewman I had grabbed and he was too busy saving the ship to worry about me.

The ship lurched and I landed hard against the fallen mast. I clung to it. Thunder rumbled and another streak of lightning lit up the sky. The last of the fire seemed to have finally been smothered but the ship was definitely sinking. It creaked and groaned, then lurched again. The stern dipped lower into the water.

"Isis!" My voice was filled with terror. "Save me. Don't let us drown. Let me finish my task."

One by one, the crew seemed to be abandoning their efforts to bail out the water. Most of them were on their knees, praying to whatever gods they worshipped. One man stepped up to the bulkhead. He raised his arms up to the sky and shouted something that sounded like a challenge. Then he dove off the ship and into the sea. If his fellows even noticed, it didn't divert them from their urgent prayers.

As we waited for the ship to sink, the rain finally abated. Dark clouds parted, revealing the tiniest patch of dawn sky. The sun peeked through and its light fell on my skin as I clung to the mast.

"Aten," I whispered. "I know you can see me. Save us. For my father's sake, if not my own. He was ever your most faithful servant."

But if Aten heard me, he didn't respond.

The ship lurched once more and began to sink. Water

lapped around my ankles. Intef would tell me to stay calm and think. There was always a solution. I just had to find it.

I spotted a smaller piece of the mast which had broken off from the main part. Perhaps that would float. If I could hold on long enough, the currents could take me to land. I let go of the mast and reached out, but the ship lurched and threw me off balance.

I landed on my hands and knees with my face in the water. I inhaled at the wrong moment and emerged coughing and spluttering. I couldn't quite catch my breath.

With one final creak, the ship sank beneath the waves. I floundered, reached for something, anything that might float. But there was nothing. My hide pants and coat became unbearably heavy. The waves surged and I sank beneath the surface.

I held my breath for as long as I could. I had a vague idea that swimming involved moving both arms and legs, but although I thrashed and kicked, I continued to sink. The babe kicked hard, as if sensing danger. My spell bottle was a coal against my chest.

There was no way out. I was too far below the surface. I couldn't swim. And I was out of breath.

I stopped thrashing and cradled my belly. Sleep, little one. I am so sorry you never met your father.

Then I couldn't hold my breath any longer. I opened my mouth, gasping, and in rushed the sea water.

Drowning didn't take as long as I had expected.

SIXTEEN

I knew nothingness. Blackness. Stillness. Peace.

Time passed. Or maybe it didn't. I didn't care.

I opened my eyes to a twilight world.

I lay on a sandy shore, staring up into a strange sky. There were no clouds, no sun. Just a grey expanse that stretched as far as I could see. Water rushed over my feet.

It would take too much effort to get up, so I didn't bother. I lay on the sand with the water lapping at my feet. Eventually I realised that sooner or later, the tide would rise. I should move. I had to roll onto my side and get onto my hands and knees before I could get up, but eventually I was on my feet.

It was only then that I realised my gown was dry. Surely it should be soaked through, or at least covered in sand. I ran my hands through my hair, but it too was dry. I couldn't see past my belly to my feet, but even they didn't feel sandy and they certainly weren't wet, despite the waves lapping over them only moments before.

On one side of me lay the ocean. A vast grey expanse,

almost the same colour as the sky. Waves rushed in and out but, strangely, made no sound. On my other side was sand. Nothing but grey sand as far as I could see. No dunes. No shrubs. Not even a bird wheeling through the sky.

There was no breeze, no sound. Nothing but grey sky and grey sea and grey sand.

I walked. I didn't know what else to do. I had to find... something. I wasn't sure what and my head started to hurt when I thought too hard, so I didn't think and simply let my feet take me where they would.

I walked for a long time. Hours, at least. Days perhaps. In all that time, I felt nothing. Neither hunger nor thirst. No pain or fatigue.

I walked along the shore. The sea stretched to my left, the sand to my right, the sky overhead. There was nothing else.

At some point I realised that somebody walked beside me. He had the body of a human, but when I looked up at his face, a falcon's eyes glittered at me.

"Horus?" My voice was croaky, but it worked. It was only after I spoke that I wondered how I knew his name.

He nodded once but made no other reply.

"What is this place?"

He looked out at the sea, then towards the sand, then up at the sky. It seemed to take a long time before he replied.

"It is the other place," he said.

I continued to walk.

"Where was I before I was here?" I asked at length.

"Does it matter? You are not there any longer."

I supposed it didn't matter. Nothing existed in this moment other than this place. Grey sand, grey water, grey sky. And Horus walking beside me.

"Where am I going?"

"Where do you want to go?"

"I don't know."

"Then does it matter?"

I lapsed into silence again, and still we walked.

"I feel like… there is something I need to do."

He turned toward me, but I looked away when he spoke. It was too disconcerting to hear human words coming out of a falcon's beak.

"You can walk for as long as you wish. When you no longer want to walk, you can decide what to do next."

"It is that simple?" Yet my feet kept moving.

"It is your choice."

We walked for days. During that time, I tried to remember what had come before. At length, my feet came to a stop.

"I no longer wish to walk."

Beside me, Horus also stopped. "I can take you to the Hall of Osiris."

"What would I do there?"

Something tugged at my memory, but it was elusive and disappeared before I could grasp it.

"Eat. Drink. Be content."

"No judgement?"

Why could I remember this but nothing else? I was supposed to have my heart weighed at Osiris's court. Say the Negative Confessions. Then I could go to the West.

"One cannot be judged if their body has not been embalmed."

"Why haven't I been embalmed?"

He looked at me steadily. I searched my memory. What had happened to me?

"You were a queen once," he said.

I searched my mind again. Still there was nothing.

"Was I a good queen?"

"Good, bad, indifferent. Does it matter?"

I supposed it didn't. Surely I would have remembered if it was important.

"This is not Osiris's Hall," I said, at last.

"No, it is not."

I waited.

"This is the place where you have the opportunity to choose."

"Choose what?"

"Life," he said. "Or afterlife."

"You mean I could go back?"

"If you wish to. It would be extremely painful, though. Nobody has ever chosen to go back."

"How did I get here?"

"You drowned. In the tenth hour of the night, I collect the souls who drowned."

I had no memory of drowning. Surely that was something I should remember.

"Why?" I asked.

"Why not? How else would you have the chance for an afterlife without your body?"

"So I can go to the Field of Reeds?"

What exactly was the Field of Reeds? I knew the name, but nothing else. It seemed, though, that it was something I should desire.

"You can go to Osiris's hall. You can have an afterlife there, although not a full one. You will feast and relax. Be treated like a queen again."

"But I cannot go to the Field of Reeds." For some reason, this seemed important.

"No." His tone was still patient. How many people had he explained this to before me?

"What if that isn't what I want?"

"What do you want then? To go back?"

Back to what? Perhaps if I could remember what I had left behind, I could decide.

"What would I have to do?"

"You would drown again." His tone held no emotion, as if this was perfectly reasonable. "It will be painful. Drowning is a terrible way to die. Nobody would choose to endure it a second time. Not when they can go on to the Hall of Osiris."

"Why are you giving me the option then? If it is so terrible and nobody ever wants it?"

"You are permitted to choose. Since you cannot have a full afterlife, I give you the choice to return. You can live out the rest of your life, whatever that may be. And maybe when you die again, your body will be embalmed and you will have the chance for a full afterlife."

"But it will be painful."

"Very."

I closed my eyes and probed the blankness in my mind. Surely the memory was still there. How could I forget something so terrible?

"I don't remember. How can I choose if I don't remember?"

Falcon eyes glittered at me. "I can help you, if you wish. Once you remember, I cannot take it away again, though."

"Cannot? Or will not?"

He simply looked at me.

"I want to remember."

He reached for me. "Take my hand."

It was a human hand. Sun-browned, five fingers, cool skin.

The memory rushed back over me like a wave. Sinking down into the water. Holding my breath. The knowledge that I was about to die. Regretting that my babe would never meet her father. My babe! How had I forgotten her?

"If I choose to go back, what will happen to my babe?"

"She will return with you. You are choosing for both of you."

"Is she dead?"

He shrugged, seemingly unconcerned.

"She is as dead as you are."

Whatever that meant.

"I haven't felt her move since I got here."

He looked steadily at me but made no reply. This was of no concern to him.

"If I go to Osiris's Hall, will she come too?"

"She has no life yet. No soul."

"No afterlife?"

Again, he just looked at me.

"Do I have to decide right now?"

"No, we can walk."

"Can we sit down?"

"Best to keep walking. You don't want to stop for too long in this place."

We walked. Days later, I thought of another question.

"How painful is it to go back? Will it be the same as drowning the first time?"

"It is ten times more painful."

I walked a little longer.

"I don't remember how painful it was. The memory you gave me was only the realisation that I was drowning."

"Are you sure you want to remember the pain? I cannot take it away again."

"How can I judge whether I can withstand ten times that if I don't remember it?"

The memory that flooded me this time left me retching. As it receded, I found myself on my knees in the sand, the water lapping halfway up my thighs. My whole body trembled. I tried to push the memory away, but it kept coming back. Over and over I remembered the pain of drowning.

"We should keep walking," Horus said, eventually.

I staggered to my feet. He didn't offer to help me.

We walked until I composed myself. The memory was a little less sharp now. I supposed we had walked for a long time.

"How can I handle ten times that pain?"

"That is why nobody ever chooses to go back."

"How long have I been here?"

"There is no time in this place."

"Are there other people here? People like me who have drowned?"

The falcon eyes glittered at me, but he didn't answer.

"If I decide not to go back, will you take me to Osiris's Hall immediately?"

"Immediately. Later. Some time. Like I said, time does not exist here. You will go when you go."

"But if I go, my babe will not live?"

He didn't respond. He had, after all, already answered this question.

"If I choose to go back, will my babe suffer? Will it be ten times as painful for her as well?"

"It will be for her as it is for you."

How could I put her through that? How could I make this

decision for both of us? Either I had an afterlife and my babe did not, or we both experienced pain beyond anything I could imagine.

"Do I have a reason to go back?"

"You have as much information as you are permitted."

"How can I decide without knowing that?"

He tilted his head to the side as he considered me. His face showed no expression and I had no sense of what he thought. At length, he looked away and didn't respond.

I wanted to cry or shout or stomp my feet. Anything to provoke a reaction in him.

"This is not fair. You have all of the information I need. I cannot make a decision until you share it with me."

"We will walk until you decide."

"Surely there are others who have drowned? Others who need to make a decision?"

"Keep walking."

I hadn't realised I had stopped. If I had drowned, I had obviously been in water. But what kind of water? A pond? A river? An ocean? I reviewed the memory he had given me. I had sunk down, deep down. Too deep for a pond or a river. So I must have been on a ship. Perhaps it had sunk or I had fallen overboard. Perhaps I had been thrown off. But if I was on a ship, I had been travelling somewhere. I had been going to do something. A task that would never be completed unless I went back. Had it been important? I was a queen so it likely was.

In the end, it was the babe that decided it for me. She would have neither life nor afterlife if I didn't go back. I could only hope she wouldn't remember the tenfold pain we would endure. Or that if she did, she would forgive me.

"I want to go back."

Horus stopped walking and turned to face me.

"Are you very certain?"

"I am."

He inclined his head towards me.

"Very well, then."

As the water rushed in over me, I held my breath for as long as I could.

SEVENTEEN

I lay on a sandy shore, staring up into a blue sky. Gulls wheeled overhead and their screeching was deafening. The sun was too bright. My eyes watered. Everything hurt. Cold water rushed over my feet.

A shadow fell over me and a man obscured my view of the sky. He spoke rapidly, but I understood none of it. He looked around, called out to someone, his hands waving as he spoke. Then I was surrounded by people. Their chatter was too loud. I couldn't see the sky anymore.

The babe kicked, suddenly and hard. I wrapped my arms around my belly. It was only then that I realised I was soaked.

"Ssh, little one," I whispered. "It is done now. We are well."

Arms reached for me and pulled me to my feet. My legs couldn't bear my weight so a man on either side held me up and helped me to walk. They took me to a nearby house where I was lowered onto a bed mat. Someone removed my sodden clothes and wrapped a blanket around me. They placed a cushion beneath my head. I stared up at a whitewashed ceiling. The room spun and I closed my eyes. When I woke, a woman sat cross-legged on the floor beside me.

"How do you feel?" she asked.

I was surprised to find I understood her. Still it took me some time to make my mouth work.

"I... hurt. Everything hurts."

"Where did you come from? How long had you been lying there before anyone noticed?"

"I don't know."

Already the memory was fading. Had I really walked on a sandy shore with Horus? Did I really drown? Or had I dreamed it all?

"Were you swimming?"

It wasn't a dream. The memory was almost gone, but I still remembered the pain. I had drowned. Twice.

"The ship sank."

She shook her head, confusion on her face.

"What ship? And why? We have had perfect weather of late."

"It was a Greek ship. Sailing for Crete."

"Surely you don't mean the *Artemis*? It sank during a storm. We found wreckage and bodies washed up on the shore. There were no survivors."

"I don't know what it was called. They didn't know I was on board. Nobody knew."

"It cannot have been the *Artemis*. That was weeks ago."

My lungs hurt and I couldn't seem to manage both breathing and talking at the same time. I didn't know whether the ship I stowed away on was the *Artemis* or not. It didn't seem to matter anyway. The ship had sunk and I survived. That was all anyone needed to know.

There was more to it, though. Something about what I had done to survive, but the memory was gone. I closed my eyes and tried to find it again. Sand. All I could remember was sand and the eyes of a falcon.

EIGHTEEN

The day was late before Intef arrived. I had been lying on the mat, trying to rest. The babe was unsettled and constantly kicking. It felt like she had an elbow lodged on my bladder. She had grown, seemingly overnight, and my belly was bigger than ever.

He must have made some small sound that alerted me to his presence. I opened my eyes and there he was. Standing in the doorway, tears rolling down his cheeks. He dashed them away with the back of his hand.

"Intef."

My mind was suddenly blank. I should have spent the time planning what I would say. Why I had left without telling him.

"Where have you been?" he asked.

"Come in. Sit beside me."

"Not until you answer my question."

The coldness in his voice took me aback. I had expected he would be pleased to see me safe. Maybe a little angry, but not this. After all, I was well, wasn't I? So was the babe, and we had come back to him. That must have been my plan all along anyway. My memory of deciding to leave Sardis was hazy, but surely I had planned to retrieve the Eye and then come back for my friends? I wouldn't have gone on without them. Not without Intef, and not with a babe on the way.

"I don't know," I said.

"You're not going to tell me? You disappear without a word, and then weeks later you come back and you won't say where you went?"

"I would tell you if I could."

Sand. Falcon eyes. I had to hold onto those images. They could tell me where I had been if I could make sense of them.

"Dear Montu, you're still playing at being the queen, aren't you? Thinking you don't need to explain yourself to the lowly servants who trudge along after you?"

"Intef, you're not being fair."

"Fair? What is fair about what you did?"

"How long was I gone?"

He took so long to answer that I thought he wasn't going to.

"Eight weeks," he said, at last.

"Eight weeks? How is that possible?" No small wonder then that the babe had grown.

"You tell me. Did you find it then? Was it worth it?"

"Find what?"

"The Eye. I presume you went off to find it on your own."

"I don't remember where I was, Intef. I swear it."

He sighed.

"This isn't making any sense, Samun. Just tell me the truth about where you've been. I cannot promise I won't be angry, but I will at least try to understand why you left me."

"Please come in and sit down. I will tell you as much as I remember."

He did, although reluctantly. I told him about stowing away on the ship. The storm. The realisation that I was going to drown. Waking up drenched on the beach. The fading memory of sand and a falcon's eyes. It was almost gone now. I wasn't even sure if it was a memory or a dream or just a thought. He was quiet for a long time after I finished.

"The falcon eyes. Do you think it has anything to do with Horus?"

Had I met Horus? Asked him about the Eye? Had I forgotten some precious piece of information we needed?

"Was I really gone for eight weeks?"

Intef looked away, maybe blinking back more tears.

"Why are you still here then? Why didn't you go on to Crete?"

"We were waiting. In case you came back."

"How long did you intend to wait?"

"Until you came back to me." His voice broke. "I thought… I was sure that if you had died, I would know. I would have felt it. So I knew you were out there somewhere and I hoped you would come back when you could."

"Intef, I am sorry."

"Istnofret tried to tell you and you wouldn't listen."

She had said I wanted the Eye for myself. Months ago, when we had barely started on our journey, I had promised that if she told me that, I would listen. But I hadn't.

"I will listen now. I promise. Something happened to me, Intef. I don't know what, but it was something big."

"And the babe? Is she well?"

"She has been kicking ever since I woke up on the beach. She is fine as far as I can tell. Here, put your hand here. You can feel her kick."

He smiled, although it was a sad smile. I wasn't sure why.

"She must be very close to being born," he said. "Your belly is much bigger than I remember."

I rubbed my hands over it. "I feel like a hippopotamus."

"You look exhausted. Let's get you home. Do you think you can walk or should I find a cart?"

"I can walk." Maybe.

He managed to haul me up, although it was no easy task with me being so heavy and him only having one arm. At last, I was on my feet. My knees buckled and he grabbed my waist to steady me.

"Is it far?" I asked.

"Just a couple of blocks."

Supported by his arm around my waist, I hobbled to the place they had called home for the last eight weeks. Twice I had to stop and lean against a wall. There was nowhere to sit other than the road itself. I wouldn't have minded so much had there been a less embarrassing way to get to my feet than being bodily hauled up by Intef.

The others waited in the house's main chamber. It was small, only two chambers in all, and Istnofret later told me they were paying an exorbitant amount for it. But since they had tracked me here before my trail disappeared, Intef had insisted they stay in Smyrna.

"He was sure you would come back," Istnofret said, through tears. "Even when the rest of us thought you had been murdered, he knew you would return."

"You thought I had been murdered?"

"Well, not me. I thought…"

"Tell me, Ist."

"I thought you had gone to find the Eye by yourself. That the wanting had gotten so bad you couldn't resist it."

Had I been that obvious? My cheeks heated as I searched for a response.

"You tried to tell me, but I didn't listen."

She gave me an appraising look. "Will you listen next time?"

"I will try. I didn't know, Ist. I had no idea how powerful it was. But something inside of me suddenly *wanted* the Eye so badly, I would have done anything to get it. It didn't matter who I hurt along the way."

An image flashed into my mind. Myself offering up my babe to Osiris. Did the Eye make me do it? I had always assumed I would make the decision, but maybe the Eye gave me no choice.

"It might get worse the closer we get to the Eye. If you cannot resist it now, how will you resist it when we reach Crete? Or when you actually have the Eye?"

"I don't know. I can only be more aware of how it affects me."

"We can help you with that, if you will actually listen."

"I will try."

She gave me a sceptical look. "I know you think that now, but you seem to keep forgetting."

"I promise, Ist. I really will try."

She shook her head and changed the subject.

"Intef was devastated when we realised you were gone."

"Do you think he will ever forgive me?"

"He is going to have to. After all, the babe must be due any day now."

"A couple of weeks yet, I think. If I was really gone for eight weeks."

"So what now? We were going to wait in Sardis until the babe was born."

"I need to get to Crete as soon as possible. Maybe I can rest for a day first, but then I must go. Once the babe is born, it might be some time before I can travel. If I go now, maybe I can find the Eye before she comes." I hesitated before saying more, but she deserved to know. They all did, but so far Intef was the only one I had told. "I think I met Horus."

"You did?" She gave me an odd look, as if wondering whether to believe me.

"When I woke up on the beach, I remembered seeing a falcon's eyes."

"Did he tell you where the Eye is?"

"If he did, I have forgotten."

"How could you forget something like that? We have been searching for it for months."

"Maybe I wasn't supposed to remember. Or maybe it wasn't Horus at all. It might just be my mind playing tricks with me."

"And you remember nothing else of where you've been?"

"Sand. That's the only other thing. Sand and falcon eyes. I think I remembered more when I first woke up, but it is gone now."

"Maybe you were there on the beach all along. Maybe Horus hid you while you were talking to him."

"For eight weeks? What could he possibly have to say to me that would take so long?"

"If you cannot remember, I suppose we will never know."

"I don't think Intef will ever trust me again. He is always going to be watching me out of the corner of his eye. Waiting for me to slip away again."

"You think he doesn't already?" she asked with a laugh. "He has been doing that since you were, what, five years old?"

"But before he did it to keep me safe. Now it is because he

thinks I am going to disappear and take his daughter with me."

"Well, the babe will be here before we know it." Her tone was suddenly brisk and all business. "So you need to decide quickly whether you're going to stay here in Smyrna until the birth."

"I've already decided. I need to find the Eye before the babe is born."

Could I avoid the fate in which I offered her up to Osiris if I already had the Eye? Or would it merely push me back to the other fate, the one I thought I had avoided when I escaped the Hittite army?

"I'll tell Renni to go find out when the next ship is departing for Crete then. You'll have to tell Intef yourself. He is not going to be happy."

NINETEEN

Istnofret was right. Intef was furious when I told him I wanted to set out again for Crete as soon as I recovered. He tried to hide his anger behind a mask of reason, but I knew him well enough to see through it.

We probably would have argued about it all night, except that Renni returned with news of a ship heading to Crete in two days. As I was preparing for bed later that evening, Behenu slipped into the chamber. Her face was pale and her eyes red.

"I am not sure we should take Mau to Crete." Her voice wobbled.

"Behenu, we cannot leave her here."

"She is not well."

"She is a little skinnier than when I saw her last, but I am sure she will be fine."

Indeed, I had been alarmed when I saw Mau today. Her hip bones jutted out sharply and each rib was visible. She seemed to have little energy and even less appetite. I had pretended not to watch the way Behenu tried to coax her to eat.

"She has gotten much frailer over the last few weeks. Maybe we should find someone here who will look after her. Someone kind."

"I don't know if I can bear to leave her behind. She was Sadeh's cat."

"I don't think she will survive another sea voyage."

I closed my eyes, which had suddenly filled with tears. I seemed to be crying all the time these days.

"Let me think about it overnight. I cannot... It is not a decision that should be rushed."

Behenu headed for the door but paused to look back at me.

"I am only thinking about what's best for Mau. It will hurt terribly to leave her, but I think we must."

I barely slept for worrying about Mau. As dawn arrived, I decided that despite Behenu's words, I couldn't leave her behind. Mau would come with us to Crete and then we would take her home. I would not leave Sadeh's cat in a foreign land.

"I have decided," I said to Behenu as we sat down to breakfast. "About Mau."

Tears trembled on her lashes. "I am not sure that it matters. She didn't come to sleep with me last night. I haven't seen her since dinner."

We searched the house. Mau must have found a cozy place to hide and fallen into a deep sleep. She was a bit deaf these days and likely didn't hear us calling for her.

It was Renni who found her body. He brought her to us, carefully cradled in his arms.

"She found a spot in a warm barn not far away," he said. "She looked so peaceful."

We buried her in a sunny spot in the little garden behind the house they had been living in. I wanted to have her embalmed, but although Renni asked around, there seemed to be nobody here who knew how to do such a thing. I stood over her grave and cried for a while, grieving as much for the loss of Mau as for feeling that I had betrayed Sadeh by leaving her cat here.

"Sadeh wouldn't think that," Intef said. He stood with his arm around me and waited patiently while I cried.

"She might. I let her down in so many ways. This is just one more."

"You're too hard on yourself. We've been through this before. I thought you had let it go."

He was, of course, referring to the way Sadeh died, when she had dressed up as me and gone to face Ay in my place. He had ordered her to be killed and Intef had done it himself so that it would be quick. I too thought I had long since made my peace with it, but Mau's death stirred up old feelings of anger and inadequacy.

Behenu disappeared shortly after we finished burying Mau and we didn't see her again until evening when she slipped back into the house, her eyes red and swollen.

"Behenu, I was worried about you." Istnofret's tone was very gentle, as if she thought the girl would break. "I know Mau was dear to you."

Behenu seemed to shudder a little as she swallowed a sob. "I thought her time was near. Just not quite this near."

"She had some marvellous adventures," Istnofret said. "I wonder if there has ever been another cat in the whole history of the world who travelled as far as Mau did."

"That is true," Behenu said, with something that could have been either a laugh or a sob. "She was a very well-travelled cat."

"We should drink to her memory tonight." Renni wrapped his arm around Behenu's shoulders. "To her and to Sadeh."

Our meal that evening was a somber affair, despite Renni's attempts to lift our spirits. Intef said little and I wondered whether Sadeh was on his mind as much as mine. Did he feel guilt over her death, despite his honourable reasons? I still felt guilty for killing Thrax sometimes, although I did it to save him from a worse fate and to save those he might have taken to the West with him. As Intef and I lay together on our mats, sleep seemed a long way away.

"You are thinking so hard I can almost feel it," Intef said, eventually.

He rolled onto his side to face me. I could barely see his outline in the chamber's darkness. I was reluctant to share my thoughts, even with him.

"It is nothing."

"Don't shut me out, my love. Last time you did that, you disappeared for eight weeks. Tell me what you are thinking."

"I am just..." I sighed. Where did I begin? "I am sad about Mau."

He waited in silence. I should have known he wouldn't let me off that easily.

"I've been thinking about Sadeh a lot tonight."

"Me too. She would be pleased that Mau has been so well cared for."

"It was all Behenu. I hardly ever did anything for her."

"Behenu loved her. She was happy to look after Mau, and I think it kept her from feeling too alone when you and I had each other, and Renni and Istnofret had each other."

"I always felt a little guilty."

"About Mau?"

"That I didn't pay much attention to her. But Behenu was always there, fussing over her. So I didn't really think too much about it. Now I wish I had given her more attention."

"I think Mau was quite happy with what she had. She was very much a one-woman cat, and it was Behenu's lap she always went to."

"Behenu…" I searched for the right words. "She must be terribly sad."

"I am sure she is."

We lapsed into silence for a while and I tried to find the courage for what I needed to say.

"Intef."

"Mm."

"Would you hate me if… if I knew something was going to happen and I didn't tell you."

"Something will happen to you?"

"No."

"To me?"

"No."

"I am too tired for guessing games, my love. What are you talking about?"

I already regretted having said even that much.

"Samun?" he prodded, when I didn't reply.

"If I knew that something would happen, and it would really upset you. Would you hate me if I didn't warn you?"

"You have seen something in your dreams?"

I nodded, forgetting for a moment that he couldn't see me.

"Yes."

"You have said before that you don't like to talk about them. That you see two futures but that it goes wrong when you try to push towards one. Has something changed?"

"No, it always goes wrong."

"Then why are you fretting about it? If the gods have already determined what is to pass, there is no point in lying awake worrying. What will come, will come, and we will face it better if we are well rested."

He seemed to fall asleep soon after, but I lay awake long into the night. The fate in which I passed my newborn babe over to a green-faced god seemed closer than ever. Would Intef hate me when he realised what I would have to do? Was there any choice left? Had I escaped the other fate when I ran away from the Hittite army? That fate — the one in which I saw myself bound in a dark chamber — had always had a sense of death about it. I had thought that neither me nor the babe survived.

I had only seen the merest glimpse of my babe in the other dream, but if she survived her birth, if she drew breath — however briefly — she had the chance of an afterlife, whatever her fate in this world was. Would Intef ever understand that? The babe stirred and I rubbed my belly to soothe her.

"Sleep, little one," I whispered.

I had no idea what could happen to make me give my babe to Osiris. Why would a mother do such a thing? What could possibly be so important that I would give her up? I pushed away the growing suspicion that perhaps I traded her for something. For the Eye.

I suddenly *wanted* this child. I wanted her to survive, to live, to grow up. To do all the things that poor little Setau never had the chance to. I had never really thought about the babe like this. She had been an inevitability, with her future fixed in one of two fates, but something had happened to me while I was gone. I felt like I had made a momentous decision, only I had forgotten it. The urge to protect my babe was strong and I wrapped my arms around my belly.

I won't let you go, I whispered to her. Damn the gods and their dreams. Damn Osiris. I will be the one who decides your fate, and I am not giving you up.

TWENTY

The ship we departed Smyrna on was solid and well-built. Like the *Artemis,* she was crewed by Greeks who understood nothing of what we said. But an Egyptian man had translated a conversation between them and us, and they understood we wanted passage to Crete. It seemed they needed to know nothing else, for they paid us no further attention once the terms of our voyage were established. *Hestia* their ship was called and the name rang vaguely in the depths of my memory.

It wasn't until we were well away from Smyrna and out on the open sea that I recalled where I knew the name from: Thrax had mentioned Hestia as the goddess his mother worshipped. Definitely an omen of some sort, but I wasn't yet sure whether it was good or bad.

We had clear weather as we sailed, although I watched the sky nervously. I took comfort in the spell bottle around my neck which remained ice cold. Those brief flashes of memory I had woken with on the beach were gone. The sand, the falcon eyes. I kept reminding myself of them, but the memories themselves were gone. Were they important? Had I really spoken with Horus? Had he told me where the Eye was?

As we approached Crete ten days later, I was surprised to discover it was an island. I had known, of course, then somehow forgot. After so long travelling through vast landscapes, it was startling that our final destination was no more than a few leagues across.

"Surely if the Eye is still here, we will find it," Istnofret said, as she and I stood at the bow, staring out at the island ahead of us. "It is not that big. We can search every cubit of it, if we must."

"We must be careful not to underestimate this last stage of our journey." I meant to remind myself as much as her. "Maia said the gods would put obstacles in our paths. There may be more yet to come."

"But once we reach Crete, surely there are few obstacles that can come between us and the Eye." Her tone was all stubbornness and defiance.

"Who knows?"

I was reluctant to be drawn into speculation about what the gods might yet do to us. If they happened to be listening, I didn't intend to give them any ideas.

We fell into silence after that. The sea around us was not the dark, almost black, water that I was accustomed to from our previous voyages. Instead it looked like lapis lazuli. Crete was a rocky promontory rising out of the Mediterranean, stern cliffs covered with patches of forest. Overhead, sea birds flew, their chatter loud enough to reach my ears even over the rushing of the waves.

We arrived at Katsamba, a busy harbour town like any of a dozen others we had seen. Past the town, the island appeared uninhabitable, all mountains and forest. But then, surely I knew better than to make assumptions based on what was visible. After all, we had passed through the land of the Hittites via an extensive series of underground tunnels.

The people were mostly Greek in appearance, although as with Smyrna, there were others from all over the world. My ear picked out at least three different languages, although none that I understood, a situation I was becoming sadly accustomed to. We found a quiet place to set down our various bags and packages a little away from the hustle of the harbour.

"Well then," Renni said. "I suppose we need someone who speaks Egyptian."

It took him a long time to find someone he could communicate with, but at last he returned with an old Egyptian woman. She wore a brightly-coloured dress, tailored to sit tightly over her waist before flaring out like a bell. The skirt was accentuated with layers of ruffles. The weather had warmed in the time I had been missing and I had once again traded my hide pants for a loose gown which was surely more comfortable than what this woman wore.

"This is Nebtu," Renni said. "She knows of a house that is vacant. She will take me to the owner and I'll see what I can arrange. Do you want to wait here?"

"Let's all go." Intef was already picking up our packs. "We don't know whether they are home and you might need to wait for a while. Best that we stay together as much as possible."

Nobody looked at me, but surely it was I his words were aimed at. He still hadn't forgiven me for leaving. Or rather, he hadn't forgiven me for being gone for eight weeks.

The path on which Nebtu led us was packed dirt and lay alongside a rocky shore. Here there were no sandy beaches, just an expanse of pebbles which led all the way down to the water. This was not the place where I had met Horus. I tried yet again to force the memory back into my mind. Sandy shore, falcon eyes. Something important had happened to me there.

I was distracted from my thoughts only when I sneezed. On the other side of us lay a field of flowers, a vast expanse of yellow dotted with occasional patches of red. A tree-covered hill loomed behind them.

"I have never seen a place like this before," Istnofret said to me.

Although she spoke quietly, Nebtu heard.

"It is very beautiful, is it not?" she said. "This is the perfect time of year to visit Crete. The worst of the winter rains are behind us and the island is blanketed with flowers. They won't last long. You are fortunate to be here while they bloom."

"It is indeed beautiful," I said.

"How did you come to be here?" Istnofret asked. "How long have you lived here?"

"Oh, many years. Too many to count," Nebtu said. "My father was a sailor. He sailed all over the world and every time he came home, he would tell my mother that there was no place more beautiful than Crete. He always intended to bring us here to live, but he was lost at sea during a storm."

Floating. Or perhaps sinking. Surrounded by blackness. The pain in my chest from holding my breath. Knowing that my daughter would never live. Istnofret's hand on mine brought me back. I blinked, suddenly stunned by the day's brightness.

"We didn't learn of his death until a year later, when one of his crew mates came home to tell us," Nebtu said. "He brought my father's final payment and a little extra as compensation from the owner of the ship. My mother didn't spend any time grieving his loss. I think she already knew he wasn't coming back this time. She sold everything we owned and bought passage to Crete. That was, oh, thirty years ago, at least. Maybe more. I stopped counting a long time ago."

Nebtu's voice held a haunting sadness. It might have been a long time ago, but it was clear she still grieved for her father.

"Here," she said as we reached a place where the dirt path forked. "We turn here and the village is not much further. My friend died a few months ago. Her daughter already had a bigger house of her own so she lends this one to travellers. She is always glad to see the place being lived in."

"I am not sure how long we will be here," I said. "We are looking for something and we don't know how long it will take."

Nebtu glanced towards my belly.

"You don't have much time to be hiking all over Crete. Best that you start your confinement."

Her tone was mild, but I felt the sting of judgement.

"I don't intend to be confined. The babe will come when she is ready and I have things to do in the meantime."

"I am surprised you have managed to walk this far," Nebtu said. "It is not a long walk, but it must feel so in your condition."

Before I could reply, Intef caught my eye and gave his head the tiniest of shakes. I looked away, into the field of flowers. I breathed in the perfumed air and tried to let go of my irritation.

The house was modest, only three chambers in total, but it was private and quiet. We unpacked our bags and Istnofret inspected our remaining supplies. Behenu already scrutinised the oven, which was outside in the courtyard, and muttered about bread and beer.

I unrolled my bed mat in the chamber that Intef and I would share. Istnofret and Renni claimed one of the other chambers and offered for Behenu to sleep in there with them. She accepted a little tearfully and it was only then that I realised she had always had Mau for company at night.

The loss of both Mau and Sadeh hit me all over again and tears ran down my face. I scrubbed them away impatiently. Sadeh had been gone for months. Why was I suddenly grieving her just as much as I had in those first few days? The babe kicked and I rubbed my belly.

"Ssh, little one," I whispered. "I am well. Just a little sad."

She wriggled and seemed to find herself a new position with an elbow lodged against my kidney.

"My love?" Intef entered the chamber in time to catch my grunt of discomfort. "Is the babe restless?"

"She is wriggling a lot today."

He came over to place his hand on my belly and waited to feel her kick.

"I cannot wait to meet her. Our daughter. I wonder if she will look like you?"

I pretended to smile although it probably looked more like a grimace. I had to find a way to avoid handing her over to Osiris.

"What are you not telling me?" He moved his hand to my chin to tip up my face, forcing me to look at him.

I shook my head and stepped back out of his grasp.

"I am tired. Nebtu was right. It was a long walk for me."

He studied my face for a moment. I was sure he didn't believe me, but he didn't push.

"Istnofret and Behenu are preparing a meal from the last of our supplies," he said. "You should rest. Tomorrow might be a big day."

"We need to figure out how we're going to find my Eye."

It was only when he gave me an odd look that I realised what I had said. I quickly corrected myself.

"The Eye."

"My love—"

"I know. I heard myself. I will be conscious of it, I promise. As long as I stay aware of it, I will be fine."

"What does it feel like?" he asked. "When you say something like that."

"I don't notice feeling any different. It is like the Eye is supposed to be mine and that it is a perfectly natural thing. It is only when someone looks as if I said something strange, that I even realise."

"It would be very easy to fall into that. To let yourself get swept away with the belief that it belongs to you."

I had to look away. His stare was too intense and I feared blurting out the thing I didn't want to tell him.

"I am trying, Intef. I promise."

"It seems to happen particularly when you are tired."

"I suppose if I am tired, I have less willpower to resist."

"This burden does not fall solely on your shoulders, my love. We all need to be alert for it."

He couldn't understand. None of them could. It was me the gods had chosen to wield the Eye and I was only just starting to realise that it would be me they made to suffer for it. Me and perhaps my daughter.

TWENTY-ONE

Istnofret, Behenu and Renni went out early the next morning to secure supplies. I had slept restlessly, plagued by dreams in which I saw myself finding the Eye and clutching it to my breast. It was the same thing over and over: I reached into a crevice and pulled out the Eye. When I woke, I tried to remember what the Eye had looked like, but either the memory was gone or the dream had never showed me. It wasn't a true dream, anyway, for I had seen only one ending.

I would have gone to help with the supplies, but Intef insisted I lie in bed a while longer. He lay there with me. His eyes were shadowed and he looked as if he had slept as little as I.

"Did I keep you awake?" I asked.

"Maybe. You tossed and turned a lot. Was the babe kicking?"

"No, she is fine."

"She will come any day now, won't she." His voice was casual, but I knew him well enough to hear the anxiety he tried to hide.

"Within the next couple of weeks. Maybe we should see if there is a midwife nearby."

"I assumed Istnofret and Behenu would help you. They were with you for Setau's birth."

"Neither of them has ever birthed a child themself. I want…"

"What?" he prodded when my voice trailed away.

"I want someone who knows how it is done. In case something goes wrong."

My old fears about childbirth suddenly emerged. After all, two of my sisters had died birthing babes. For many years, I had feared the same fate. The fear changed after Setau, who had been born several months too early and never even had the chance to draw breath. I had never considered the torment of surviving when the babe did not.

"When this is all over, I want us to settle down somewhere and be a family," Intef said. "You and me and the babe. A nice little house. I'll get work, soldiering or labouring or whatever I can find. After all this travelling, I need to wake up in the same bed every day and eat vegetables from my own garden. Sit in the shade of my own dom palm tree. Watch my daughter grow up."

"It sounds lovely."

"You don't believe it will happen."

I avoided his eyes. "I cannot think that far ahead right now. There's too much to do yet. We have to find the Eye. Get it back to Egypt. I don't even know how I am supposed to use it, only that I need to find a way to stop Ay. Put this war between Egypt and Hattusa to bed."

"And before you do any of that, our daughter will be born."

His words felt like a rebuke. After all, where was our daughter in my plans? Where was he?

"I want this child, Intef. I hope you know that."

"Do you?" His gaze searched my face. "You never mention her when you talk about the future."

"I cannot yet see past what I need to do. Once that's done, there will be time for us. For a family."

"What do you see our future as? After this is over?"

"Much the same as you. A little house somewhere. Not far from Istnofret and Renni. She wants to live by the sea, so I suppose we will have to as well. I don't see myself baking bread or brewing beer, though. The gods know I am hopeless at tasks like that."

"I think you would be happy living near an archive. Pottering around old documents all day. Coming home streaked with dust to tell me about whatever marvellous new tales you've discovered."

The picture he painted made me smile. I had been happy back in Babylon when I went to the archive every day. Frustrated, perhaps, at not finding what I sought, but I had enjoyed being surrounded by scrolls and clay tablets.

"That does sound wonderful."

The front door opened with a crash, making us both jump.

"Are you still in bed?" Istnofret called. "Lazy sods. Come and help us unpack the supplies."

"Time to get up, I suppose," I said.

Intef reached out to stroke my belly. I supposed he imagined he was stroking our daughter. Could she feel his hand? Could she feel the love he already had for her? He rose and reached down to haul me up.

They had finished laying our supplies on the shelves by the time Intef and I dressed and went out to the main chamber.

There was wheat for bread and beer, various lentils and pulses for soups, olives, leeks, asparagus, pomegranates, figs, and a pair of fish of a species I didn't recognise. It was silvery with dark speckles along its back.

"Trout," Behenu said when she caught me examining them. "Very tasty."

"Dinner tonight, I presume?" Intef came to lean over my shoulder and inspect the fish.

"I haven't decided yet whether to cook them over coals or in a stew," Behenu said.

"Over coals would be nice," Istnofret said around a mouthful of what was undoubtedly figs. It never took her long to find the fruit. "With asparagus."

"I can do that," Behenu said.

I took a few figs in case Istnofret ate them all before I came back and wandered outside. The sky was dark with rainclouds.

"We should go now," I said as Intef followed me out. "Ask around about the Eye. If the weather turns, we might not be able to do much this afternoon."

"We need a plan first."

Intef had brought a pomegranate with him and set it down on a stone while he tried to slice it in half. It wobbled around and he couldn't get his dagger into it.

"Let me do that." I swallowed the last of my figs, then took the dagger from him. I cut the pomegranate open and offered it back to him, glancing up in time to catch the look on his face. "I am sorry. You were having trouble and I only thought to help you with it."

"I need to learn how to do things for myself. There won't always be someone nearby to cut open a pomegranate for me."

"You were getting frustrated. I was just trying to help."

He took a deep breath and seemed to exhale away his annoyance.

"I know, my love, but I am going to have only one arm for the rest of my life. Let me be frustrated while I try to figure things out. If I need help, I will ask for it."

"Or you won't eat the pomegranate," I muttered.

"Or I will eat something else," he said, with forced cheerfulness. "And if that's what I need to do, I will survive."

"But you wanted the pomegranate. And I want you to have what you want."

"Are we still talking about pomegranates?"

Once again I remembered sand and a falcon's eyes. Myself on my knees before a green-faced god. Offering him my newborn babe.

"Is there more to this quest than you've told us?"

Even after all these years, his intuition still surprised me sometimes. I didn't trust myself to speak. If I spoke right now, I would likely blurt it all out and I couldn't tell him. Even though I had resolved to find a way to avoid giving the babe to Osiris, Intef would hate me if he knew. Because I had gone this long without telling him. Because I had travelled so far with the knowledge that I might hand the babe over. It wouldn't matter that I had no intention of complying. Renni's arrival was a welcome relief.

"What's the plan for today?" He must have sensed something of our conversation from the looks on our faces. "Am I interrupting?"

"Not at all." I spoke quickly before Intef could send him away. "I suppose we need to start asking around. Find out if anyone knows of either Djediufankh or Antinous."

"We don't have much to go on," Behenu said as she and Istnofret strolled out to join us. "Just two names."

The scroll I found at the library in Babylon was written by a man who called himself Antinous, son of Antinous, son of Herodianus. He had written about being given the Eye by his friend Djediufankh.

"Antinous was a priest," Istnofret said. "We could start at the temples. See if anyone knows of him."

"Ist and I will go find out where the temples are," Renni offered. "No need for everyone to go until we know where we're going."

"I am not an invalid," I said, a little testily.

He looked to Istnofret, obviously seeking rescue.

"Am I the only one who's tired after our journey here?" She gave an elaborate yawn. "I am getting too old for all these travels."

I shot her a dirty look, but she only yawned again.

"Are you feeling well, Samun?" Behenu asked. "You seem rather…"

"Testy?" I snapped.

She shrugged, seemingly unwilling to be drawn into an argument.

I took a deep breath and tried to push down my irritation.

"I am sorry. I've been feeling strange ever since we arrived. I suppose it is just that we're so close to the end of the journey."

"And the babe's birth." Istnofret gave my belly a pointed look. "You shouldn't push yourself too hard over these next few weeks."

"I cannot sit around all day. I will go out of my mind. The babe will come when she is ready and me sitting with my feet up won't make that happen any sooner."

"Shall I go see Nebtu?" Behenu asked. "Ask her where the temples are. She might even know Antinous."

"Good idea," Intef said. "We will rest here while you do that, and once you have some information we will decide what to do next."

"You mean, decide who will stay and babysit me," I said.

"I'll go now." Behenu ignored my comment. "Renni, do you want to come with me?"

As she left, Intef pulled her aside to speak with her. He kept his voice low and I could hear none of their conversation.

"Sending her in search of a midwife as well, I suppose?" I said after she had gone.

He gave me an apologetic shrug.

"She may as well ask Nebtu while she is there. No harm in being prepared in case the babe comes early."

His words made my heart hurt, reminding me of how early poor little Setau was born. He had been so tiny. I could still remember how little he weighed when I cradled him to my chest. His tiny fingers and toes.

"I am sorry, my love. I didn't mean to make you sad. I just want to be prepared."

I nodded, unable to speak through the lump in my throat.

"There's a very pretty beach not far from here," Istnofret said. "Would you like me to show you?"

The beach was only a few minutes' walk and Istnofret was right. It was a pretty spot. No pebbles, just white sand stretching all the way down to the water, which was the same brilliant shade of lapis lazuli as I had admired from the ship. Where the sand ended, a field of yellow flowers began. At the far end of the field rose a tree-covered mountain.

"I have never seen a place like this before," I said.

"It is an odd combination, isn't it?" Intef shaded his eyes to better see the mountain. "The sand and the flowers, the mountains and the cliffs."

"Can you imagine what it would be like to live here?" Istnofret's voice was dreamy as she dug her toes into the sand. She breathed deeply of the salty air and sighed. "I would like a house here. Right here on the sand."

"I am afraid you would get rather wet every time the tide came in." Intef came to stand beside me and wrapped his arm around my waist. I leaned against his shoulder and tried to let go of my worries.

The breeze suddenly gusted from behind us and my hair was in my eyes. As I brushed it back, I caught sight of Istnofret. She had turned her back to the sea so that she faced into the wind. It swept her hair back behind her and when she looked at me, she laughed.

"I love this place," she said.

"This is it. This is where you are meant to be."

"I know. I feel it. I wonder if I can convince Renni to stay."

"No, I mean this is the place I saw you. I dreamed about you here, standing with your back to the sea like that and laughing at me."

"Oh." Her laughter quickly died. "Is that still the only time you saw me in your dreams?"

I nodded. "I wish I had known this was right at the end of our journey. I would have worried less if I had known you would still be safe at this point."

"I was making beer in the other dream, wasn't I?"

"I was never sure. Maybe."

"I thought that had already come to pass. I sometimes helped Behenu with the brewing while we were in Babylon."

"I never saw anything that was exactly like what I dreamed."

"Huh. I wonder when that was supposed to happen then."

"I am not sure it matters. This is the fate that came to pass. You were meant to be here."

"Maybe once all this is over, we'll come back. Renni and I. There's something about this place that calls to me."

I smiled but my heart was heavy. I couldn't see myself living anywhere other than Egypt and I didn't understand why Istnofret would want to do such a thing. Egypt was home. Just because I had dreamed about her being here, didn't mean she was supposed to stay here. Just that she was meant to be here, now, in this moment.

TWENTY-TWO

W e didn't stay on the beach for much longer. Istnofret seemed to know I was unhappy, even if she didn't realise that she was the cause of it, and she soon suggested we returned to the cottage in case Renni and Behenu had returned.

"Do you think Antinous is still here?" I asked as we made our way back.

"I think it unlikely," Intef said. "It would be too easy, wouldn't it? We arrive on Crete, find the man we knew last had the Eye, and he tells us where he hid it? I cannot imagine the gods would make it that easy."

It had been no more than I was thinking myself, but I had hoped he might say that yes, this was it, our journey was almost at its end. For once, I had hoped he would lie to me.

The cottage was empty when we returned. Istnofret decided to use the time to mend a tear in her gown and Intef made himself busy with some chore of his own. Left alone, I wandered through the three chambers of our new home until

Istnofret suggested that I stay away from where she was working or she would find me some stitching to do. I went out to the garden. It wasn't much, just a couple of trees and a grassy patch. Mau would have liked the sunny spot in the corner.

I shed a few tears as I stood there. For Mau. For Sadeh. For little Setau. For my daughter who was yet to be born. Why had I never seen any future for her after I offered her up to the green-faced god? The closer the time came for her to be born, the more difficulty I had in believing my dream. No mother would hand her babe over like that. Perhaps the other future — the one in which I was bound in a dark chamber — might yet come to pass.

"They're back," Istnofret called from the doorway. "Samun, come inside. They have news."

I wiped away the last of my tears and took a couple of deep breaths to compose myself.

"Samun!" Istnofret called again.

"I am coming."

With a final steadying breath, I headed back inside. One look at Behenu and Renni's faces told me the news wasn't what we had hoped for.

"We found someone who knew Antinous." Behenu shot me a look. "He said Antinous died four weeks ago."

I sighed heavily. That put his death during the time I had been missing. Walking on a beach with Horus, or whatever I was doing.

"Are you sure it is the right Antinous?" Istnofret asked. "It could be a common name."

"There are indeed at least three men by that name," Renni said. "But there was only one who was a priest and whose father was named Antinous."

"What about his father's father?" I asked. "If he was not Herodianus, it is not the right one."

"The man we spoke to didn't know. He only knew him as Antinous, son of Antinous."

"So it might not be the man we're looking for?"

It was a ridiculous thing to cling to and Renni quickly shattered my hope.

"We are certain he is the right one. The man we spoke to recalled Antinous having spoken of living in Babylon some years ago."

"The good news is that he has a daughter," Behenu said. "We know where she lives, but there was nobody home. We thought we would come back here to rest for a while and then we could all go see her."

Hope surged so quickly, it left me light-headed. This was the breakthrough we needed. Antinous would surely have told his daughter about the precious object entrusted to him. She would know where he had hidden it. All we had to do was locate it and we could be on our way back to Egypt. My daughter might yet be born on Egyptian soil. But within the hour, the rain began.

"We could still go," I said. "I don't mind getting a bit wet."

"Not in your condition." Istnofret gave me a stern look. "You'll get chilled and that would be no good for either you or the babe."

"Speaking of the babe," Behenu said. "I almost forgot. There's a midwife who lives not far from here. She said to send for her when you need her."

"Is she experienced?" I asked.

"She is very old," Behenu said. "And she lives with her daughter and her daughter's children. There were at least five of them running around."

"I suppose she is suitable then."

One less thing to worry about, not that I intended to still be here by the time the babe came. We could well be on the next ship back to Egypt. But when the rain stopped a few hours later and we made our way to Eritha's house, I quickly realised this was not the breakthrough I had hoped for.

"I am not sure I can help you," Eritha said on learning we wanted to know about her father's life before he came to Crete. "He spoke rarely of Babylon."

She had invited us to sit out in her garden. There was a pretty spot where a tree with wide-spread branches had protected the grass beneath from the worst of the rain and we sat there on woven mats. We sipped beer and ate from a plate of olives. It would have been relaxing if I hadn't been so anxious about what Eritha could tell us.

"Did he ever talk about his friend, Djediufankh?" I asked.

Eritha considered my question but eventually she shook her head.

"I don't recall it. My father may have mentioned him, but perhaps not by name. There were one or two friends that he spoke about, but he usually called them things like *my friend in Babylon.*"

"Did he ever tell you why he left Babylon?" Intef asked.

Eritha's face became shadowed.

"That was a very sad time for him and he spoke of it rarely. He met my mother there, of course. She died when I was born and it broke his heart. I don't believe he was ever the same man again after that. We moved here while I was still very young. I don't remember living there."

"Did he talk about Djediufankh giving him something?" I asked. "Something he brought with him to Crete?"

"Like I said, if he ever mentioned someone of that name, I

don't remember it. If he brought something with him, he kept it a secret. What exactly are you looking for? I might be of more help if I knew."

I didn't need to look up from my mug to know they all looked at me. It seemed this was my decision. I hesitated, but Eritha's face seemed honest and I had no sense that she tried to hide anything from us.

"We don't know what it looks like," I said. "I believe it is small and it may have some connection with Horus, but that is as much as we know."

"Horus?" she asked.

"One of our Egyptian gods. Do you not know of him?"

She shrugged and didn't seem terribly interested.

"We have enough gods of our own without worrying about others. Perhaps we know him by a different name."

"Maybe. Do you know if your father kept anything from his time in Babylon? Something small that might have been significant to him?"

Eritha took her time in answering.

"Nothing that I can think of. The thing that was most precious to him was this ring." She held out her hand to show us a silver band engraved with a winding vine. "He gave it to my mother when they learned she was with child. He wore it himself after she died and only gave it to me shortly before his own death."

I held my breath as I leaned in to examine the ring. Could this be it? It wasn't anything like I had expected, but it was small and Antinous had brought it with him from Babylon and had kept it safe for the rest of his life.

"Could I take a closer look?" I asked.

Eritha hesitated. "I don't take it off. It is very precious to me, you understand. It is the only thing I have that belonged to my mother."

"I will be very careful."

But she shook her head and when she tucked her hands back into her lap, her other hand covered the silver ring.

I shot a pleading look towards Intef, although I wasn't sure what I expected him to do. He could hardly wrestle Eritha to the ground and remove the ring from her finger. He caught my eye and shook his head just the tiniest bit. Did he mean that I shouldn't press Eritha or that he wouldn't help me? We sat in awkward silence for a few moments until Renni spoke.

"What kind of man was your father? Perhaps if we knew more about him, we might be able to figure out what he did with the item we are looking for."

Eritha seemed relieved at the change of topic.

"He was very intelligent. Always learning. Very dedicated to Ares."

"Is that one of your gods?" Renni asked.

"The god of war. Son of Zeus and Hera. A strange god for a man like him, perhaps, but his family had always worshipped Ares and tradition was very important to my father." She paused, her gaze distant. "He liked to go off on his own. Sometimes he would be gone for days at a time. I never used to worry, but as he got older, he started to forget things. When he didn't come home at night, I would worry he had forgotten where he lived. Had forgotten he had a daughter who was waiting for him to come back."

"So sad," Istnofret murmured. "It is very difficult to see your elders like that."

Eritha gave her an appreciative smile.

"Yes, it was hard, especially since my father was so learned. It pained me to see him forget things he used to know."

"Where did he go when he went away by himself?"

Intef's tone was casual, but I sensed the tension behind it. My heart started to race.

"Various places," Eritha said. "He liked to go up to a mountain top to worship. Sometimes he spent a couple of days up there, completely exposed to the weather but so immersed in his worship that he barely noticed if he was cold or wet. Other times he would go stand on a beach and stare out into the sea. There was a cave he went to occasionally. He was there for a full month once. The gods only know what he ate in that time. Whatever he found in the rock pools, I suppose."

"We would like to have a look at the cave." Once again, Intef's tone was studiously casual. "Could you give us directions?"

"It is quite a walk from here." Eritha glanced towards my belly. "Go back down to the beach and follow the shoreline around to the north. Keep going until you reach the place where the beach ends and the cliffs come right down to the water. The cave is about halfway up. You cannot see it from the ground and the climb is perilous. Those cliffs have been weathered by the sea for thousands of years. They may seem solid enough, but there are parts that will crumble as soon as you look at them."

We thanked her politely and left. I glanced back as we walked away and she was looking after us with a worried expression. Perhaps she was concerned I would try to climb up to the cave myself. I supposed I had no choice. After all, Maia had said the Eye could only be touched by the one who would wield it.

TWENTY-THREE

"Are you sure you want to walk so far?" Istnofret asked quietly as we headed back to the beach.

The babe kicked, hard, and I rubbed my belly.

"I am the only one who can touch it. What if you find it and I am not there? Someone would have to walk all the way back to get me and that would be a waste of time. I may as well go."

A woman's voice came from behind us, interrupting our conversation.

"Intef?"

Intef whirled around, almost knocking me over in his haste.

"Tey? What? How?"

The woman who approached was obviously Egyptian born, although she wore no kohl and was dressed in the manner of the local women with a tightly fitted dress which bellowed out into a ruffled skirt. Her skin was darkened by the sun and her long hair fell freely to her shoulders.

"Are you looking for them?" Her gaze drifted down to his

missing arm and if she was shocked at his appearance, she gave no sign of it. "Have you come to take them back?"

She glanced at me then and quickly frowned at Intef.

"You brought her here?" she asked. "Why?"

I suddenly realised who she thought we were looking for and my breath caught in my throat.

"You know where my sisters are? Take me to them immediately."

Intef grabbed my wrist.

"Wait," he said to me, then to her, "We didn't know you were here."

"You mean to tell me you haven't come to retrieve them? That you are here by some accident?" She shook her head. "Oh, Intef, you should not have come. If she is here" — she gave me a dark look — "then others will not be far behind. This place is no longer safe."

"Where are my sisters?" I tried to shake off Intef's hand, but he grasped my wrist even more firmly. "Tell me, please. I must see them."

The woman shook her head. "Intef, you don't know what you have done."

"I swear I didn't know you were here," he said. "And nobody here knows who we are. We will be gone as soon as we have found what we are looking for. I swear we will not endanger them."

"No." I was crying now, although I couldn't have said why. Shouldn't I be happy about this? Being so near to my sisters. Finally knowing where they were. "Please, you must take me to them. Don't keep them from me, not when they are this near."

The woman stared at me for a long moment and I thought

she was actually considering my request. Then she shook her head and my heart broke.

"It is too dangerous. My sole duty is to keep them safe and I cannot do that if they encounter you. Although nobody here may know who you are, there may be many searching for you."

"Please." I was sobbing and likely incomprehensible through my tears. "We have travelled so far. I swear to Isis I will never come back here again, if you just let me see my sisters."

"Goodbye." She ignored my pleas and directed her words to Intef. "We will be gone from here by nightfall."

"Please," I begged. "If you will not let me see them, at least give them a message. Tell them I was here. Tell them I love them, that I wrote to them every week even though they never received my letters."

She turned and walked away. Intef held my wrist, preventing me from chasing after her.

"Tell me you will tell them," I called.

She made no reply and didn't even indicate she had heard me.

"Will she tell them?" I asked Intef.

I tried to wipe the tears from my face, but they were falling too fast and I couldn't manage with one hand. He released my wrist to pull me in against his side. I rested my head on his shoulder as I cried.

"I don't think so, my love." His voice was gentle. "There would be no benefit to them."

"They would want to know. They deserve to know I was here."

"But you weren't here for them."

"But-"

"Think of what it would do to them. If they miss you as much as you miss them, it would only distress them to know you were so close. No good can come of their knowing."

"No good?" For a moment, I was speechless. I pulled away from him and scrubbed the tears from my face. "How can you say that? It would be good for them to know that... That..."

There was sympathy in his gaze as he waited for me to continue.

"That I am alive. Surely they would want to know that."

"Do you think so? You sent them away from Egypt. You took them from everything they knew, from their home, their family, and sent them away. Maybe they don't want to know anything about you."

"I was protecting them. They know that. They would want to know I was here. I am the only family they have left."

"They've been gone for many years. They may well have started their own families by now. The present is likely more important to them than the past."

I had often wondered if my sisters had married, whether they had birthed children.

"Who is she? How does she know my sisters?"

"That is Tey," he said, and his pride was evident. "My sister. I told my father that I had been given the task of finding someone to send with your sisters. Tey overheard and volunteered."

"I always assumed you sent a soldier with them. Someone who could guard and protect them."

He laughed a little.

"I did. Tey is the best soldier I have ever met."

"But she is a woman."

"And a damn fine soldier."

I suddenly recalled an old conversation.

"You told me once that you knew a woman who could bring you to your knees faster than she could look at you. Or something like that. Is she who you meant? Tey?"

"She used to train with my father. The only thing she ever wanted was to be a soldier. He taught her everything he knew, but it wasn't enough for Tey. She used to go and watch the soldiers train, then copy what they did. She'd always stay far away from them, of course, although I doubt they were unaware of her. But she learned from them and she trained hard on her own. When other girls her age were dreaming of husbands and babes, she was hiking in the desert or running laps of the city or sparring with my father."

"But why did she go with my sisters? Why would she give up her life to look after two girls she didn't even know?"

Intef stared out at the ocean.

"She was never an ordinary girl. She wouldn't have been happy with an ordinary life. She wanted… I don't even know what she wanted. But when she heard me telling our father about the two princesses that needed to be hidden away, she didn't even hesitate. It took most of the night for her to convince our father. He eventually agreed, but I think he knew she would do it whether he approved or not. I smuggled your sisters out of the palace before dawn that morning and Tey left with them. She took nothing but her dagger. Not even a change of clothes or any provisions."

"I always assumed that the person who had gone with them had been paid handsomely. I couldn't imagine what else might persuade someone to give up their life."

"I made sure your sisters had a few gems each from your mother's jewellery. I figured they were their birthright anyway. But that was to support them all, not to pay Tey. She wouldn't have accepted anything else and I never offered. I couldn't exactly submit a requisition for payment for her. She knew there would be no reward other than the satisfaction of living her own life."

"And you really never knew where they went?"

He finally pulled his gaze from the water.

"I didn't ask where she was taking them and she didn't say. I am not sure she even knew where she was going when they left."

"You told me once that if the person who had gone with my sisters was still alive, they would be too."

"And now you know the truth of it."

"I wish you had told me it was your sister who went with them."

"You have never believed that a woman could be as good a soldier as a man. You would have worried even more had you known it was Tey who went with them. But I swear to you, I sent them with the best soldier I knew. Nobody could protect them better than she."

"We should leave some gems with her," I said. "She can take all of my share. I want to know that she has enough to provide for them."

"Tey will be just fine without your gems," he said, with a bit of a laugh. "And besides, we don't know where they live and it is unlikely we could catch up to them before she takes them away. Best that we focus on the Eye and leave Tey to do her job."

"I wish I could see them. Even if just from a distance and only for a moment. I need to see that they're well."

"You know they're well. As long as Tey is alive, your sisters are safe, and if she says you may not see them, I for one do not intend to cross her. Now, we need to keep moving if you want to find the cave today."

TWENTY-FOUR

Nobody spoke as we walked away. My feet were unwilling and my heart kept telling me that we should be chasing after Tey, not walking in the opposite direction. My mind spun with the knowledge that it was Intef's sister who had ushered my sisters away all those years ago. That they had been here on Crete, only a week's sail from Egypt. Was it a coincidence that both my sisters and the Eye were on Crete? Did I dare assume the gods intended me to find them both?

Long before we reached the place where the cliffs met the sea, I realised that the walk was indeed too much for me. My legs were tired, my back ached, and the babe kicked vigorously. At least the discomfort distracted me from thoughts of my sisters.

"My love, are you well?" Intef asked. "You seem to be breathing very heavily."

I shook my head, too out of breath to respond.

"You should sit. Wait here. Istnofret can stay with you while the rest of us go on to the cave."

"You need me," I managed, between gasps.

"We might not find the cave, or there might be nothing there. There is no need for you to exert yourself. If we find it and the Eye is there, we can return in the morning. We will bring a cart or something. Find a way to get you there without you walking so far."

I hadn't intended to stop, but my legs suddenly came to a halt. I pressed my hands into the small of my back, which ached fiercely. Thankfully the babe had stopped kicking at last. The others were a little ahead of us, but eventually they realised we had stopped and came wandering back.

"Is it the babe?" Istnofret called to us. "She is not coming already, is she?"

Intef gestured for them to stay where they were.

"Please," he said to me. "Stay here and rest. This cannot be good for either you or the babe."

"I can do it. I just need to go a bit slower."

"My love—"

"I said I can do it."

I somehow forced my recalcitrant legs to move and I tottered along the beach. Behind me, Intef sighed heavily as he followed.

The others set off again, although Istnofret kept shooting worried looks back over her shoulder. I gritted my teeth and tried to pretend I couldn't see her.

By the time we reached the place where the cliffs met the water, I was drenched in sweat. My legs wobbled and I couldn't quite catch my breath. The cliffs towered over us, much higher than I had expected. They didn't look climbable. Surely this was not the place Eritha had meant for us to find.

"Sit down," Intef said. "While we figure out how to get up there."

My legs abruptly stopped holding me up and I fell, rather than sat, in the sand.

"Are you sure this is it?" Istnofret asked.

"She did say we wouldn't be able to see the cave from the ground," Renni said. "I suppose one of us will have to climb up and see."

He and Intef looked at each other. Once, it would have been Intef who volunteered for such a task, but scaling the cliff would be hard enough for a man with two good arms.

"I will go," Behenu said.

Intef immediately shook his head. "It is too dangerous."

"I have some climbing experience," Renni said. "Not much, but it is better than nothing."

"You're too heavy," Behenu said. "Eritha said the rocks could crumble. I am the lightest of all of us. I have the best chance of making it up."

"We should have brought ropes," Intef said. "We can come back tomorrow. Figure out a way of securing you so you don't fall."

"We have already walked all this way," Behenu pointed out. "I don't think Samun will be able to walk back again, and we don't even know if there's anything up there worth coming back for."

Intef and Renni both hesitated. Each seemed to be waiting for the other to make the decision.

"I will be careful," she said. "I will test each step before I put my weight on it. Besides, what would you do even if you had a rope? Someone would have to be on top of those cliffs to secure it from up there. There is nothing on the way up to tie it to."

"I still don't like it," Intef said.

"Do you have a better idea then?" she asked. "One that

doesn't involve Samun exhausting herself unnecessarily. You know she will insist on coming if we have to return tomorrow. She shouldn't be doing this much so close to the babe's birth."

Intef shot me an alarmed look. "I thought we still had a couple of weeks."

"It could be any day now, or she might hold on for another month yet."

"We are too far from the midwife," Intef said. "Behenu, go carefully. If you fall, you will crack your head open on the rocks."

"I will be careful."

Behenu stepped straight up to the cliff and placed her hands against it in preparation for climbing.

"No." For a moment I didn't realise the words had come out of my own mouth. They all looked down at where I sat in the sand, my legs spreadeagled to allow my belly to rest between them. I reached out my arm to Intef. "Help me up."

"Stay there, my love." He didn't even move to help me. "Behenu is probably going to be a while. You can rest in the meantime."

"Behenu is not going up there," I said.

They all looked at me quizzically.

"I will do it."

Blank looks on their faces.

"I will climb up to the cave."

Intef's expression became cautious, as if I was a wild animal that might attack at any moment.

"My love—"

"We are wasting time. Will somebody come and help me up?"

Nobody moved.

"Oh, come on. You know I cannot get up by myself."

Still they didn't move.

"Intef!"

His mouth opened and closed as if he was searching for the right response. It was Istnofret who spoke first.

"Samun, I need to say something and you need to listen."

"Later. Intef, get over here and help me up."

"No, it must be now," Istnofret said. "You promised last time that if I told you this, you would listen. Will you honour your promise now?"

"What are you talking about?" I didn't even try to hide my irritation. "Forget it. I can get up by myself."

I tried to get my legs under me, but the soft sand provided too little support. Somehow, I managed to get onto my hands and knees, but I couldn't figure out how to stand up from there.

"Samun, remember that Maia said you might want the Eye for yourself. Remember you promised you would listen if I told you it was happening again."

"Do we really need to do this now? Can someone just come over here and help me?"

"Nobody is going to help you up until you listen to me."

I floundered in the sand for a while longer but eventually had to concede that I wasn't going to get up without help. I sank back onto my heels.

"Fine, I am listening."

"Are you really? Or are you just letting me talk at you?"

"Does it make a difference? Say what you need to."

She crossed her arms over her chest and shook her head.

"Not until you promise to really listen."

"Come on, Ist. Just say it and then help me up. We don't have much light left."

Already the sun slid towards the horizon and the shadows around us lengthened.

"We can wait here all night if we need to," Renni said.

I glared at him. "Of course you're going to back her up."

"I am in no hurry," Behenu said.

I looked to Intef. "Are you going to side with them also?"

His face was conflicted. "My love-"

"Oh, for Isis's sake, stop saying that. Will *somebody* just tell me what you want?"

"I already did." Istnofret's irritation started to seep into her voice, although she still tried to hide it. "You didn't listen."

I sighed, then took a deep breath and tried to rein in my annoyance. If only I was still queen and they were my servants. I would only have to tell them what I wanted and they would do it. In fact, if they were good servants, I wouldn't even need to say it. They would anticipate my desires. Like they used to. But once I had the Eye, we could go back to that. I would be queen again and they would have to do what I told them to.

The babe kicked, hard, and I rubbed my belly.

"Ssh, little one," I said. "Everything is well."

I looked up at my servants. They still waited for me to agree with them. To listen to whatever it was they wanted to say. I only had to tolerate them until I found my Eye.

"Fine. What is it you want to say?"

"Tell me you're really listening," Istnofret said. "Listening with your heart open. Not just letting me speak."

"I am listening."

"No, you're not. I can tell."

"Speak, Istnofret. It is not like I can avoid hearing your words."

"You need to listen with your heart. Until you are ready to do that, I will not speak."

I glared up at her and she glared back.

"That's your imperious look. The one you used to use when you were queen and someone displeased you. You are no longer queen, Samun, and I don't have to bend to your will. We are friends. You will listen to me because you know I love you."

Her words hit me like a blow. Tears welled in my eyes.

"You love me?" I tried to sound nonchalant.

"Of course I do. We all do. Do you think we would stay with you if we didn't?"

I looked away, out into the waves. Their endless motion still fascinated me. Called to me. Once again, I found myself sinking down into them. Darkness all around. My hair streaming out above me. The realisation that my babe would never draw breath. I had drowned. That was the only thing I was sure of. But somehow I had come back. Something here, in this life, had called to me so strongly that I came back. I only wished I knew what it was. I took a deep breath and opened my heart.

"I am listening. Speak, Ist."

"Maia said you would want the Eye for yourself. That you needed to be able to tell the difference between your own desires and what you must do."

I wanted to argue, to tell her she was wrong. But I had promised to listen with my heart, so I swallowed down my angry words and let hers sink in.

"It happens when I am tired, doesn't it?" I said, at last. "Sometimes, it is like everything gets twisted and all I can think about is how much I want the Eye. How I want it so I can be…"

"Be what?" Intef asked, when my words trailed away.

"Be queen again. Be the one who gives orders. Who everyone runs to obey. Sometimes all I can see is what I could *do* if only I had the Eye."

"You're the only one who feels the Eye like that," Istnofret said. "I don't feel anything. Do you?"

She looked around at the others and they all shook their heads.

"It wants you, Samun," Behenu said. "But you need to decide how much of yourself you will give to it."

I flinched at her words but made myself listen with my heart.

"I may not have a choice," I said. "I don't know what the Eye will want from me. Maia said there might be a price to pay. I have no idea what the gods could possibly want from me."

Even as I spoke, I realised my lie. I did, in fact, know exactly what the gods wanted.

"Remember you can only use it once," Istnofret said. "If its power is that insidious, you will need to be constantly on your guard when we find it. Otherwise you might use it too soon."

I had so far failed to resist the Eye at all and it wasn't even within my grasp yet. How would I resist long enough to get it back to Egypt?

"We will help," Behenu said. "We can wrap it in something. Maybe that will help to shield you from its power."

"And we will put it in a crate or a bag or something," Renni added. "You must avoid touching it directly."

"And we must ensure you never get too tired," Istnofret said. "It seems like being tired saps your ability to resist it."

"We will all help you, my love," Intef said. "If you will let us."

It had been so easy to imagine myself as queen again. And my friends as servants who were required to do my bidding. I hadn't even noticed the wrongness in my thoughts. How could I stop myself if I didn't realise when I was doing it? And what would the Eye make me do to them if it thought they were a threat?

"Thank you. I cannot do this alone."

The relief on their faces told me they hadn't been at all sure how I would react.

"Now, will you help me up?" I stretched out my arms and this time Intef stepped forward. "I really need to stand up."

"Are you sure you wouldn't rather sit?" he asked. "It might take Behenu a while to climb up."

"I will sit if I need to."

Meanwhile, Behenu had stepped up to the cliff and explored its surface with her hands.

"It is very smooth. I am not sure I can climb it." Her voice was doubtful. "There is little to hold onto."

"The rocks down here have been polished smooth by the waves." Renni stood next to her and pointed to a spot up above her head. "See up here. You will be able to get your fingers into this crack. And a little higher up there is a small protrusion. It is not much but it is wide enough to get your toes on. You will need something to hold onto to keep yourself there, but that little ledge should support your weight."

He pointed out a series of spots she should aim for, then put his hand on her shoulder.

"Are you sure about this? Once you are out of our reach, we cannot help if you get stuck. And if you fall, you will be injured. Perhaps it would be better if I go."

"Eritha said the rocks would be fragile," Behenu said. "It would be even more dangerous for you."

"It will be harder to climb down since you won't be able to see the next handhold."

"You will guide me."

He stepped back to give her more room. "Take off your boots. You need to feel what you are doing."

Behenu pulled off her shoes. She set her hands against the rocks again and seemed to take a moment to steady herself.

"Good luck," Istnofret said quietly. "May the gods protect you."

TWENTY-FIVE

I could barely breathe as I watched Behenu make her way
up the rocks. I couldn't imagine doing that myself, even if
I wasn't so heavy and unwieldy. The Eye had twisted my mind
indeed if it had made me think I could. The first few cubits
were easy enough and Behenu moved with confidence. But
then she hesitated.

"Renni." Her voice was shrill.

"Breathe," he said. "Your left hand. About half a cubit
straight up from your hand, there is a bit of rock sticking out."

She edged her hand up, sliding her fingers over the rock
until she located the protrusion.

"I've got it."

"Right hand," Renni said. "About the same distance. You
should be able to get your fingers into the crack."

She swept her hand along the rock. Bit by bit, she crept
upwards with Renni guiding her.

"I cannot see any higher," he said, at last.

"I cannot do this by myself."

"Just go slowly. Make sure you have a good grip before you move."

Cubit by cubit, she edged up. Then she took hold of a rocky protrusion and it broke right off. I held my breath as she swayed a little, sweeping her hand desperately over the rock until her fingers caught something she could grip.

I placed my hand over my heart, which beat hard enough to burst right through my chest. The babe was kicking again, but I couldn't spare her any attention.

"Isis protect her," Istnofret whispered.

Behenu crept up a little further. She was at least the height of three men now. Then the rock beneath her foot crumbled. She slid and lost her footing entirely. Only the grasp of her fingers kept her up there as she scrambled to find another foothold. For a long moment, I was sure she would come crashing down, but her toe caught on something I couldn't even see. Then she had a grip with the other foot.

"You're doing well," Renni called.

"I cannot do this." She breathed heavily, almost hyperventilating. "I need to get down."

"You're almost at the cave," Renni said.

"Can you see it?"

"Not from down here. Look up. It cannot be far from you."

"There's nothing up here. Eritha was mistaken. I am coming back down."

"Keep going. Just a little higher. One more cubit. Then you'll see the cave."

"I cannot. I am too scared."

"You can do this, Behenu. You're the only one of us who can. Go slowly. One hand. Just reach out and you'll find something to hold."

I held my breath, waiting. Would she slip and fall? Would

another rock crumble beneath her and send her tumbling down? Would she panic and simply let go? Istnofret cleared her throat several times and when I finally looked at her, she tipped her head towards Behenu.

"You're doing great, Behenu," I said.

Istnofret gave me a pleased nod.

Behenu reached up, grabbed the next protrusion, then eased herself a little higher.

"I see it. It is to my right and not much higher."

We waited as she edged sideways. At last the moment came when she was able to release her perilous grip and step into the cave. She disappeared.

My heart pounded harder and harder. I could hardly hear the waves anymore. My legs wobbled and I collapsed down into the sand. I couldn't catch my breath. Intef leaned down to steady me. His mouth moved, but over the pounding of my heart I heard nothing of what he said.

Behenu seemed to take a very long time, but eventually she called down to us.

"I don't think it is here."

"Are you sure?" Istnofret called back.

"Tell us what it is like inside," Intef said.

"Just an ordinary cave. The rocks are much the same as what you can see down there, only they are rougher and not smoothed by the waves. There are a couple of recesses which I don't think are natural, but there is nothing in them. On the floor is a blanket and a few pieces of firewood. Nothing else."

"Look again," I called, finally finding my voice. "It is in there somewhere."

"I will, but I am quite certain it isn't here."

She was quiet again for some time. I chewed my nails,

needing something to busy myself with while we waited. Finally, she called out again.

"It really isn't here. I have checked everywhere."

"Check the recesses again," Renni called. "Feel all the way to the back if you can. It could be tucked into a little crevice right at the back."

"I already did."

"Shake out the blanket," Istnofret said. "The Eye could be wrapped up inside it."

"I did that too."

"Are you sure there are no other recesses?" I asked. "A tunnel? A second cave? Maybe there is some hidden place that you cannot see until you are right on top of it."

"I have been over every cubit at least twice."

Behenu's tone was a little curt. I knew she was getting exasperated, but I also knew the Eye had to be in there.

"There is really nothing here. The cave is small. Barely the length of one man, and not much more than that in width. There are no hidden places. I am sorry but it is not here."

"You should probably start coming down then," Renni said. "The sun is close to setting and you don't want to be climbing down in the dark."

"No." If she left now, I might never find the Eye. It was in there. I knew it. "Behenu, go look again. You must be missing something."

"Samun." Intef crouched down beside me. "You know Behenu. If she says she has checked, then she has. We must accept that the Eye is not here."

"It has to be. We know Antinous used to come here."

"It is not here."

"But it is the perfect hiding spot. A place that cannot be seen from the ground. High enough to be safe from the tides. A perilous journey to reach it. Who would bother to climb up to a cave they cannot even see? It has to be there."

"But it isn't. Now, Behenu is coming down and then we will go back to the house. I am worried about whether you can walk that far."

"I did it before and I'll do it again. I have walked much further than that."

"But not while so close to giving birth."

I hated that his tone was so reasonable. It made me even more aware of how irrational I sounded. I was so easily irritated these days and the closer the babe's time came, the worse it seemed to get.

Behenu had already started her climb down. The rocks crumbled away beneath her twice. Her feet were almost level with Renni's face when she finally lost her grip. He managed to catch her as she fell and they both tumbled to the ground.

"Ow." Renni's voice was muffled with his face in the sand.

"Yes, ow," Behenu rolled off him and lay on her back panting. "But thank you for breaking my fall."

"Any time."

Intef allowed them only a few moments to recover before he offered his hand to help them up.

"We have a long walk yet," he said. "We should be moving."

Once Renni and Behenu were both on their feet, Intef came to haul me up as well.

"Are you sure you can manage?" he asked, quietly.

"I really have no choice, do I? I either walk back or spend the night here on the sand."

"I could run back to the house and get some blankets and food. We could build a fire. It will be a cold night, but we have survived much worse. Then in the morning, we could figure out how to get you back. Maybe someone has a donkey that could carry you, or a cart we could pull."

"I will not be dragged in a cart like a sack of wheat. Besides, you were the one who said we needed to get back in case the babe comes. You said we were too far from the midwife."

He shot a worried glance towards my belly. "I know. I am trying not to think about it."

"Intef, I will be fine. We're wasting time standing here talking about it. Let's just start walking. If it becomes too much for me, we will figure out what to do then."

He didn't look at all reassured. As we finally set off, my legs wobbled. The walk back was going to take every bit of strength I had.

TWENTY-SIX

I stopped counting how many times I needed to stop to rest. I might have been embarrassed if I had enough strength to care. As it was, everything I had was going into keeping me on my feet. There was nothing left to be embarrassed with. I didn't even have enough energy to think about the discovery that my sisters were somewhere on Crete, or at least they were a few hours ago. Every time I tried to think about them, my thoughts seemed to slide away.

The sun was long set by the time I staggered up the path to our house. Behenu offered to run on ahead to light the lamps, but she looked like she could barely stagger another step, so Istnofret went instead.

Intef and Renni were on each side of me, their arms around my waist holding me up. We finally stumbled into the house and they lowered me onto a cushion.

I felt awkward lying there while everyone else rushed around, preparing our meal, closing the window shutters to keep out the insects or swatting the ones that had already gotten in because the shutters were left open too late. How odd this feeling was. When I was queen, I expected to be the one who lay back on soft cushions and did nothing. Now I felt lazy and fat and embarrassed.

"Samun, are you well?" Intef crouched beside me.

"My legs hurt."

The rest of my thoughts were too embarrassing to share.

"Is the babe all right?" He rested his hand on my belly. "I was so worried she would decide it was time to be born while we were walking back."

"She has been quiet for a while. I think she is sleeping."

"Any day now, yes?"

"Any day."

"Why did you sigh before you said that? Are you not looking forward to meeting our daughter?"

"I didn't realise I did. I am just tired. Everything seems to take so much effort at the moment. I was…"

"Was what?" he prompted.

"I was hoping we would find the Eye quickly once we reached Crete. I thought perhaps our daughter might yet be born on Egyptian soil."

"Oh, my love. Nothing about this quest of yours has been easy. Did you really think the gods would make these final days any easier? I think that whatever lies ahead will be the most difficult part of our journey yet."

"I hope not. I don't have either the time or the energy for difficult. Intef, I so want our daughter to be born in Egypt. It doesn't seem right for her to be born on foreign soil."

"We could go home. It is only a week's sail from here. We could get you back to Egypt for the birth."

"And then what? I come back here, with a babe in arms, and resume the search? I won't be able to travel immediately. I'll need to rest, at least for a few days, and by then, who knows what might have happened. Someone else could find the Eye. We might never find its trail again. And then it would have all been for nothing."

Would little Setau have been born too soon if I hadn't overexerted myself with travel and the shock of cutting off Intef's arm? One thing I knew for certain is that Intef would still have his arm if we had never left Egypt. And his father, Setau, would have lived if we had never gone to Thebes.

"I don't believe the gods would lead us all this way and then allow someone else to snatch the Eye away at the last moment," Intef said. "They are testing us. Testing you. But surely they would understand if you needed to put this search on hold to deliver our daughter."

"I think this is all part of the test." I hadn't considered this before, but it became clear to me as we talked. "If this last part of our journey will require physical feats, how could they make it more challenging than by waiting until I was heavily pregnant to lead me this far?"

Once again I thought of a sandy shore and a falcon's eyes. I had spoken with Horus. Of that, I was certain. If only I could remember what had happened. There had to be some purpose to our meeting. Perhaps he had told me where the Eye was. If I had forgotten something like that, I had to find a way to remember.

"I have to keep going," I said. "I think that if I stop now, they will never let me find the Eye."

Intef looked deep into my eyes as if searching for some truth that perhaps I didn't even know myself.

"Will you promise me something?" he asked.

"What?"

"Once you find the Eye, and you take it home, promise me we will have a chance at a normal life after that."

"Istnofret wants to come back to Crete."

And my sisters were here. I had even more reason than Istnofret to return, if I only thought they would still be here by then.

"We could do that, too. If you could bear to be away from Egypt. I am finding I quite like Crete myself."

"I cannot think of things like that. Not yet. There is too much I need to do first."

"Do you have a plan?"

"A plan?"

"For when you find the Eye. What exactly do you intend to do? You have always been rather vague about it."

"I don't know what it can do. We've heard a couple of stories, but how much is true? I suppose I was hoping that once I have the Eye, it would tell me what to do. I only know that I need to take it back to Egypt. Use it to claim the throne back from Ay. Restore peace with the Hittites before they turn Egypt to dust, if they haven't already. The treasuries were empty when my father died. They are still not what they should be, or at least they weren't when we left. We cannot afford war with the Hittites, and I cannot bear to think of the blood that would be shed. And all because their prince was killed."

"It is no small thing for them."

"Of course not, and I didn't intend to make light of it. But is it really worth war between two countries? Is the life of one man worth the hundreds, maybe even thousands, that will be lost? The devastation to families and livelihoods and crops? We need a peaceful resolution. We cannot live the rest of our lives looking over our shoulders and wondering if the Hittites are sneaking up on us yet."

"This is the first time I have heard you mention peace."

"I have said before that my intention is to avoid war."

"You have talked about war. You have not talked of peace."

"Isn't it the same thing? Avoid a war. Make peace."

He considered his reply for a long moment.

"No. I don't think they are the same. Avoiding war could still mean battles. It could still mean death and destruction."

"So could peace."

"I suppose. Peace can be hard-fought and not necessarily desired by both parties. I am just pleased to hear you talk of it."

"I bear a responsibility towards both Egypt and Hattusa for what happened. I need to make it right."

Istnofret came into the chamber then, bearing a plate of food for me.

"Intef, you can go and serve yourself," she said. "I am not waiting on you when you have two good legs to carry yourself out there."

"I only have one arm, though." He gave her a cheeky grin. "Does that not entitle me to be waited on?"

"No," she said, curtly. "It doesn't. Here, Samun. Fish broth. It is rather tasty, if I say so myself."

I restrained a smile at their banter. It was good to see Intef able to joke about his missing arm. When we had first cut it off, he wanted to lie down and die. I hadn't been sure he would ever be himself again.

The fish was sweet and tender. I hadn't felt hungry until that moment, but my stomach growled and I devoured my share.

We were all rather quiet that evening. I was too exhausted to speak further and I supposed the others were too disheartened. Nobody mentioned either my sisters or the Eye. We went to bed early and I quickly fell asleep. I dreamed of sandy shores and falcon eyes, although when I woke, I wasn't sure whether my dream was memory or imagination. Over breakfast, we discussed our next moves.

"We should talk to Eritha again," Istnofret said. "Find out where else Antinous used to go."

"We talked before of going to the temples," Renni said. "There must still be priests here who knew Antinous. Perhaps he mentioned having a special artefact, or something that he needed to hide. He might have asked for advice on a suitable place to put it."

"We can do both," Intef said. "You and Istnofret go talk to priests. Behenu and I will speak with Eritha."

"And I suppose I am to stay here and lie on my mat like a calf being fattened for slaughter?" I asked, sourly.

Intef started to reply but I cut him off. I wasn't in the mood for one of his perfectly reasonable responses.

"I am not an invalid. I want to contribute. If the babe comes before we find the Eye, I might have to stay in bed but for now, while I can, I want to go with you."

And perhaps I would see my sisters. Maybe they hadn't yet left Crete. Just a glimpse of them would be enough, or so I told myself.

"You exhausted yourself yesterday," Intef said. "You need to rest."

"What I need is to find the Eye."

We glowered at each other until Istnofret intervened.

"It is only a short walk to Eritha's," she said. "Samun can go with you and Behenu. You will only worry about her if she doesn't."

Intef looked like he wanted to argue, but he said nothing. It seemed I would be permitted to go.

TWENTY-SEVEN

W hen we left for Eritha's home, Intef set a slow pace. Even so, I struggled to keep up with him and Behenu. The babe seemed to have doubled in size since yesterday and I felt fatter and more unwieldy than ever.

Eritha didn't look surprised to see us.

"I take it you didn't find what you were looking for," she said, mildly.

"You knew it wouldn't be there," I said.

"If indeed my father had something he wanted to hide, he would be too clever to put it in a place he was known to frequent."

"Then how are we supposed to find it?" I asked.

"Isn't that the point? He didn't want anyone to find it. My father was a wise man. If he thought that whatever he had was too dangerous, you should take heed of that. Leave it where he put it, wherever that may be."

"You don't understand how important this is," I said.

"Eritha." Intef intervened, likely sensing my increasing irritation. "Where else did your father go when he wanted to be alone? There must be other places that were special to him."

"He used to wander through the mountains," she said. "Sometimes he would be gone for days. I never knew exactly where he went. He didn't offer such information and I didn't ask."

"What if he didn't take it to a secret place?" Behenu said. "Maybe he put it in plain view. If it didn't look like anything special, he might have felt there was no need to hide it away."

I tried not to let my gaze drop down to the silver ring on Eritha's finger. Surely it couldn't be that simple.

"But that means it could be anywhere," I said. "How are we ever going to find it on this gods-damned island if it could be anywhere?"

"It could be anywhere whether he hid it or not," Intef said in that reasonable tone that never failed to irritate me. "We still have no information about where he might have taken it."

He turned back to Eritha. "Are you sure you don't know where he went when he was off in the mountains?"

She thought for a long moment and I began to grow hopeful, but when she finally shook her head, my heart sank.

"He really never said. I don't know whether he went a short distance away and then found shelter for a couple of days, or if he walked a long way and didn't stay long. He never said and I never asked."

"So what now?" I asked. "Do we wander aimlessly through the mountains and hope to stumble over it?"

"Is there someone he might have confided in?" Intef asked. "A friend perhaps? A fellow priest?"

"He was friendly with a lot of people, but I cannot think of anyone he might have confided in. His friends were back in Babylon. He didn't really get close to anyone here."

We were mostly silent as we walked home. I tried not to look like I was watching for my sisters, but Intef gave me a few sideways glances as if wondering whether I was about to run off and search for them.

"Maybe Istnofret and Renni found something," Behenu said. She didn't sound hopeful, though.

The house was empty when we returned. I lay down for a nap, still fatigued from yesterday. My back ached again and I couldn't find a comfortable position, so I ended up tossing and turning and trying not to wonder where my sisters were. Had Tey already taken them from Crete? Would I ever find their trail again? I was still awake when Istnofret and Renni returned, but when Intef came in to haul me off my mat, the look on his face said clearly that they had found nothing useful, so I waved him away.

I eventually fell into a shallow half-sleep, where I wasn't quite sure whether I was dreaming or merely imagining. I saw myself walking on a sandy shore in a strange shadowy world. Somebody walked beside me, but I never turned my head to see who it was. *You should be careful of the jackal,* whoever it was said. *He is a trickster.*

Dinner that night was glum. Istnofret and Renni had already told the others about their day, but they relayed it again for my benefit. The priests had spoken of Antinous as a polite but quiet man who mostly kept to himself. He liked solitude and seclusion, as we already knew from Eritha. He prayed a lot and he liked telling old tales. One of his favourites was about the minotaur, a creature half-man and half-beast which was supposedly kept in the tunnels beneath the palace at Knossos.

"Maybe he hid the Eye in the palace," Behenu said.

"It is in ruins," Renni said. "Destroyed by an earthquake a

few years ago. If he put it there, it is either buried beneath the rubble now or stolen by looters."

"What about the tunnels?" I asked.

"Inaccessible, and likely caved in anyway," he said.

"The priests said the location of the entrance to the tunnels was kept a secret," Istnofret said. "Nobody is permitted on the site anymore. It is too dangerous."

I lay awake long into the night after we went to bed. My back still ached fiercely and the babe wriggled constantly. I kept thinking about the ruined palace.

"Intef," I said.

"Mm."

"How far away is the palace? The one Renni spoke of?"

"I don't know."

"It is probably too far for me to walk. Maybe we could hire a cart."

"Can we talk about it in the morning?"

"I want to go there. I feel like I need to see it. Maybe it is nothing, but if Antinous kept talking about the palace, he might have been trying to leave a clue in case someone came looking for the Eye."

Intef rolled over with a sigh.

"He wasn't leaving clues. He wanted to hide the Eye. That was what he promised, to hide it away somewhere no one would ever find it again."

"But maybe he thought a day might come when it would be needed."

I couldn't give up now. Not after everything we had gone through to get here. There was a clue somewhere. We just weren't seeing it.

"I thought Eritha would be our best chance, but it is clear she knows nothing about the Eye," Intef said.

"Maybe she knows more than she is telling us."

"I don't think so. She doesn't look like she is trying to hide something. She looks straight at us. She speaks calmly, doesn't fidget, doesn't act like she is trying to avoid answering. She simply doesn't have the information we need."

"Somebody must know something," I said.

"Maybe not. I think Antinous did exactly what he said he would. He hid it away in a secret place and he never spoke of it again."

"Then how am I supposed to find it?"

He didn't answer and I supposed I couldn't blame him. He knew no more than I did. Intef's breathing deepened soon after as he fell asleep again. I must have dozed at some point myself, for when I woke, the sun had risen and the birds outside chirped loudly. My back still ached, but at least the babe seemed to have settled for now.

"I think we should go to the palace," I said over breakfast.

"The ruined one?" Istnofret asked. "I hope you don't intend for us to be shifting rubble all day."

"I just want to look around. See if there's anything worth following up on."

Intef set down his bowl with a sigh. "I will go see if I can find a cart."

TWENTY-EIGHT

I ntef returned with a cart and an ox.

"It is only a couple of hours away," he said. "We can be there and back before sunset."

The cart looked rather rickety and the ox was surely too old to walk so far.

"Won't the cart be too heavy?" I asked.

"Not with only you in it," Intef said. "The rest of us will walk."

"Oh no. I am not going to ride if you're all walking."

"Then you can stay here. This is the only beast that anyone was willing to loan me and it doesn't have the strength to pull a loaded cart. So you can ride in the cart or you can stay here, but you are certainly not going to walk."

I glared at him, but he met my gaze evenly. I knew that look: he would not be persuaded of anything else. Was it better to feel awkward at being the only one riding or to stay here while everyone else went? What if they missed something? What if there was a clue that only I could see?

"I will ride," I said, at length. "But do you think the ox is strong enough to pull the cart with two people in it? If someone else gets tired, maybe they could ride with me."

"Two might be fine, but no more," Intef conceded. "The rest of us should walk as long as possible first, though. We don't want to tire the poor beast too early."

Istnofret tried to make the cart more pleasant for me with a blanket and some cushions. They did little to ease its jolting on the rough path, although when she asked if I was comfortable enough, I thanked her nicely. I was still embarrassed at being treated differently and old fears of whether they would stay with me if I made demands rose again. But if anyone was annoyed at my riding while they walked, they didn't show it. They chatted easily amongst themselves and even tried to include me in the conversation every now and then, although I could hardly hear anything over the rumble of the cart's wheels and the ox's hooves.

The sun was high overhead by the time we reached the palace. I had expected it to be a somewhat modest building — certainly nothing like the palaces I grew up in — but the ruins stretched over a very large area. Maybe not a league in length but certainly bigger than I had anticipated. The entire site was a mess of jumbled stones, cracked beams and shattered plaster. Strewn through it all was broken pottery and smashed jars. An occasional partial wall or brightly painted column gave a hint of what it must have looked like.

"Such devastation," Istnofret said, quietly. "I didn't expect it to be so completely destroyed."

"I am glad you said that," I said. "I was feeling foolish for thinking the same thing."

"What now?" Renni asked.

They all looked to me.

"I don't know. I thought there would be areas we could

search but this" — I gestured at the ruins — "there is nothing left. If the Eye is in there somewhere, it is buried and I don't know how we would ever find it."

Intef shaded his eyes as he stared out at the ruins.

"Do we walk all the way here, only to look at it for a few minutes, and then go home?"

I studied his face. He hadn't been at all encouraging of my desire to see the ruins, but now he sounded like he thought we should stay longer.

"What can we do?" I asked. "We dare not climb over the ruins in case they collapse down into the tunnels, so we are limited to inspecting only what we can see from back here. Is there any point to that?"

He shrugged, although his face was calculating.

"It just seems a waste to come all this way only to turn around again."

"Fine then," I said. "We will walk along the perimeter and see if we can see anything useful."

"It is something," he said. "I would rather we did something."

"You should get back in the cart, Samun," Istnofret said. "Perhaps you will be able to see something we cannot from up there."

"You're only saying that because you think I cannot walk. You know I will see nothing over the cart's walls."

"We can lead the ox anyway," Renni said. "That way if you get too tired, we have the cart with us."

So we set off, making our way slowly along the length of the ruins. My fatigue returned before we had even walked the length of one side, but I pushed myself on, not wanting anyone to suggest I should sit in the cart like a sack of laundry.

"Perhaps we should rest for a while," Intef suggested when

we reached the point that marked the furthest extent of the ruins.

I ignored him and set off along the next side. He followed with a sigh. I quickly realised that I should have taken heed of his suggestion. My legs wobbled and it was all I could do to keep myself moving. I wasn't even looking at the ruins anymore, just plodding along with my head down. When Renni spoke from behind me, it took a few moments for his words to penetrate the fog of my exhaustion.

"Wait a minute." He had climbed up into the cart to inspect the ruins from this higher vantage.

"What can you see?" Behenu asked.

Intef climbed up as well. He stood beside Renni and looked out at where he pointed.

"See, there," Renni said. "The ruins are lower."

"So what?" Istnofret asked. "Maybe it was a courtyard without a roof. Less to fall down than in other areas."

"I don't think so," Intef said. "It looks like a section of the ruins has sunk."

"Maybe we could get down into the tunnels from there?" Behenu suggested.

"Exactly what I was thinking," Renni said. "It would have to be you, though, Behenu. If the ruins won't bear your weight, the rest of us don't have a chance."

"Not Samun," Intef said, quickly.

"I am not waiting here by myself."

"It is too dangerous," he said. "The ruins will be unsteady. They might shift underfoot without warning. And they could collapse down into the tunnels at any moment."

"I will go last. If they take the weight of all of you, they will hold me."

Intef shook his head, a stubborn look on his face. "They

might be weakened enough by our passage to collapse under you."

We glared at each other. He was trying to protect both me and the babe, but I didn't intend to be left behind.

"I am going," I said. "I just need to rest a little first."

I leaned against the cart since getting down to the ground by myself was too much effort and I wasn't going to ask Intef for help. But Istnofret quickly suggested I sit and Renni tossed the blanket down from the cart. Istnofret and Behenu managed to lower me down onto it.

Behenu had packed some provisions and now she brought out bread and a wedge of local goat's cheese. The cheese was sharp and tasty, and I ate with relish. The babe kicked a little. Maybe she didn't enjoy the cheese as much as I, or maybe she protested the day's activities. It must be hard to sleep while being jostled around so. When I felt somewhat rested, they hauled me to my feet.

"So how do I do this?" Behenu asked.

"Slowly," Renni said. "Like when you climbed the cliff. Feel each step before you put your weight on it. Take note of where you step so you can make your way back by the path you know is safe."

"What do I do when I get there?"

"Just look. You might be able to see down into the tunnels or perhaps see a way to get down there."

Behenu stepped out into the ruins. The first few steps were easy enough. Pottery and plaster crunched underfoot. Then she had to climb over a fallen beam and make her way around a jumble of stones.

"They look too loose," she called to us. "I don't dare try to climb over them."

"You're doing well," Intef called back. "Just go slowly."

There was a heart stopping moment when her foot slid and she almost fell. She paused, her hand over her heart as she composed herself.

"Oh, be careful," Istnofret said again, but very softly this time. "I cannot bear to watch."

"Then look away," Renni said. "You will hear if anything goes wrong, but you don't need to watch. Behenu can probably feel your anxiety all the way over there."

I absently rubbed my belly as I watched Behenu's progress.

"Are you all right?" Intef asked quietly.

I had been so absorbed in my thoughts that I hadn't noticed him sidle up beside me.

"Just waiting, and trying to be quiet."

"She will be fine. You don't need to worry."

I sighed and didn't reply.

"Samun?" he prodded.

"I am fine. I just feel a bit odd."

"Is it the babe? Is she kicking again?"

"No, she is quiet. It is nothing. I am probably just being silly."

I doubted he would have let the matter drop except that Behenu had almost reached her destination.

"Slow down," Renni called to her. "It might be more unsteady over there."

"What can you see?" Istnofret called.

"It is definitely collapsed down into the tunnels. I can see a couple of patches of darkness but nothing more."

"Do you think we can get down there?" Intef asked.

Behenu took her time answering, creeping a little closer to the sunken area.

"I think so," she called finally. "There's a place where the foundation rocks have fallen down. They are quite large and it would be easy enough to climb down them. There is one section that will need a bit of a jump, but it doesn't look too bad."

"What do you think?" Renni asked the rest of us.

All three of them looked at me. Intef opened his mouth, but I spoke quickly.

"Don't you dare suggest I should stay here while you all go and investigate. I feel much better now after having rested. I will come too."

"Somebody should stay and keep an eye on the ox," Intef said.

"You do that then, but I am not staying behind."

He turned away but not before I saw the exasperation on his face. I felt a little bad at deliberately provoking him but didn't seem to be able to stop myself. The closer we came to the babe's birth, the more over-protective he became. If only I could tell him that both the babe and I would survive the birth. But I couldn't tell him that without sharing the rest of my dream. Besides, I was going to find a way to keep the babe from Osiris, so there was no point in worrying him.

"The ox will be fine," Renni said quietly to him. "It won't get far with the cart attached and I doubt it will try to make its way over the ruins."

Intef replied, but his voice was too low for me to hear.

"Should we take the rest of the provisions?" Istnofret asked. "What if we get lost in the tunnels?"

"We should have brought a lamp," Intef said. "There is no point exploring down there if we cannot see. I brought flint in case we needed a fire, but I didn't think of lamps."

"You're getting rusty, old man," Renni said. "It is not like you to forget something useful."

"I know." Intef sounded abashed. "It has been too long since I trained properly. I am getting soft."

"Do you miss soldiering?" Istnofret asked as she retrieved the sack with our provisions from the cart. "I know Renni does."

"I miss parts of it," Intef said. "The camaraderie, the training. I don't miss the endless hours of standing guard and waiting for something to happen."

"That's what Renni said," Istnofret said. "He wouldn't want to go back to standing guard at someone's door, but he misses the exercise and the men he worked with."

It was my door they used to guard and I felt oddly chastised at the memory.

"We likely won't get far anyway," Renni said. "Let's just see what sort of state the tunnels are in. If they seem safe enough, we can come back tomorrow with lamps."

We set off across the ruins, trying our best to follow Behenu's path. She called out helpful tips, letting us know that a particular section was slippery or unstable. I had only taken a few steps before I realised what a bad idea this was. It was difficult enough for the others but even more so for me, since my balance was less than steady and I couldn't see past my belly to where I put my feet. I walked behind Istnofret and tried to step only where she did, although I was never sure if I stepped in quite the right place or not.

I tried to keep my mind on my footing, but I kept thinking of what Intef had said. It had never occurred to me to wonder whether he missed being a soldier. I had assumed our travels would be enough to satisfy anyone, but it seemed this wasn't what he wanted. He had told me he wanted to settle down, but I hadn't really understood. It wasn't just about a house, was it? He meant a lifestyle. A life where he had a job and an income. Where he had men he trained with and worked with. Where he was once again the expert in his field. I wasn't sure I could ever offer him that kind of life again.

Distracted by my thoughts, I slid as plaster moved beneath my foot. I was knocked off balance and landed heavily on my hip against a waist-high pile of rubble. Intef was a few paces behind me, but it took him only a moment to reach me.

"Are you all right?" He grabbed my arm, even though I didn't need steadying by that point.

"I am fine. Just a bit embarrassed."

"You need to be more careful. If you had landed on your belly, the babe could have been injured."

"I am well aware of that," I answered, frostily.

I shook off his hand and set off again. Intef was right at my heels this time. I tried to shake off my annoyance. He didn't need to walk quite so close behind me. *But look at what happened when he didn't,* a little voice inside me said. *The babe could have been hurt and it would have been your fault for not paying attention.* I pushed the thoughts away and focussed on my feet. The babe was safe enough — at least until she was born.

TWENTY-NINE

As I made my way across the rubble, I glimpsed bits and pieces of the broken palace that gave hints of what life here had been like. Chunks of plaster no larger than the size of my palm revealed fragments of murals. Dolphins, goats, a strange winged creature I didn't recognise. A shattered frieze with a woman, or maybe a goddess, tending a flock of sheep. Half of a person's head, carved from stone that had shattered neatly in two. The surviving eye looked out balefully at the ruins it now inhabited.

"This place has a disturbing feeling," Istnofret said as I reached her. She wrapped her arms around herself. "I don't like it."

"It feels haunted," Behenu said. "Somebody's spirit still resides here."

My skin crawled, although I had been too intent on my passage to notice, or perhaps I hadn't been bothered until they mentioned it. Whatever the reason, I suddenly felt uncomfortable. This was a place we shouldn't trespass in.

"See, there." Behenu pointed to where the fallen rocks

formed a staircase of sorts, leading down into the tunnel. "Shall I go first?"

"Go carefully," Renni said. "I am still not convinced it is safe."

Behenu slowly climbed down the rocks. Her passage looked easy enough and the rocks must have been stable because she steadied herself against them several times.

"I will have to jump from here." She leaned out to peer down. "It is not that far."

"Should have brought a rope," Intef muttered.

"Too late for that," Renni said. "Wait there, Behenu. I will come down to you. I'll jump."

"And then how do we get you back up again?" Istnofret asked, tartly. "You are too heavy for us to haul back up. Better that Behenu goes."

"She might sprain her ankle," he said. "I am more used to that sort of thing."

"Not anymore. As Intef pointed out earlier, it has been a long time since either of you trained properly. Let Behenu go."

"And how will she get back up again?" he asked.

"How will you get back up?"

"I'll find a way."

"So will she."

They glared at each other, neither willing to back down, until Intef intervened.

"Let Behenu go. We will find a way to haul her up if we need to and she is lighter than Renni."

Renni shrugged at Behenu. "I guess you get to go."

She looked like she wanted to say something — perhaps ask him to go with her — but in the end she merely shrugged back at him.

"Be careful," Istnofret said.

Behenu lifted one hand in acknowledgement but didn't respond.

"Let her concentrate," Renni said quietly. "She doesn't need us distracting her."

"It is too dangerous," she said. "Maybe you should go after all."

"A minute ago you said she should be the one to go."

"I've changed my mind."

"Contrary woman."

He wrapped an arm around her shoulders and she leaned against him.

I glanced at Intef, wondering if he, like Renni, thought he should have gone himself. He watched Behenu carefully but if he was at all upset, his face didn't show it.

"Here I go," Behenu said. She jumped before anyone could respond.

"Behenu?" Istnofret called. "Are you all right?"

"I am fine. It was hard to judge the distance in the dark, but it is not as far as I thought. There's a couple of big rocks down here. If Renni could come down, I think we might be able to push one of them over and then the rest of you won't need to jump."

Renni was already making his way down the rocky staircase before she had finished.

"What are the conditions like?" Intef called.

"Dusty but the passage is clear from what I can see. And you won't believe it, but there is a lamp hanging from a hook. There are others that are shattered, but this one looks like it is still useable."

Istnofret only wrang her hands and didn't seem reassured. Renni had jumped down by now and I heard the grinding of rock on rock and much puffing and panting.

"Can you manage?" Intef asked me.

At least he didn't ask if I would stay behind.

"I will be fine," I said, briskly. "Let's not waste any more time. We should at least take a quick look down there this afternoon. If the tunnels really are clear and stable, we can come back tomorrow with more supplies and search properly."

"Let's go then," he said. "I will go ahead so I can steady you."

I wanted to tell him I was perfectly capable of getting down there by myself, but I swallowed my pride and held out my hand. Now was not the time to be careless and risk falling. His feet were nimble and he always seemed to know exactly where to step. He had come a long way since those first months after we cut off his arm, when he had to learn how to use his body all over again.

It was only as I made my way down that I realised why Behenu had been so confident. The rocks couldn't have been more perfectly positioned if someone had *wanted* us to climb down.

Renni had already located the unbroken lamp and Intef tossed him the flint. With the lamp lit, we set off slowly, stopping often to listen for any sound that suggested the tunnels might be unstable. My fear from the tunnels in Asia Minor came back to me, that moment when I became aware of the weight of the earth above us. Intef urged me on with a light touch to my arm. I tried not to think about the rubble and rocks and beams piled up over our heads. Now I understood just how safe and solid the last tunnels were. This felt much more precarious.

The tunnels seemed to follow an orderly pattern with regular intersecting passages. Intef said we should always turn left so we could find our way back. It would be easy to get lost in here and we didn't have enough supplies to spend days trying to find our way out again.

At length we came to an area where the roof had caved in and a pile of rubble provided a convenient enough staircase up to the surface.

"We have been in here for a while." Intef shot me a worried look. "Maybe we should go back up. We have a long walk home ahead of us."

"We haven't seen enough yet," I said. "There must be leagues of tunnels down here. If there is any possibility that Antinous hid the Eye down here, we need to search them thoroughly."

"But not today. We will go home and figure out a plan. Perhaps we come back tomorrow prepared to spend a couple of days down here. We need a way of marking our progress, and blankets and more supplies. And perhaps we should see if the midwife would come with us."

I sighed. In a way I almost wished the babe would hurry up and arrive. Once she arrived, surely Intef would stop fussing as much. Or at least he would have a new target for his fussing.

"As long as we can come back tomorrow," I said.

Intef nodded and held out his hand to help me up the rubble steps.

The sun had started to set by the time we emerged from the tunnels, or at least that was what I assumed. The sun must have dipped down behind the surrounding trees and hills, for everything was shrouded in shadows.

"Where is the ox?" Behenu asked. "Shouldn't it be over there?"

We all looked in the direction she indicated, but Renni pointed slightly further to the east.

"I think it is that way. But still, I don't see it. It must have wandered."

"It cannot have gone far," Istnofret said.

We set off in search of the ox, although not without a brief disagreement over whether I should walk that far or sit and wait for the beast to be located and the cart brought to me. I soon regretted insisting I would walk, for it seemed we had gone much further than we realised. Ahead of us, Renni came to a halt.

"It should be around here," he said. "It really cannot have gone very far."

"Maybe it made its way over to those trees?" Behenu gestured towards a stand of tamarisk some distance away.

"With the cart attached and nobody to drive it?" Renni asked. "I doubt it, but there is nowhere else it could hide."

"Stolen, perhaps?" Intef suggested. "After all, an ox and a cart have considerable value. We should have left someone behind to guard them."

I kept my mouth shut, not wanting to remind anyone that it was me they had thought should stay.

"I can run over and check," Behenu suggested. "There is no point in everyone walking all that way if it isn't there."

She didn't look at me, but I knew who *everyone* was.

"Good plan," Renni said. "Off you go."

Behenu had only taken a few steps when Istnofret gasped.

"Stop," she said.

Behenu froze. "What is it?"

"Just hold still." Istnofret slowly walked up to her.

"Tell me," Behenu whispered.

Istnofret turned back to the rest of us.

"Do you see it?"

She pointed at Behenu's feet.

It took me a few moments to see what she saw. It wasn't Behenu's feet she looked at. It was her shadow. And it was moving by itself.

THIRTY

I ntef swore. "Montu!"

"How is that possible?" Renni asked.

"What's wrong?" Behenu whispered. "You're scaring me."

"Do you see it, Samun?" Istnofret asked. "Tell me I am not crazy."

I slowly shook my head. "I don't think you're crazy."

"Please." Behenu was almost in tears. "Somebody tell me."

"It is your shadow," Istnofret said. "It is moving."

Behenu turned very slowly and looked down at her shadow. It froze, but when she looked away, it slowly moved again. It wasn't much, just a ripple, a slight stretching, a twitch of the fingers. Her shadow was moving when Behenu wasn't.

"Ist, yours is moving too," Renni said.

My own shadow moved only when I did, or at least so it seemed. When I looked away, I caught the slightest movement out of the corner of my eye. I glanced back in time to see it grow still again. Intef's moved, too. A slight wriggle that was barely noticeable unless you looked right at it. So did Renni's.

"What is happening?" Istnofret whispered. "What do we do?"

Was she whispering because she thought the shadows could hear her? Could they?

My shadow stilled as soon as I looked at it. Somehow it knew when I was watching.

Behenu's shadow slowly grew larger.

Intef's wriggled vigorously.

Then there was something that felt like a pop, although I heard nothing, and Renni's shadow separated from him. It took a step or two, cocked its arms and seemed about to run. Renni moved before it could, stomping on its leg. His shadow twisted and turned, trying to escape, but it couldn't get away as long as his foot was on it.

I felt another soundless pop and suddenly Behenu chased her shadow across the grass. They were evenly matched for speed and she couldn't quite catch up to it. Then Behenu leaped and flung herself on her shadow. She hit the ground with a groan, but she landed on her shadow and, like Renni's, it was trapped. It writhed but couldn't get away.

I glanced at my own shadow and my heart beat in double time at how it had grown in the few moments I hadn't been looking at it. Another soundless pop and my own shadow hurried away.

"Samun, quick," Renni shouted.

I took a giant step and just managed to catch my shadow's heel. It was trapped. While I was distracted, Istnofret and Intef had each pinned down their own shadows. We looked at each other.

"Now what do we do?" Istnofret asked.

"We cannot let them leave," I said. "You know we cannot be resurrected without our shadows."

"They don't seem to be able to leave as long as we are touching them," Intef said. "We just have to keep doing that until we figure out what to do."

"What is happening?" Behenu asked. "I don't understand."

"Oh, but you didn't grow up Egyptian," Istnofret said. "Of course you don't know. A person has five essential components. The body, the *ka*, the name, the personality..."

"And the shadow," I said. "Without your shadow, you aren't a complete person. You cannot be resurrected without all five essential components."

"What about Intef?" The look on Behenu's face suggested she wasn't sure she wanted to know. "Can he be resurrected without his arm?"

"I have my arm," Intef said. "Renni kept it for me and had it mummified. I carry it in my pack. When my time comes, my body will be complete."

"I had no idea." Behenu looked down at the shadow beneath her. "We Syrians do not have any such stories. I've never even thought about my shadow."

She had barely finished speaking before her shadow began wriggling even more violently than before.

"Can you feel it?" My shadow had been perfectly still since the moment I caught its heel. Perhaps it thought that if it pretended it hadn't tried to run away, I would forget and step away.

"It feels like nothing more than a light breeze," she said. "I can see it is fighting me, but I don't feel its struggle."

"How very curious." Istnofret was sitting on hers. It still wriggled a little but seemed resigned to being subdued.

"What do we do now?" I asked. "How do we reattach them?"

"It is only a couple of hours until dark," Renni said. "Even if we left now, we won't get home before the sun sets. We don't know what will happen then. Maybe our shadows will become more powerful. Maybe we won't be able to control them in the dark. After all, how do you hold onto something you can neither see nor feel?"

Horror filled me as I stared down at my sullen shadow. Was I about to lose it permanently? I would never be reunited with my sisters in the Field of Reeds.

"I don't know where we are, but we're not in our own world," Intef said. "Nothing looks quite right. Look at the sky. It is just slightly the wrong shade. And where is the sun? The grass, the trees. Nothing looks as it should."

"The remains of the palace are the wrong colour," Behenu said, as we all looked around. "The grey stones are too dark."

"And the ox is gone," Renni said. "That should have told us something was wrong."

"How did we get here then?" I asked. "And how do we go back?"

"I think it might have been when we climbed out of the tunnel." Intef's tone was thoughtful. "I thought for a moment that something was wrong, but I couldn't immediately see what and there was no obvious danger. I shouldn't have dismissed my unease. Perhaps if we had gone straight back down, we could have gotten back without losing our shadows."

"So do we go back down into the tunnels then?" Istnofret asked. "Try to find the right entrance to lead us back to our own world?"

"What do we do with our shadows?" Behenu asked. "I don't think we can carry them and it hardly seems likely they will cooperate."

"And we only have the one lamp," Renni said. "We don't

know if the shadows can impact on the world around them. What if they can put out the lamp and escape?"

"If there is no light, we cannot see them," Intef said. "I think it is logical to assume that without light, we cannot control them."

"Can they be reasoned with, do you think?" Istnofret asked. "After all, we have been together with our shadows for our whole lives. Maybe if they could tell us what they want, we could find a way to make them happy?"

"Do you think they have names?" Behenu asked.

"Maybe their names are the same as ours," I suggested.

My shadow seemed to shake its head.

"Or maybe not."

My shadow had its hands on its hips. It seemed to be tapping its foot. If it had eyes, it would have been rolling them at me.

"Hello, Shadow," I said. "Can you hear me?"

Its foot stopped tapping and it seemed to cock its head towards me.

"I think it does," Istnofret whispered.

"Can you talk, Shadow?" I asked.

There was no reply, or none that I could hear at any rate.

"Is there something you want? Are you so unhappy that you would leave me?"

Its foot started to tap again.

"If I have upset you, I am sorry."

The foot stopped tapping. I took that as an encouraging sign.

"I admit I've never paid much attention to you. I've never thought about how that made you feel. You're always there with me and yet I've never noticed you, have I? I am sorry, I am a terrible… partner."

My shadow nodded and I felt the sting of chastisement.

"Do all shadows feel like this? Do they all feel ignored and taken advantage of and not noticed?"

My shadow shrugged. Perhaps it could draw only on its own experience.

"Can the other shadows hear me?"

But if they could, they didn't respond.

"Maybe you should try talking to your own shadows," I said. "Perhaps only you can communicate with yours."

I turned back to my shadow. I needed to find out what it wanted. If I knew that, I might be able to negotiate with it. I might be able to convince it to reattach itself to me.

"I realise that I am standing on you," I said. "Does that hurt you?"

My shadow nodded. I hesitated. This might be a way to build trust — or it might take the opportunity to flee. I saw how fast Behenu's shadow moved. I would not be able to catch mine if it ran.

"I will take my foot off if you promise you won't try to run away."

My shadow cocked its head again, considering.

"We need to trust each other. Now that I know you understand, that you hear things and can feel, you can trust me to look after you. But can I trust you not to run away?"

It seemed frozen. Had something happened to it?

"Shadow? Can you hear me?"

It nodded slowly.

"What do you think about this? Can we agree to trust each other?"

My shadow turned so that its protruding belly was visible. Of course, I should have expected that its belly would resemble mine.

"You are with child?"

My shadow rubbed its belly.

"Is that your child? Or mine."

Its hand stopped moving and it turned its back to me. I had offended it.

"Shadow, I am sorry. Forgive my ignorance."

Its head turned slightly. Looking at me out of the corner of its eye, I supposed. Assuming it had eyes.

"You will have to teach me. Help me to understand what you need."

It slowly turned back to face me. Interesting that my foot on its heel didn't seem to stop it from turning in whatever direction it wanted, only from leaving.

"I am going to step off you. Can I trust you?"

One hand went to its hip. It wasn't going to give me any indication either way. I hesitated. This could be the worst decision I had ever made. If I lost my shadow, I would never go to the Field of Reeds. I would never again see my sisters who were already there. I pushed away thoughts of my living sisters. There was no time for that now.

I took a deep breath, but before I could move the babe kicked.

"Oh." I rubbed my belly, then realised my shadow had done the same thing. "Did your babe kick too? At the same time as mine?"

Was that my own babe's shadow inside it? By giving my shadow the chance to flee, did I doom my daughter before she was even born? I took a deep breath and prayed to Isis that I wasn't making the wrong decision.

"I have decided I am going to trust you. And I hope you will trust me. I am going to move my foot away."

Perhaps if my shadow was as heavily pregnant as I, it

couldn't run very fast anyway. Maybe it could go no faster than I could. I pushed the thought out of my mind. I had to establish trust, and I couldn't do that if I was already making a backup plan.

"I am moving my foot now."

My legs trembled as I stepped back. My shadow hesitated. It turned to look behind itself and shifted a little as if preparing to run. But then it turned back to face me and seemed to study me intently. Its hand moved to its belly, rubbing it in the same way I rubbed my own. Eventually, it nodded.

"That's good." I suddenly realised I had been holding my breath and I let it out with a rush. "We can learn to trust each other."

THIRTY-ONE

I pushed away my thoughts about how I didn't quite trust my shadow. Could it tell what I thought? I should think nothing negative about it, just in case. Yet even as I turned to see how the others fared, I tried to keep watching it out of the corner of my eye. They all still had their shadows pinned down and no one seemed to be having much success in communicating. I suddenly noticed how the sky had darkened.

"We don't have long before sunset," I said.

Alarm flashed across Intef's face as he noticed I wasn't standing on my shadow.

"We have decided to trust each other," I said.

"How? Mine won't listen. I am not even sure it can hear me."

"It hurts the shadows when we stand on them. Mine has been feeling neglected and unseen. I have promised to learn what it needs."

"I wonder if they need us as much as we need them. If I knew what it needed, I might be able to get it to listen to me."

"Have you asked it how it feels?" I asked.

"What's the point? It cannot respond."

"Maybe not, but you are demonstrating that you *see* it. That you are trying to understand. I think that's what they want."

He looked back down at his shadow. "I suppose you feel ignored. You're unseen, like a good soldier should be."

His shadow seemed to lean a little closer.

I turned back to my own.

"Shadow, can you communicate with the other shadows?"

It seemed to shrug and I wasn't sure whether that was a *yes* or a *what of it*.

"Could you tell them we're trying? That we have no experience in talking with shadows and we don't know how to go about it or what we should say?"

It cocked its head and raised one hand. A question perhaps? What's in it for me?

"I have shown you trust by releasing you. Perhaps you could return that trust by telling your fellows that we are trying to understand."

It waved its hand around. Perhaps saying that it had already repaid my trust by not running away.

"Please. I would be very appreciative if you would do this for me."

It seemed to sigh then turned away. Except for Behenu's, the shadows leaned in towards it. They were communicating even if I could hear nothing. Renni's shadow shook its head. Istnofret's crossed its arms and turned its back. Only Intef's seemed to listen without becoming aggravated. It turned back to him and seemed to study him carefully.

"I wonder if your mind works the same way as mine does," he said to it. "After all, you and I have endured the same training. Do you notice everything around you? Are you always alert for threats? Do you constantly check for anyone who looks suspicious, for who is carrying a weapon, for exits in every building we enter?"

His shadow gave no sign that it understood.

"We could work together. You and me. We could be a team, if we could find a way to communicate. While I look for danger ahead of us, you could look behind us. Imagine what we could achieve. How safe we could keep her if we could watch in every direction at once."

He glanced over at me at the same time as his shadow looked towards mine. Did they have feelings for each other? Was that even possible? At length Intef's shadow turned back to him. It had obviously reached a decision, for it nodded and held out its hand. Intef held his out too until it met his shadow's. A deal had been struck.

The others had been watching and now they renewed their attempts to communicate with their shadows.

"I have only ever wished to serve," Istnofret said. "I have no wish for fortune or attention for myself. I only wanted to serve my lady, to anticipate her every need, as a good serving woman should. Is that what you wanted too? Do you feel as adrift as I, now that we no longer serve her?"

Her shadow seemed to sigh.

"I understand," Istnofret said. "Once I was defined by my position. Now, I don't know what I am."

"You are my beloved," Renni said. "Is that not enough?"

Startled from her thoughts, Istnofret glanced up at him. "No, I don't think it is. For me or for her." She gestured towards her shadow. "We need a purpose, and that has nothing to do with how much we love you."

Renni didn't answer but turned back to his own shadow. "You are the unseen one. Not the star recruit. Not the one with almost miraculous abilities. The one who always has to push that little bit harder and further to keep up."

Intef frowned at him. "I work just as hard. Have you forgotten what I went through when I first trained to be a soldier? The way the men thought me too young to be competent? I had to work twice as hard at everything they did, and still it was several years before they took me seriously."

"You also have talent," Renni said. "I am not debating that you worked hard, but your talent aided you. I have none of that talent. I've always had to work that bit harder than you, train that bit longer and further than you, just to keep up, and even so, I am always still a step or two behind you."

"I got to where I did by always being the one who worked the hardest. If you had worked harder than me, it would have been you who was captain of the queen's guard."

"That isn't true, and you know it." Renni looked sad rather than angry. He turned back to his shadow. "You know what I mean, don't you?"

Behenu was the only one who seemed to be making no headway in communicating with her shadow.

"We have never had control over our destiny," she said. "There has always been someone else to decide our fate. A queen, a noble man. Earlier, our father. The priestesses. Do you long to control your life the way I do?"

Her shadow resolutely ignored her.

"It is not an easy path, to be the one on which so many expectations are laid. The one who was expected to live a certain life, right from birth. At least once we were taken from Syria, we were free of that. Free to live without anyone knowing what was expected of us. And yet, I long to go back, even though…"

Her voice trailed away and I thought she might have shed a tear or two. At length, she looked up at us.

"I have tried everything. Compliments, bargaining, persuasion. Why does mine refuse to listen?"

"Maybe it cannot hear you," Istnofret suggested. "Maybe there is something wrong with it."

If she tried to provoke Behenu's shadow, it didn't work.

"Shadow, can you help?" I asked. "We need to get back to our own world, but we cannot leave without Behenu."

My shadow merely shrugged. Whether it wouldn't help, or it couldn't, I didn't know.

"What stories do your people tell of shadows?" Istnofret asked. "Maybe there is something in them that might help."

"Maybe there are stories that I have forgotten, but I can think of nothing useful."

"You didn't know the Egyptian language before you were taken from Syria," Intef said. "Maybe your shadow doesn't understand you."

"You think I should speak to it in Syrian?" Her face brightened. "Why didn't I think of that?"

She turned back to her shadow and spoke. The sky grew darker as we waited.

"Perhaps I should return to the tunnel and get the lamp?" Renni suggested. "This doesn't look promising."

"But what if you go into the tunnel and come back out somewhere else?" Istnofret asked. "We don't know that you will be able to get back to us."

"I will go with him," Intef said. "I won't enter the tunnel but will watch him from the surface. If I can still see him, surely he cannot disappear into some other world."

"We don't know that," Istnofret said. "Renni, I don't think

you should risk it. What if you accidentally go somewhere else and we never find you again?"

"Someone has to go," Renni said. "I will be as fast as I can, but we cannot afford to lose the light. Not while Behenu has yet to reach an agreement with her shadow."

He glanced down at his own and, like me, probably still wondered if we could really trust them. My shadow glanced up at me sharply, as if it had caught my thought.

"You and I will wait here, I think," I said to it. "There is no need for all of us to go and I am sure you're as uncomfortable as I am."

Indeed, the babe seemed to be lying on top of some organ or other. My kidneys perhaps, for something ached low in my belly, almost a cramp. My shadow nodded and rubbed its belly.

"You too? I don't think it will be long before our babes arrive."

Intef overheard our quiet conversation.

"We need to get you home. We are too far from the midwife."

"We cannot leave Behenu and there is nothing we can do to hurry things up. It will take as long as it takes for her to make a connection with her shadow."

"We still need to figure out how to reattach them," Istnofret said. "We cannot just walk around and expect them to follow behind us. Besides, it will look odd and people will notice. They might think we are cursed."

"Maybe they will think we are magicians," Renni said, with a grin.

"You and Intef perhaps," she retorted. "Nobody will think we women are magicians. They will likely think the two of you have cursed us, and then we will all be in trouble."

"We need to make a decision," Intef said. "If Renni and I are going for the lamp, we should do it now. The sky is darkening with every minute we stand here arguing about it."

"Go," I said. "But be careful."

Intef and Renni jogged away, their shadows following close behind them. My shadow waved, catching my attention.

"Do you need something?" I asked.

It gestured towards the departing men.

"I am worried too, but they have to go."

It pointed at them again, more urgently this time.

"You want to go with them? I am not sure that's a good idea."

It shook its head and I sensed sadness.

"Why are you sad?"

It just looked at me.

"Because you think I don't trust you?"

It nodded and I thought carefully before I spoke next. Our bond was still tenuous and the wrong words from me could destroy that connection.

"You and I have never been apart. A person and their shadow are supposed to be together. We have no idea what will happen if we are too far apart. Will it hurt you? Will you cease to exist? And what will happen to me?"

My shadow shrugged, perhaps indicating it didn't know, or that it didn't care.

"Why do you want to go?"

They were almost at the tunnel now and my shadow seemed increasingly anxious. It shifted from foot to foot, looking between me and the men. I felt just as anxious but tried to hide it. After all, we had no idea how we had gotten here, not really. What if even close proximity to the tunnel was enough to rip them away and deposit them in some other world?

"Is it their shadows you're worried about?"

Did my shadow feel the same way about Intef's as I felt about the man himself?

It nodded and gestured after them again.

"You won't get there quickly enough. Not in our condition. Stay here with me. We can sit and rest while we wait." I lowered myself to the grass with a groan. "Come, sit beside me. We can watch them from here. If anything happens, we will see it."

My shadow seemed to sigh and its shoulders drooped. It sat down as awkwardly as I had. Side by side, we watched our men.

THIRTY-TWO

Intef stayed at the entrance to the tunnel, just as he promised. He had his back to us so I couldn't tell whether he spoke, but it was clear that he watched Renni carefully.

We had left the lamp at the foot of the pile of rubble. It should only take a few moments for Renni to get down there, grab the lamp, and come back to us. It was taking too long.

Then Intef dashed down into the tunnel. I could barely breathe as I waited for him to reappear. An icy touch on my hand drew my attention. My shadow had edged a little closer and placed its hand on mine.

"I can feel you," I said. "Did you know that would happen?"

It shrugged but didn't look at me, too focused on the tunnel. We waited, but neither Intef nor Renni reappeared.

"Something is wrong," Istnofret said. "Where's Renni? Why is he taking so long?"

"I don't know."

Beside Istnofret, her shadow also looked off in the direction of the tunnel. Behind them, Behenu still tried to reason with hers.

"Is she having any success?" I asked, with a nod towards Behenu.

"I cannot understand a word of it, but I don't think so. I don't know what to do. Something has happened in the tunnel, but we cannot leave Behenu here alone."

"Is there anything you can do?" I asked my shadow. "Can you explain to Behenu's shadow that we need to leave this place?"

It shook its head. Perhaps it couldn't communicate with the Syrian shadow, or perhaps it simply chose not to interfere.

"We have to do something," Istnofret said. "I cannot stand here and do nothing. I will go see what has happened. You wait with Behenu."

"We don't know whether it is safe to be that close to the tunnel."

"We have to go down there sooner or later. It is likely our only way of getting back to our own world. Maybe Renni has fallen and hurt himself, and Intef is trying to help. I will just go to the entrance and see if I can see something."

"Promise me you won't go down there. No matter what you see. Even if Renni is lying on the ground and Intef is gone, promise you will not go down."

She didn't meet my eyes.

"If something has happened to them, you and I must not get separated," I said.

"I know. But it is Renni. I don't know if I can just walk away if I see him in trouble."

"He and Intef are together. We have to trust them to cope with whatever is happening down there, but you and I and Behenu must stay together."

She leaned down to give me a quick hug, then set off for the tunnel. Her shadow trotted beside her.

"Be careful," I called.

She acknowledged my words with an upraised hand.

My shadow paced back and forth, rubbing its belly.

"Shadow, let's see if we can help Behenu. If nothing else, it might take your mind off what is happening over there for a few minutes."

"It is no use," Behenu said as we approached. "It won't listen to anything I say."

"Does it not understand or is it refusing to listen?"

"I don't know. It responds to neither Egyptian nor Syrian. I am starting to wonder if it understands speech at all."

"Perhaps Syrian shadows are different to Egyptian ones. Maybe you cannot communicate with it."

"Then how do I convince it to come back to me? I cannot sit on it forever."

"We will think of something."

An icy chill touched my hand. My shadow pointed towards the tunnel. Istnofret had reached the entrance and leaned down to look in. A faint noise reached my ears as she called to Intef and Renni. She looked back towards us and I knew she wondered whether to go down there.

"Come back," I called to her.

My shadow paced again, increasingly agitated. Could it communicate with Intef and Renni's shadows even from this distance?

"Shadow, do you know what is happening?"

It flicked a hand at me, as if waving away an annoying fly, and didn't stop its pacing.

"Shadow, what do you know?"

It shook its head.

Istnofret called down into the tunnel again. Could she see them? Were they both lying injured at the bottom?

"Maybe we should all go over there. If something has happened, she won't want to leave them to come back and tell us."

"You should go then," Behenu said. "I will... I don't know. I have to stay here until I make my shadow listen to me."

"What if something happens to Istnofret and I? We could get pulled down into the tunnel. You would be here all alone."

"I have endured worse," she said, grimly. "Go. Make sure they are well. Then come back to me if you can."

"Maybe you could carry your shadow over there?"

She gave me a puzzled look. "It has no substance. I cannot even touch it."

"Have you tried? I feel it when my shadow touches me."

"I am already sitting on it and I feel nothing."

"Just try. Please."

Behenu's face was doubtful, but she obediently reached for her shadow. Her fingers touched the grass.

"Nothing. I wouldn't know it was there if I couldn't see it."

But her shadow turned its head towards her.

"It felt something," I said. "Try again."

Again she reached out. Her shadow shook itself, as if ridding itself of an unwelcome touch.

"See that, Behenu? It feels you."

Over and over she reached for her shadow. It grew increasingly irritated, but then she had a handful of it. It was no more substantial than mist, but somehow she held onto it.

"Let me help you up," I said.

"No, no. Stay back. You are just as likely to fall over on top of me."

I held my breath as she got slowly to her feet. Her shadow

seemed to stretch, still pinned beneath her, but its shoulder twisted and the arm Behenu held lengthened. As she stepped off her shadow, it began to wriggle furiously.

"Hold on, Behenu."

"I am."

She held her shadow with both hands as it thrashed around, trying to pull itself from her grip. Despite its furious actions, it seemed to have no more effect on Behenu than papyrus fluttering in a breeze. At length the shadow seemed to exhaust itself and hung limply from Behenu's hands.

"Will you behave yourself now?" she asked sternly.

She gave it a little shake before repeating her question in Syrian. The shadow didn't acknowledge her words.

"Well, then, let's go," she said. "If it is going to ignore me, there's no point waiting any longer."

The walk back to the tunnels seemed endless. The babe had shifted, sitting lower than ever in my belly. I started to worry she would decide to be born before we could find our men and get back to our own world.

"Did you manage to communicate with it?" Istnofret asked Behenu as we reached the tunnel.

Behenu dragged her shadow along by its arm. It tried to dig its heels into the ground, but if Behenu even noticed its efforts, she paid it no attention.

"It is stubborn," Behenu said. "It will learn to listen."

"Where are they?" I couldn't wait any longer. "Has something happened?"

Istnofret looked back towards the tunnels and gestured helplessly. "I don't know. They are gone. Something must have happened to Renni and Intef went down to help him."

"So what do we do?" I asked. "Do we wait here or go after them?"

"We need a lamp," Behenu said. "It is one matter to keep hold of this thing in the daylight, but what will happen once the light is gone?"

"Then we have no choice but to go down there." I looked towards my shadow. "Shadow, do you agree? Should we go after them?"

My shadow nodded vigorously, then gestured towards Istnofret's shadow. It too nodded.

"We are all in agreement then," I said.

"Except for my shadow which has no say in anything until it learns to behave." Behenu repeated her words in Syrian and her shadow began trying to pull away again, but quickly subsided.

"I think it does understand you, Behenu," Istnofret said. "At least when you speak to it in Syrian."

"Then why won't it respond to me like yours does?" Behenu's voice was filled with frustration. "What have I ever done to make it hate me so much?"

"I think all of our shadows hate us," I said. "We have ignored them for our whole lives. Imagine how that would make you feel."

An icy touch to my hand brought my attention back to my shadow. It put its hand to its chest. I thought it maybe touched the place where its heart was. Perhaps telling me it had forgiven me.

"Thank you, Shadow. I will try very hard in future not to ignore you, but you must remind me if I forget."

It nodded.

"So we are in agreement?" Istnofret asked. "We are going back into the tunnels?"

"I suppose so," I said.

"Shall I go first?" she asked. "That way I can help you, and

Behenu can follow us."

She set off down the rubble staircase with her shadow following closely behind. They reached the bottom without incident.

"Can you see them?" I asked.

"No, there is very little light down here and the lamp is gone."

"Where are they?"

I didn't expect a reply, for she clearly had no more information than I did, but I was suddenly filled with annoyance at Intef. He knew he wasn't supposed to go down into the tunnel. He knew I would worry. He knew the babe was close to being delivered, and yet he left us anyway. And he took the lamp.

"Come down," Istnofret called. "Carefully. The last thing we need now is for you to fall."

"Come on then, Shadow," I said.

I started down the rocks, glancing back only once to make sure my shadow followed. It waved me on. I reached the bottom without incident and a moment later, my shadow was there too.

Behenu came down next, dragging her shadow behind her. There was one heart stopping moment when either Behenu or her shadow — I couldn't tell which — slipped, and they both tottered on the edge of a rock. She quickly regained her footing, but she moved more cautiously after that. As they reached the tunnel floor, she said something in Syrian to her shadow. It turned its head away from her.

Ahead of us, the tunnel was dark and empty of anything other than dust and small pieces of rubble that must have tumbled off the pile we had climbed down.

"Intef?" I called.

"I already tried," Istnofret said. "They aren't here."

"What would possess them to leave us?" I asked. "I thought maybe Renni was injured and Intef came down to help him, but they would still be here. They wouldn't just get up and walk away, not with one of them injured and us still up there."

"Maybe something…" Istnofret's voice trailed away.

"What is it?" My tone was sharper than usual. "I am sorry. I didn't mean to snap at you."

"When Renni and I went to talk to the priests, one of them told us this story. About a beast that roamed these tunnels."

"Yes, one of you did mention it earlier. What else do you remember?"

"We didn't put much weight on it. The priest said there had long been stories of a creature that was half-man, half-beast that lived down here. That was all really."

"Is it dangerous?" Behenu asked.

"He said no more than that, and we didn't ask. It sounded too fanciful. I don't know what Renni thought, but I assumed it was just a story. Perhaps to deter children who might want to explore the tunnels. I didn't actually think there was a beast down here."

"We still don't know that there is," I said. "We have seen no sign of violence."

"Then why did they leave?" Istnofret asked. "Renni wouldn't leave without a very good reason."

"Neither would Intef," I said. "We all know that. But we need to decide what to do. Do we go further into the tunnel and hope we find them? Or do we wait here and hope they come back?"

"I cannot go further without the lamp." Behenu shot a

worried look at her shadow which continued to try to extricate itself from her grasp.

Istnofret looked back down the dark tunnel. "Intef is the only one who thought to bring flint so the lamp would do us no good even if we had it."

"They wouldn't leave us to try to make our way through the tunnels without a lamp," I said. "Whatever happened, they meant to come back."

"Maybe we should wait here." Behenu looked up at the hole through which the last vestiges of sunlight fell. "At least we have a little light here. They could return at any moment."

"Or they might not," Istnofret said. "If something has happened, it is up to us to rescue them. Although I am not sure that we are in any shape for such a thing." She looked from my belly to Behenu's shadow. "Maybe I should go alone. I might find some clue that will help us to decide whether to stay or go."

"What kind of clue are you going to stumble over in the dark?" I asked. "Unless they are dead and lying in your path, you have no hope of finding anything."

"Then what do you suggest?" she shot back. "I cannot stand here and do nothing. They could be in danger."

My shadow touched my hand and gestured down the tunnel.

"I don't think that's a good idea," I said. "We have no light."

It shook its head, gesturing again.

"We need to stick together."

Again, it shook its head. It was hard to see what it did in the little remaining light, but it seemed to point towards itself and then down the tunnel. It pointed at me, then at Istnofret and Behenu.

"Shadow, are you suggesting that you should go? And I should stay here?"

It nodded and wrung its hands. Quickly, quickly, it seemed to be saying. Time is running out.

I tried not to let myself think about whether I could trust it. About what would happen once my shadow became merged with the darkness.

"I don't know."

I stalled, hoping to think of a better plan before I had to decide.

Quickly, quickly, it urged me. I must go.

"Wait a minute. I am trying to think."

No time, it said. I must go now.

"But where are you going? And when will you return?"

It shook its head and seemed to sigh a little.

"I do trust you. I am just afraid we may never find each other again."

I won't let that happen, it seemed to say. I must go.

"Go then. But hurry, and come back if there is any sign of danger."

It nodded and hurried off down the tunnel. In moments it was lost in the darkness.

"Are you sure that was a good idea?" Istnofret asked.

"I don't know. Perhaps it is better equipped than we to search these tunnels in the dark. Intef and Renni may be in danger, which means that Intef's shadow probably is too. Mine seems to have a connection with his. Maybe it cannot bear to stand by knowing that its love is in danger."

We would likely never know the truth of it. I turned back to Behenu.

"Are you all right?" I asked.

She gave her shadow a fierce glare.

"It is too stubborn. I don't know how to make it listen. Why am I the only one who cannot speak with my shadow? Your shadows are all receptive and cooperative. Mine is like a wilful child."

"Perhaps Syrian shadows are different," Istnofret suggested.

"How could that be possible?" she asked.

"I don't know," Istnofret said. "We know hardly anything about the shadows."

"Oh," Behenu said.

But she looked behind me, not at her shadow.

I turned and there stood my shadow.

"You are back already," I said.

It motioned at us. Hurry, hurry, follow.

"Did you find them?" I asked. "Are they all right?"

It shook its head. No time to waste, hurry, follow.

I looked to Istnofret and Behenu. Behenu only shrugged, too occupied with trying to subdue her shadow who again writhed around.

"I don't know," Istnofret said. "They will come back for us, if they are able to."

"And if they cannot? How long do we wait before we conclude that something has happened to them?"

"Can your shadow tell us nothing?"

But my shadow only shook its head again and motioned for us to follow. It edged back down the tunnel, back into the darkness. Hurry, follow, hurry.

"I think we must follow it," I said. "It has found something and it wants to show us."

"I hope you are right." Istnofret glanced down at her shadow who waited at her side like a loyal hound. "Shadow, do you agree we should follow?"

Her shadow looked to mine. If they communicated, it was done silently. Istnofret's shadow nodded.

"Let's go then," I said. "There seems no other choice."

As we started towards my shadow, it urged us to go faster.

Hurry, hurry.

"Shadow, you know I can go no faster," I grumbled. "And neither can you."

Hurry, follow. No time to waste.

Then it took another step backwards and disappeared. We stopped.

"Can you see it?" Istnofret asked.

"No. I don't know whether it has faded into the darkness or if it is gone."

"Do we still follow?"

It could be leading us into danger. Or it could be taking us to Intef and Renni.

"I have to trust it," I said, at length. "It will never trust me again if I don't."

I took a step but faltered. I wasn't as certain as I sounded. Istnofret took my hand and reached for Behenu with her other.

"We will go together," she said.

Together with Istnofret's shadow, we stepped forward. Behenu dragged her shadow behind her.

THIRTY-THREE

We stepped forward and there was nothing but darkness all around us.

"Samun," Istnofret whispered.

My mouth was too dry to speak so I just squeezed her hand.

I shuffled forward, trying to feel my way. If I tripped, I might land on my belly, perhaps injuring the babe. My heart pounded and my knees trembled.

I took one more step and lamp light burned my eyes. The sudden brightness blinded me, but I didn't need to see to recognise Intef's voice.

"Samun!"

"Intef?"

Then he was there, wrapping his arm around my shoulders. I leaned into him and inhaled his familiar scent.

"What happened? Where is Renni? Is my shadow here?"

"We are fine. Renni is right here. Your shadow found us while we were still deciding whether we should try to get back to you, or wait for you to find us. I was so thankful to see it because I knew it must mean you weren't far behind."

"I thought you would come back for us. We wouldn't have waited so long otherwise."

"We feared the tunnel might lead us somewhere else and we would get trapped there. We hoped you would find us if we waited here."

"Find you? Even if you didn't have the lamp, you had only to stand in the middle of the tunnel and we would surely have walked right into you."

"Did you pass through a place of utter darkness? Where you couldn't even see the light from the hole behind you?"

"Yes, once we had gone too far for the light to reach us."

"Renni and I think that place of darkness was somewhere else. Perhaps a place partway between our world and that of the shadows."

"I don't understand."

"Neither do I, my love. But it is the only thing that makes any sense."

"You should have stayed on the surface like you promised. Why in Isis's name did you go down into the tunnel?"

"Because I saw Renni disappear. He was carrying the lamp and went only a little way into the tunnel. Then he was gone."

"So you went after him?"

"Of course I did. You don't think I would leave him?"

"No, but..." Of course he wouldn't let Renni disappear without trying to rescue him. He wouldn't see it as a choice between Renni and me. He wouldn't see it as leaving me and our unborn daughter behind. "Renni was in trouble and you went after him, because that's what you do."

"Do you really think that's all I was doing? Saving a fellow soldier?" He gave me a disgruntled look.

"Well." I floundered. "He is not just any soldier. He is your friend."

"He is my friend, yes, and yours, but he also helps to keep you safe. If something happened to me, Renni would look after you, and the babe."

I looked away, ashamed. He was always so many steps ahead of me that I never had any chance of figuring out his plan. I should know that by now.

"Are both of your shadows well?" His shadow waited at his heels like a loyal hound. Before Intef could reply, the lamp flickered and dimmed.

"How much longer will the light last?" Behenu asked.

Her shadow wriggled furiously.

"Not long," Intef said. "We should move."

We hurried along the tunnel, following Renni as he took each right turn. The walk seemed much further than I remembered and I breathed heavily. The lamp flickered as Renni halted.

"What's wrong?" Istnofret asked. "Are we almost there?"

Renni shook his head. "We missed a turn."

"I counted the turns," Intef said. "This is where we entered the tunnel."

"There is no sign of a hole in the roof," Renni pointed out, not that any of us needed to hear it.

"If it was anywhere nearby, we would see the light," Intef said, a little crossly. "My point was that this is exactly where we entered the tunnel."

"So where is the hole?" Istnofret asked. "Where is the rubble we climbed down?"

Intef didn't answer. There was no answer. The hole simply wasn't there.

"Maybe this is not our world yet," Renni said. "Maybe we left the shadow world and went somewhere else."

The lamp flickered again and dimmed even further. It now gave only the barest hint of light. Behenu moved closer to Renni, trying to keep her shadow in the tiny bit of light remaining. It hung limply from her hand. Was it a good thing or bad that it had stopped fighting her?

"So what do we do?" Istnofret asked. "Maybe we missed it."

"We didn't miss it," Intef said. "We couldn't have missed a pile of rubble and a hole in the roof. Even without the lamp, we couldn't miss it."

"So where is it?"

"If I knew that, I would take us back there," Intef snapped.

"Let's go a little further," Renni said. "Maybe we miscounted the turns."

We walked on. I couldn't hear what Intef muttered to himself, but I could guess it was likely something about not having miscounted.

"I suppose we keep turning right." Renni shot a glance at Intef. "Even if we counted wrong, turning right every time will lead us back there eventually."

"Maybe the hole has moved," Behenu said.

"And the rubble," Istnofret added.

We walked on. Turn after turn revealed only darkness ahead. I leaned against the tunnel wall. My legs trembled and my belly felt strange.

"I need to rest for a few minutes," I said. "I cannot keep going."

"Here, sit down." Intef came to help lower me to the ground. My shadow sat beside me, seeming as uncomfortable as I was.

"Shadow, are you well?"

It seemed to sigh and rubbed its belly.

"The babe is sitting very low, is she not?"

It nodded.

"We should move on," Intef said, after only a few minutes. "While you can still walk. The babe might come any time now."

"I think her time is near. Very near. Shadow, do you agree?"

It leaned back against the tunnel wall with a sigh, too exhausted to reply.

Intef hauled me up and we walked on. My shadow staggered after us.

THIRTY-FOUR

We walked until we all agreed we couldn't possibly have gone that far the first time. The lamp gave one last splutter and died, leaving us in total darkness.

"Please don't fight me, Shadow," Behenu said. "We must stay together."

"Shadow, are you there?" A familiar icy touch to my hand confirmed my shadow was right by my side. "There you are. Are you all right?"

I had no way of knowing whether it replied.

"Now what do we do?" Istnofret asked. "We cannot wander these tunnels in the dark."

"Perhaps we should rest for a while," Renni said. "A couple of hours of rest might make all the difference."

"I am not sure we can afford to linger," Intef said. "We need to get back to the surface and find a midwife."

I had gotten turned around after we stopped and was no longer sure which way was which.

"Perhaps it is my imagination," I said. "But there seems to be some light up ahead."

"I see it," Intef said. "It is around the next corner."

"Shall I go and check it out?" Renni asked.

"Oh no you don't," Istnofret said. "If anyone goes, we all go."

I sighed at the thought of having to walk even another step.

"Do you need to lean on me?" Intef asked.

"I am fine, thanks," Renni replied, before I could answer.

I heard the thud to his shoulder, then Intef's arm was around my waist.

"Come on. We can go slowly."

I hoped his shadow helped mine but didn't have the energy to ask. We stumbled towards the light and discovered it did indeed come from around the corner. There we found a pile of rubble and a hole in the roof.

"Thank you, Isis," I breathed.

Hope gave me the strength to stagger the rest of the way. The rubble looked daunting from the bottom, but with Intef there to haul me up each step and Istnofret steadying me from behind, I made it to the top. I collapsed onto the grass. For a while, all I could do was breathe. When I finally got my breath under control enough to pay attention to anything else, I realised the sun was higher than I had expected. Had we walked right through the night? Beside me, my shadow still panted.

"Shadow?"

It flicked one hand at me. Clearly, that was all it could manage.

Eventually, I realised that the only sounds were my own ragged breathing. Everyone else looked off to our right. I followed their gaze. There stood an enormous pair of gates. They were black and glistened like wet stone in sunlight.

"I think we have a problem," Behenu said, eventually.

"This isn't our world," Intef said.

I sighed.

"I am sorry, my love," he said. "I thought I was leading you home."

"Where are we if this is neither our world nor the shadows' world?" I asked.

"Perhaps we have not yet left the shadow world," he said.

"I think we might be in the underworld," Istnofret said, slowly.

Dread crept over me, making the hairs on my arms stand up. "How is that possible?"

"I don't know." She shook her head, as if trying to dissuade herself. "But it makes sense. The rules are different in the underworld. Our shadows shouldn't have been able to separate from us, but they did. And now these gates. We know the underworld has gates through which travellers must pass. I cannot be sure from this distance, but I think those carvings on the gates are of Anubis."

I squinted, but the carvings were nothing more than a smudge to me.

"It is a dog," Behenu said.

"A jackal." Renni corrected her with a quick smile. "Anubis has the head of a jackal."

"Are we dead?" Istnofret asked.

Renni moved closer to wrap his arm around her. "I don't think so. I am not sure how we came to be here, but surely if we were dead, we would have some memory of it."

I remembered drowning. Remembered the certainty of death approaching. Sandy shores. The flash of a falcon eye. I had been dead, but I remembered nothing of the moment of my death, or of what happened afterwards except for those brief glimpses of sand and a falcon's eye.

"I thought a living person could only reach the underworld by passing through a tomb," I said.

"Perhaps that's exactly what we did." Intef spoke slowly. He was still figuring it out, but the pieces were falling into place for him. I was, as usual, several steps behind. "The tunnels may have been a tomb. Either that of a human or of the beast Renni and Istnofret heard about. Perhaps we passed straight through a tomb and into the underworld without realising."

"But how did we get *here*?" I asked. "Why is Anubis in Crete? Or how did we get from Crete to wherever this is?"

"Maybe it has something to do with the Eye. Maybe there's a... I don't know, a doorway of some sort in those tunnels, and when we passed through it, we ended up wherever *here* is. Maybe we aren't in Crete anymore."

"So I suppose we're meant to go through those." Istnofret nodded at the monstrosity ahead of us.

"It won't be that easy," Renni said. "Aren't there supposed to be challenges before a person can pass through the gates of the underworld?"

"What do we know of Anubis?" Intef asked. "We should share our knowledge now before we approach the gates. It might be helpful later."

"God of the afterlife," Istnofret said promptly. "And of mummification."

"God of lost souls." I hadn't realised I had spoken until they looked at me. "I think."

"God of the helpless and hopeless," Istnofret said.

Renni shot her a look. "How do you know so much about Anubis?"

She shrugged. "I heard someone speak of him. A priestess. It was many years ago. I remember thinking how appropriate it was that one who wandered in the underworld might be watched over by the god of the helpless."

"We could certainly do with a little help right now," Behenu said, with a sigh. She clutched her shadow, who still wriggled feebly.

"Do you remember anything else, Ist?" Renni asked.

She looked off towards the gates, but eventually she shook her head. "He has the head of a jackal, black to symbolise both the decay of death and the fertility of soil, but that's all I can remember."

"He holds the scales on which the heart is weighed against the feather of truth," I said, as an image popped into my mind. I didn't know where I had seen it, but I could picture it so clearly: Anubis holding out the golden scales with the heart of the deceased sitting on one side. Ma'at, goddess of truth and balance, set her feather of truth on the other side of the scales. If the heart was lighter than the feather, the deceased could progress to the next stage of the trials of the afterlife. If it was heavier than the feather, it would be eaten by Ammut, the Devourer.

"Good," Renni said. "That might be useful."

"We should go." Intef glanced at Behenu whose shadow had started wriggling more violently. He turned back to me. "Do you think you can manage?"

"There is no choice, is there?" I held out my hand for him to haul me to my feet. "If we are indeed in the underworld, or anywhere that is not our world, we must carry on, and pray to Isis that we find a way out of here. I fear that a babe born in the underworld may never be able to leave."

Intef shot me a horrified look and I was sorry I had said it.

"I will get you out of here." He held my hand tightly. "I swear it. Even if the babe comes and you are trapped here, even if for some reason I have to leave you here, I will find a way back to you and I will get you both out of here."

My throat was too choked for words.

We set off towards the gates. Soon enough I could see that it was indeed Anubis carved into each side. In one hand he clutched an *ankh*, the symbol of life, and in the other, a flail. It was a familiar image and I had never before wondered why he was depicted with those particular items. Why would the god of the afterlife carry an *ankh* and a tool used for threshing grain, both of which were symbols of life? Did it mean he wanted us to live? To find a way back to our own world?

Eventually we stood in front of the gates. They towered over us, glistening in the sunlight.

"What do we do now?" Istnofret asked.

"I expected a guardian," Renni said. "Someone who might give us a test of some sort, or ask for a password. Someone to open the gates and let us through."

"Why don't we just walk around them?" Behenu asked.

We all frowned at her, but she shrugged.

"If there is no guardian, what is to stop us?"

"It is too easy," Intef said. "I feel very certain that we are supposed to find a way through them, rather than around."

"Well, I am going around them," she said. "Maybe once I am on the other side, my shadow will start cooperating."

She set off, clutching her unwilling shadow by the arm. She walked. And walked. Eventually she stopped and looked back at us.

"The gates are much larger than they look," she called.

"We are not that far from the other side here," Istnofret said. "I'll walk that way."

She set off, but she too walked and walked. Eventually they both returned.

"It grows," Behenu said. "Or stretches. You cannot see it happening but no matter how far you go, you cannot get to the end."

"I suppose there has to be a way to force people to go through the gates instead of around them," Renni said.

"Maybe you need to go faster," Intef said. "I will run around them."

He set off but eventually he, too, admitted defeat. He returned, panting a little harder than he should have. He wasn't as fit as he had once been. No wonder he wanted to return to a more normal life.

"I suppose someone should knock," I said.

"I think it should be you." Intef gestured towards me.

Nobody disagreed, or offered to do it for me, so I stepped up to the massive gates, half expecting them to move back away from me. But they stayed where they were and I placed my hand against them. The surface was smooth and warm. I knocked.

My knocks boomed. I had expected to hardly hear a thing, given the size of the gates. After a moment, a voice called out.

"Who knocks at the Gates of Anubis?"

I couldn't tell whether the speaker was male or female, old or young. Their voice seemed to be everything at once. This didn't seem like a time to identify myself as Samun.

"My name is Ankhesenamun. I was once Queen of Egypt. Great Royal Wife of Pharaoh Tutankhamun, may he live for millions of years. Daughter of Pharaoh Akhenaten, may he live for millions of years. Great of Praises, Lady of The Two Lands, Mistress of Upper and Lower Egypt."

"And what do you seek, Ankhesenamun, once Queen of Egypt?" the voice asked.

I paused to consider my reply. They had asked what I

sought, not what I wanted to do. "I seek the Eye of Horus."

There was a long pause before the voice spoke again. "Why do you seek it here?"

Was there a wrong answer? How could I know what answer the speaker sought, given I didn't know who they were? It must be a guardian, possibly a minor goddess, but which one?

"I was led here. I have spent many months searching for the Eye."

"The Eye is not meant for the hand of mortals. It is too powerful. It should be wielded only by the gods. You should go home."

"If the Eye is not meant for mortals, why did Horus gift it to a woman?"

I held my breath as I waited for the reply. We had found two versions of the story that told how Horus had lost his Eye. I had no way of knowing which one was correct. Maybe they both were. Maybe neither.

"What makes you think you are worthy of the Eye?"

This time I answered without thinking.

"The gods would not have led me this far if they didn't find me worthy. I have travelled a very long way, across oceans and through many countries. My companions and I have endured much hardship to reach this place."

"A long journey and a bit of suffering do not entitle one to the Eye."

"Then tell me what I must do to prove myself."

"Do you possess the Eye?"

"I am still searching for it."

"Then you cannot prove yourself. If you find the Eye, then you may try to prove yourself."

"I seek the Eye not for my own glory." I tried to push away

the memories of the times I had done just that. Now was the time to hold fast to my integrity, not my pride. "I seek to right an injustice. To bring peace and truth and honour. Only the power of the gods will allow me to do what I must."

"You presume much."

The speaker's voice had changed a little, but I couldn't tell whether they were amused or offended.

"I am not presumptuous, but courageous. I am trying to save two countries from war. I am trying to rid Egypt of fear and corruption and hatred-"

But the speaker cut me off.

"Then where is the Eye? If the gods have found you so worthy, show it to me."

"You already know I don't have it."

"Then you have no business here. You should return home. Your babe will be born very shortly and this is not a safe place for new souls."

I rested one hand on my belly, reassuring myself that the babe was well. She was still, possibly sleeping or maybe listening to her mother argue with a goddess.

"Horus himself led me here." I couldn't be sure it was true but the image of a falcon's eye lingered in my memory. "He wouldn't have led me this far if he didn't intend for me to find his Eye."

"If he led you here, he would have told you the location of the item you search for."

"I am sure you know that is not how such things work. I must find the Eye myself."

"Then go ahead," the speaker said. "Find the Eye."

"I need to pass through your gates to do so."

"What is stopping you?"

Was it that simple? Did I merely have to open the gates to

pass through them? I glanced back at the others. The looks on their faces told me they had all come to the same realisation. I turned back to the gates and took a deep breath. I set my hands against them and pushed.

I might have expected such an enormous structure to be far too heavy for one woman alone, but they swung open with no more strength than I had to give.

The world on the other side looked the same as where we were now. Daylight. Grassy field. A few trees. There was no sign of the guardian of the gates.

"Do you think that is our world?" Istnofret whispered.

"I have no idea," I said.

I started to step forward but Intef grabbed my wrist.

"Wait," he said. "If that is truly our world, we don't know what will happen to our shadows if they are not attached to us."

I looked back at my shadow. It rested its hands behind its waist and seemed to be rubbing its back. My back ached too, fiercely as it had just before Setau was born. There was little time left. If my babe was born before my shadow and I were rejoined, would she too be separated from her shadow?

"Shadow," I said. "Will you come back to me?"

It stilled and cocked its head. One hand moved down to rub its belly.

"I promise to pay more attention to you. I will talk to you. I will consider your comfort. I will not forget that once you and I were separated, and that neither of us felt truly whole."

My shadow seemed to take a very long time to decide. It tipped its head towards the other shadows and they seemed to have a conversation that we couldn't hear.

"I, too, will pay more attention to you, Shadow," Istnofret said to hers.

Intef and Renni made similar promises. Only Behenu was silent. Her shadow still struggled in her grip.

At last, my shadow stepped closer to me and leaned right in to my face. I felt an icy touch on my cheek. A kiss perhaps? Then my shadow held out its hand. When I grasped it, there was a familiar pop and my shadow was suddenly back in its usual place, stretching its length across the ground, joined to me at our feet.

"Hello there, Shadow." I waved at it and my shadow waved back. But it was just the usual motion of a shadow with its owner, not that of an independent being choosing to wave. I suddenly felt lonely.

When I looked up, the other shadows had rejoined their people. Only Behenu's shadow remained. It had stopped struggling and hung weakly from her fist.

"What am I going to do?" she asked, a little forlornly. "I cannot go without my shadow."

"I suppose we don't know that," Istnofret said, in the brisk tone that indicated she was trying to keep her feelings to herself. "Perhaps you should step through the gates and see what happens."

"What if it kills me?" Behenu asked.

"Is there any other choice?" Intef wrapped his arm around Behenu's shoulders. "We cannot stay here."

"Easy enough for you to say." She glanced down at his shadow which mimicked each movement he made.

"True. It has to be your decision. But you know we cannot stay if you choose to. Samun's time is close and we need to get her and the babe to a safer place."

Behenu glanced at my belly, then looked me in the eyes. We stared at each other for a long moment. Was she, like me, remembering the first time we met, when a slave girl who was sitting where she shouldn't encountered a queen? When I first saw the girl I had dreamed about years before. When I made the decision to remove her from Horemheb's possession.

"If this kills me, it will be my sacrifice for you," she said. "You cannot stay here."

"I am sorry if I did wrong by you." If I had left her alone, she wouldn't be here, with such a terrible decision to make.

She gave me a sad smile. "You didn't. I could not have borne it much longer. I would have killed either myself or him. I have had many adventures since then. Even if this is the end for me, I am not sorry to be here. I would not have missed out on the things we have seen for anything. I am truly grateful that you noticed a slave girl."

With her spare hand, Behenu reached for the pouch that hung around her neck. She took it off and held it out to Renni.

"If I… if I don't survive, would you see that my father receives this? He is Adad-Nirari of Nuhasse."

Renni accepted the pouch from her. "I will put it in his hands myself."

"You were supposed to go home." My voice broke and I swallowed down my sobs. "After this was all over. You were meant to go home. You have a purpose. A destiny."

Behenu shrugged a little. "I have always known I was different. I suppose I didn't know until now just how different. Maybe people like me are not supposed to venture into the underworld."

"I don't think any living being is supposed to be in the underworld," Intef said. "I would not have brought you here if I had known."

She smiled at him, then took a step back, towards the gate.

"I have always had my own path to follow. This is no different."

THIRTY-FIVE

At the last moment before Behenu stepped through the gates, her shadow flung its arms around her. On the other side, she fell to her knees in the grass. Her shadow stretched out behind her, once again joined to her.

"Behenu?" Istnofret cried. "Are you well?"

Tears streamed down Behenu's face and she held a shaky hand up in front of her face, as if checking she was really alive. She looked down at her shadow.

"Shadow, I am sorry," she said through her tears. "I would have liked to have been friends with you if you had let me."

Renni helped Istnofret to her feet. She wiped her face with the hem of her skirt as she tried to stop crying and he brushed away a few tears of his own.

"We need to go." I felt bad about hurrying them, but the ache in my back told me the babe's time was very close.

"Samun is right." Intef held his hand out to me and I took it gratefully. He hauled me up.

"I will go next." Renni turned to Istnofret and wiped more tears from her cheeks. "If something happens to me…"

She shook her head and wrapped her arms around him. He gave Istnofret one last, long look. They said nothing, only looked at each other. Then he kissed her cheek and stepped forward.

I held my breath as Renni passed through the gates. I leaned on Intef, seeking comfort in his nearness, but his focus was entirely on Renni.

Renni stepped through without incident and when he reached Behenu, he leaned down to hug her before handing back her pouch. She hung it around her neck and tucked it under her shirt. Renni turned back to us.

"Come through," he said. "I think it is safe."

I held my breath as I walked through, my shadow at my heels and Intef at my side. Nothing happened and I felt no different. I let out a shaky breath.

"Come on, Ist," I said. "Your turn."

She hesitated, biting her lip, before she finally took a deep breath and rushed through. Once she was safely on the other side, she burst into tears again and reached for Behenu.

It was only now that I looked around, hoping to see the ruins of the palace and the ox hitched to the cart.

To the west of us, where the ruins should have been, stood a massive building complex. It towered several storeys into the air, its whitewashed walls gleaming in the sunlight.

"Oh dear Isis," I muttered.

The others merely sighed.

"I suppose we are meant to go there," I said when it became clear that nobody else was going to say it. "There is a reason the gods have brought us to this place and I cannot see anything else they might intend for us to do."

Around us, the area looked much the same as our own

world with a stand of oak trees on the far side of a grassy expanse. The palace was the only thing that was different.

"No point standing here looking at it," Intef said. "Let's go while you can still walk."

The babe kicked, hard, as if to emphasise his words.

"Don't you go siding with him before you're even born," I muttered to her.

As we set off across the grass, I glanced back to check my shadow followed. I had forgotten for a moment that we were joined again. That it was no longer its own being.

"Is your babe kicking, too, Shadow?"

There was no response and although I hadn't expected one, I was still disappointed.

The palace in its glory took my breath away. Plastered stone walls painted with murals. Tiled mosaics. A pond, filled with water although devoid of fish. Greenery everywhere with plants in tidy courtyard gardens or ceramic pots. Stairs provided access to the upper levels. Covered walkways led between buildings. A seat under a window provided an agreeable place to sit and enjoy a warm afternoon.

"I didn't expect it to be so pleasant," Istnofret said.

I murmured agreement.

"I suppose we should go in." Intef gave a heavy sigh. "Look around. See if we can figure out why we are here."

"We could cover more ground if we split up," Renni said, but Intef shook his head even as he spoke.

"We don't know what this place is. Until we get back to our own world, we should stay together."

"I agree." Istnofret gave Renni an apologetic smile, but he didn't seem bothered that she had sided with Intef.

Behenu was silent. I saw her casting several glances at her shadow. Was she wondering what would have happened if her shadow hadn't rejoined her before she stepped through the gates?

We quickly searched the ground level of the first building but found no indication of why we were there.

"Maybe we should split up after all." Intef peered up the stairs towards the second storey. "Samun cannot go up and down all these flights."

"What if you stay at the top of the stairs. Istnofret and I can go into the chambers. She only goes in as far as you can see her and I'll stay where she can see me."

"You disappeared while I was watching you earlier," Intef said. "I don't think that gives us any protection."

"But at least you will know exactly where I disappeared. You might be able to follow me."

Intef gave me a careful look and for a moment I thought he would argue further.

"You look very pale," he said to me. "Sit down on the steps and rest for a bit while we go up. Behenu, maybe you should sit with her."

I sat for a minute or two. The ache in my back grew worse and I couldn't sit any longer.

"I am going to walk around," I said to Behenu.

"Intef will be upset."

"I cannot sit here. I really need to walk."

She started to get up.

"No, you sit," I said quickly. "You should rest."

Tears welled in her eyes. "I was sure I was going to die."

I didn't know what to say. Whether it would make it worse if I agreed with her, or lied. She dashed the tears away before I could make up my mind.

"Don't go out of sight," she said. "I don't want Intef mad at me as well."

I staggered back out to the grassed courtyard. My back ached less when I walked. I paced up and down the courtyard, which was only the length of a couple of men, then decided to peek around the corner. I glanced back at Behenu. She looked up the stairs and seemed to be saying something, perhaps explaining to Intef where I was. She wouldn't notice if I went a little further. I would only be gone a moment.

Around the corner was more grass. More buildings. A pretty little garden with a plant I didn't recognise all over with buds. And beyond those was a temple.

A shiver went through me and goosebumps rose all over my body. This was why we were here. It wasn't anything in the building they searched, or any of the other buildings. It was the temple. We were meant to go in there.

"Intef?" I called.

He came running.

"Samun? Where are you? Is it the babe?"

"Look."

"Do you think-" he asked.

"That's it. That's where we are meant to go."

"Wait here. Don't move. I'll get the others."

I could hardly take my eyes off the temple. Almost without realising, I began walking towards it.

"Samun!"

I heard Intef's voice but didn't seem to be able to stop my feet. I was halfway to the temple before they caught up with me.

"What are you doing?" Intef asked, a little crossly. "We don't know if it is safe."

"This is why we are here. Whether it is safe or not is irrelevant. This is where the gods intended us to go."

"How do you know?" Istnofret asked. "It is not that

surprising to find a temple here. There was more than one temple at the palace in Memphis."

"Don't you feel it?"

She shrugged and didn't answer. Perhaps it was only I who could feel it.

We reached the entrance to the temple. It didn't look all that different from any other Egyptian temple. A stone building, columns at the front, a long hallway leading towards its centre. What was different was the way it called to me.

"I think you should all stay out here," I said.

"Absolutely not."

I knew Intef would react that way, but I needed him to stay. I couldn't explain, but it was important I do this on my own.

"Please." I rested my hand on his arm. "Intef, do this for me."

He shook his head. "We have no idea what's in there. You could disappear into some other place and we might never find you again."

"If something happens to me, I know you will find me." Hadn't we had this conversation before?

"I am not letting you go in there on your own."

"Intef, I have to. I can feel it. There's something about this place. This is meant for me."

He gave me a sideways look, as if assessing my mood. Whatever he saw on my face must have convinced him, for he gave a great sigh.

"Be quick. And if I hear anything that worries me, I am coming after you."

I glanced at the others. Istnofret looked worried. Renni frowned at Intef, but I wasn't sure whether he disagreed or was worried about something else. Behenu was pale and seemed to wobble on her feet. I wasn't sure she was even listening.

I felt like I should say something. Perhaps a promise to be back quickly, but I didn't know what waited for me in there, and I didn't want to lie to Intef. Not if this might be the last time I saw him. I leaned my head against his shoulder for a moment, then went into the temple.

THIRTY-SIX

The passage leading into the temple was dark and it wasn't long before I could hardly see where I walked. Then my belly bumped up against a stone wall. I turned back, confused. I had felt so drawn to this place, but it was a dead end. I started back to the entrance but spotted a branching passage I had missed in the dark.

I reached another turn and ahead of me the tunnel lightened. Fluid dripped down my legs and I paused to lean against the wall, suddenly breathless and filled with dread. The babe was on her way.

I remembered little of Setau's birth, but I knew well enough what lay ahead. I peeled myself off the wall. I had to move on while I could still walk. I wasn't so deep into the temple that Intef wouldn't hear me if I called for him.

I rounded one last corner and found a chamber. The light was dim and the chamber was empty with no exits other than the one in which I stood. Another dead end. A wave of pain gripped me and I leaned against the wall as I waited for it to pass. I must be missing something. There was a reason I had been led here.

When the pain subsided and I could think again, I examined the chamber. The walls were stone, as was the floor and the ceiling. There were no murals or inscriptions. It was just an empty stone chamber. I had been mistaken.

But then I spotted a small recess set into the wall. Inside the recess was a box. With trembling hands, I reached for it. It was wooden and carefully made, with smooth sides and tidy joints. A pin secured the lid. On the top of the box was a symbol etched in blue paint: an eye.

My heart felt like it had stopped and I only realised I held my breath when my head began to swim. I leaned against the wall and tried to breathe. Was this it?

I fumbled at the pin, but my fingers trembled and before I could get the box open, I became aware that someone else was in the chamber.

A green-faced man stood behind me. He wore a long white tunic and the conical white crown of Upper Egypt. He studied me with his arms crossed over his chest. His impassive face gave no hint of his feelings. My mind was blank and I could only wait for him to speak.

"Are you certain?" he asked.

Of all the things I might have expected him to say, this wasn't one of them.

"Of what?"

My throat was clogged and the words were no more than a whisper.

"Your path."

"My- my path?"

He nodded towards the box in my hands.

"I don't know what's in it."

I itched to open it, but I couldn't with him watching.

Another contraction gripped me and I almost dropped the box. When it was over, I found myself leaning against the wall, panting. Osiris — if that was really who the green-faced man was — continued to observe me.

"Once you take it, it will insist on being used. Are you strong enough to save it for the moment you intend?"

"I know it can only be used once."

"Knowledge is one thing. Comprehension is another."

My fingers fiddled with the pin, working it out of its holder.

"I would suggest you do not open it. Once you see it, you will be filled with the desire to use it. You will not be able to resist it."

I wanted to argue with him, to tell him I was strong, but this conversation may well determine whether he allowed me to leave with the Eye.

"I assume you are aware there is a price to be paid," he said.

"Yes."

"And you are willing to pay it?"

I hesitated. "I don't know what the price is."

His lips curled very slightly. "You have come all this way without knowing? Perhaps you should not have come."

"Tell me what it is. I will pay it if I can."

"There is no *if you can*. You either pay the price or you don't. You either leave with the power you seek or you don't."

"If I have the capacity to pay the price, I will."

"And if not?"

I only looked at him, unwilling to answer. I wouldn't give him the box, even if he demanded it. I clutched it more tightly, my fingers sweaty and slippery.

"Will you tell me what the price is?" I asked, since he seemed quite happy to continue talking in riddles without giving me any real information.

"It is the thing you desire most."

"But that is what I need the Eye for. I want to restore peace to Egypt. The Eye can help me do that. How can I give that up in exchange for using it?"

Osiris looked at me steadily.

"That is what you intend to use it for. It is not the thing you most desire in this world."

"I don't know what you mean."

Another contraction. Moments lost when I knew nothing but the pain. When it passed, I was breathless and sweaty. The box was somehow still in my hand.

"Please tell me. I cannot stay here much longer. My babe is about to be born."

"If you wish to leave with the box, you must pay the price first."

"But I don't know what the price is," I snapped. "If you would just tell me, I will know whether I can pay it."

"The thing you desire most in this world."

"You've already said that."

His gaze dipped down to my belly. Cold realisation filled me.

"No."

"You pay the price or you leave without the box."

"You intend to take my child in exchange for the Eye?"

"It is the thing you want most. That is the price for such power."

"And that's why it can only be used once." Understanding suddenly dawned. "You can only give up the thing you want the most once."

Still there was no expression on his face.

"Please. There must be some other way I can pay. Anything."

"I will give you until the child is born to decide."

The box vanished from my fingers.

"What?"

I stared down at my empty hand. The box had been returned to the recess where, presumably, Antinous had placed it years earlier. I reached for it again.

"Do not." His voice was a command and I found myself frozen, unable to reach any further. "You may not touch it again until you have paid for it."

"I cannot give you my child. I will not."

"You will stay here until the child is born. I will return to hear your decision."

Then he was gone.

THIRTY-SEVEN

Another contraction gripped me and when it was over, I found myself sitting on the floor. I leaned back against the wall, letting it support me.

"Intef!" I called.

But my voice was too weak and I already knew he wouldn't hear me. Even if I could call loudly enough, Osiris would stop him from coming to me. He intended for me to suffer this alone. He could have at least provided a mat for me to lie on, or a birthing brick. Instead, I lay on cold stone in an empty chamber.

With each contraction I felt more and more alone. My fatigue grew, as did my fear. What if I didn't have enough strength to deliver the babe? What if something went wrong? Would I even know, given how little I remembered of Setau's birth? What if the babe was in the wrong position? Or the cord was wrapped around her neck? What if she got stuck and I couldn't push her out?

By the time the next contraction came, I could barely think for my panic. Somehow my hand made its way to my throat, to the spell bottle I wore on a cord around my neck. It was cold. I was in no imminent danger myself, but what about my daughter?

Then my fingers tangled with something else, a necklace I had almost forgotten I wore. It was the acacia seed pod, given to me by the *ka*-seer. I had no knowledge of what goddess she worshipped, but it was a protective amulet nonetheless. Focusing on it gave me strength and somehow through the pain came a memory of Istnofret telling me to breathe. Perhaps it was from Setau's birth. I kept her image in my mind as I fought for calm. Focusing on her helped and I pretended she was in the chamber with me.

As the birth progressed, I told myself the things I thought Istnofret might say. How well I was doing, that it wouldn't be much longer now, that I would soon meet my babe. Every time Osiris came into my mind, I pushed him away. I would not think about him right now. I needed to focus on my daughter.

I had no sense of time. The light in the chamber never changed and I never saw its source. The stones eventually warmed beneath me. Although they were too hard to provide any comfort, at least they no longer sent a chill through me.

The babe took a long time to arrive. I endured wave after wave of pain. I had some vague memory that I shouldn't try to push her out too soon. Perhaps this, too, was a memory from Setau's delivery. But eventually the time came when I couldn't resist pushing any longer. I desperately wished for a birthing brick to sit on. How was I supposed to grasp the babe as she came out while I lay on the stones?

I managed to drag myself up to sit leaning against the wall. As another contraction washed over me, I reached between my legs and found the babe's head had emerged. I endured two more contractions before she was out and in my arms. She was covered in mucous and blood, and she was the most beautiful thing I had ever seen. I wrapped my skirt around her and held her to my chest.

It was only then that I saw beside me a knife. It was not there before. I took up the knife and cut the birth cord, pulling a few threads from my skirt to tie it off.

My daughter had dark eyes like Intef's. Her face looked so much like his that I couldn't see anything of myself in her. I placed my finger in her hand and as she wrapped her fist around it, my heart swelled.

Eventually I remembered the cord that still led between my legs. I managed to cut off enough of my skirt to wrap the babe in and set her gently on the stones while I dealt with the remains of the cord.

I had just picked the babe up again when I realised that Osiris had returned. His gaze swept over the bloody evidence of her birth and went straight to the babe in my arms.

"Have you made a decision?" he asked.

"I will not give you my babe."

"Then you may not leave with the box."

"Surely there is some other way. Something else I can pay you with. I have gems. You may have them all."

"I have no use for your wealth."

"Then something else. Tell me. Anything."

"You know the price. There can be no substitutes."

Tears dripped as I studied my daughter's face.

"Please. You cannot take her from me."

He seemed unaffected by my emotion. "The price is the price. You pay it or you do not."

"You don't know what you are asking. Have you ever loved someone?"

He only looked at me.

"Isis. Surely you love your wife? Would you give her up if someone asked you to?"

Still he merely looked at me.

"Give me another way to pay. Please, I beg you."

"The price is the price."

I looked down at my tiny daughter. Could I justify one life against the thousands that would be lost if I didn't restore peace? In my dream, Suppiluliumas had sworn to destroy Egypt. And more than lives was at stake. I could rid Egypt of the anger and hatred Ay injected into everything. I could bring fairness back to the throne. Truth. Justice. Ma'at.

"But this is my child. My daughter."

And she was one life.

One life against many.

If I didn't give her up, everything we had endured to get this far had been for nothing. Sadeh. Intef's arm. Little Setau. Was all of that worth the price of my daughter?

Was it even my decision? She was Intef's daughter as much as mine. But I knew without asking that Osiris wouldn't allow me to speak with him. This was to be my decision alone.

"I cannot." My voice broke. "If you had ever really loved someone, you would understand."

Yet even that provoked no response from him.

"Why lead me all this way?" I was crying now and he probably couldn't even understand me through my sobs. "Why put me through all of that? Why put all of us through it, if only to refuse to let me take the Eye?"

No response.

"I want to speak with Horus."

"Have you made your decision?"

"I will not give you my daughter."

"Is that your final decision? Shall I take the box away?"

I desperately wanted to say, yes, take it. I would find another way to achieve my goal.

My daughter was sleeping now, her fingers still curled around mine. My heart was broken.

Maia had warned that the price might be too great. I had known I would have to hand my daughter to Osiris at some point. I had barely admitted to myself my suspicion that she would be my payment for the Eye.

I couldn't let it all be for nothing. As Queen of Egypt, my life was dedicated to my country. My people came before any will of my own. Even when that will was the desire for my daughter to live.

I didn't have to tell Osiris I had decided. When I looked up, his face finally showed a flicker of compassion.

"Are you ready?" he asked.

"Wait," I said, through my tears. "Just give me one more minute."

"You must offer her up to me. I will not take her from you."

I knew what he meant. In my mind I again saw my dream. The one in which I knelt before a green-faced god and offered him a newborn babe.

I set the babe gently on the stones, still wrapped in the linen of my skirt, and hauled myself to my knees. The floor was slippery with birth fluids and what was left of my skirt was immediately soaked.

Once I was on my knees, I reached for the babe. She woke and looked up at me. Her fingers opened and closed, searching for mine. I placed my finger in her fist and she clutched it.

I inhaled a shaky breath. Once I gave her to Osiris, there was no turning back. I knew without asking that he wouldn't return her to me if I changed my mind.

"It is time," he said, very quietly.

I closed my eyes for a moment, steadying myself, then took one last look at my daughter. At the mostly bald head with just a few wisps of dark hair. At the face that looked so much like Intef. At her dark eyes and her tiny, perfect fingers. I kissed her forehead, and I named her. Meketaten, for my sister.

Then I bowed my head and offered my babe up to Osiris.

He took her from my hands.

"Will she…" My voice broke and I paused to compose myself. "Will you keep her safe?"

"She is no longer your concern."

I desperately wanted not to cry. Meketaten wouldn't remember this moment, but I didn't want my last view of her to be through a veil of tears. What would I tell Intef? He would never forgive me.

"You may take it." Osiris nodded towards the box.

My head swam and I steadied myself against the wall as I rose. I took the box from its recess. It was light, its wood warm to my touch.

"Are you sure this contains the Eye of Horus?" I asked.

"You think I would deceive you?"

"Of course not." I could hardly say yes. "But I thought maybe… tricked. My child for an empty box."

"Open it then." His tone was careless. "See if it contains what you seek. If it doesn't, you may take the child and leave."

He had said before that I shouldn't look at it. That I wouldn't be able to resist it once I had seen it. Was this a trick? With trembling fingers, I managed to unhook the pin and open the box. An amulet lay on a bed of faded linen. It was made of clay, or perhaps carved from wood. I couldn't tell without touching it. It was painted in a reddish-brown colour that reminded me of dried blood. Already it called to me to use it, like he had said it would. I closed the box.

"All to your satisfaction?" Osiris asked.

"Why do you guard it? Why not Horus?"

"Does it make a difference to you?"

"I just wondered."

"You would be advised to keep your wonderings to your-self. Now go. Take the Eye and leave this place. Do not return. The child will not be here once you depart."

"Please. Can you at least tell me that she will be allowed to live?"

He didn't answer. I hadn't expected he would.

THIRTY-EIGHT

My hands trembled so much that I could hardly hold the box. I left the chamber slowly, with many backward glances towards my daughter. Osiris held her carefully enough, but perhaps that would only last as long as I watched. I had no certainty that she would live, or if she did, that she would be cared for. Perhaps she would be killed as soon as I was gone. An unwanted offering to the gods. Perhaps she would be kept alive to endure some punishment that I should have suffered for my arrogance in thinking I could wield a tool of the gods. She might spend her life being tormented and abused.

I had gone barely two steps before I changed my mind. What was I thinking? I couldn't give up my daughter. I rushed back into the chamber, but they were already gone. Gone, too, was the evidence of her birth. There was nothing left to signal what had happened in here. It was just an empty chamber.

"Osiris," I called. "Give her back to me."

I waited but there was no answer. Of course there wouldn't be. One could hardly expect to make a deal with a god and then change one's mind. The deal was done. My daughter was gone.

I leaned against the wall and sobbed. By the time I managed to stop, my eyes were swollen and my nose was blocked. I slowly made my way out of the temple. Dread welled within me as I reached the entrance. How would I tell Intef? He had wanted this child so badly. There was nothing worse I could have done to him. He would hate me for this.

"Samun!" Intef was standing right by the entrance when I emerged, squinting against the brightness. "What happened?"

"The babe." Istnofret's gaze went straight to my belly, which still protruded even though it was empty. "Where is the babe?"

Intef followed her gaze and his face filled with confusion. "Samun?"

"I am sorry." My voice broke and it was all I could do not to fall apart. I clutched the box more tightly. After everything I had done, I didn't want to drop it and break the Eye. "She was the price."

He looked at me for a long moment. I knew that look. He was figuring it all out, letting the pieces of the puzzle drop into place before he spoke. When he did, his voice was cold.

"I think you should explain yourself. And tell me where my daughter is."

"She was the price. I have the Eye."

"You traded our child for, what? A superstition?"

"It is real. I can feel it. It calls me to use it."

"And you paid for it with our daughter. Tell me I am misunderstanding this."

I couldn't look him in the eyes. There was none of the disappointment I might have expected. He was all cold fury.

"Intef, let me explain."

"That is what I am waiting for."

"The price was that I had to give up the thing I wanted most. I could only take the Eye if I gave her to Osiris."

"Osiris?" Istnofret's voice revealed her doubt. "Was he real or a hallucination?"

"I always knew it would end like this." I tried to wipe away my tears, but they fell too fast. "I just didn't realise that this ending went with these events."

"You knew you were going to give away our daughter?" Intef asked.

There was no way I could answer which didn't end in him hating me.

"Intef, please."

He didn't answer, only turned his back on me and headed into the temple.

"She isn't there," I called after him. "They are gone."

He disappeared inside. Of course he would search for her, but he wouldn't find her.

We waited in silence. I expected they might have asked why I did it, but nobody spoke. Had they not wondered why I was in there for so long? Had nobody come looking for me? But perhaps time had not passed at the same speed as it had out here. I let my hair fall forward over my face and kept my gaze focussed on the grass. My breasts ached, filled with milk for a babe they would never feed.

It was a long time before Intef came back out. Nobody asked if he had found our babe. He wouldn't have left her if he had.

"Well, what is done is done," Istnofret said eventually.

"She had her reasons," Behenu said. "Even if we do not understand them. I am sure they were... valid."

"We need to concentrate on finding a way home," Renni said. "We can talk about the rest later."

"There's nothing to talk about," Intef said, his voice more bitter than I had ever heard. "She has already given my daughter away."

I glanced up in time to see Renni's fingers flash as he spoke to Intef in their silent language. Intef gave him a dark look.

"I don't suppose Osiris told you how to get home from here?" Renni asked.

I shook my head, unable to speak through my tears. Intef stared at the ground, the sky, the gates. Anything to avoid looking at me.

"Maybe we go back through the gates?" Istnofret suggested, but Renni frowned.

"That takes us to another place, but it is not the place we need to go."

"Walk in the other direction then?" she suggested. "I suppose if we walk long enough, we will find a way out." She looked towards me. "Samun, can you walk?"

I wanted to say that of course I could, but suddenly my head spun and I could barely keep myself upright. Renni grabbed me before I could collapse and helped me to sit down.

"I suppose that answers my question," Istnofret said. "So we need to find a way home, but we cannot walk there. What now?"

"Can you use that" — Renni gestured towards the box in my hands — "to get us home?"

I tried to answer but started crying again.

"She can only use it once," Istnofret said. "I don't suppose she wants to waste it on getting us home. Especially after…"

They all avoided looking at me. Intef stood a little way off with his back to us. Istnofret, Renni and Behenu looked at each other, seemingly all waiting for someone to come up with an idea.

Again, the memory came to me. Sandy beaches. A falcon's eye.

"I died." I had told nobody but Intef of this.

Istnofret gave me a sharp look. "When the babe was born?"

"No, before. When I was gone for all those weeks. There was a storm and I drowned."

"You didn't really-" she started, but I cut her off.

"I remember falling into the water and sinking, down, down. All around me was blackness and I was so sad because I knew my daughter would never live. I held my breath for as long as I could, but eventually I drowned."

Intef still had his back to us but he had turned his head very slightly. He listened, even if he pretended not to.

"Then what happened?" Istnofret asked.

"All I remember is a sandy beach and a falcon's eye. I don't know what happened. I woke up on the beach, and I was alive."

"You came back to life?" Istnofret's tone was uncertain and it was clear she hadn't yet decided whether to believe me.

"Maybe that's how we get out of here," I said.

"We need to drown?" She looked even more confused.

"Not drown, but maybe we need to die. Maybe that's the way back to the world of the living."

"And how exactly do you propose we test that theory?" Intef finally turned to face us. The look he gave me was both pitying and disbelieving. "Who's going to die first so we can see if you're right?"

"At least I am trying to come up with a plan."

He gave me a scathing look, but Renni saved me from whatever biting reply he intended.

"What we need right now are ideas," Renni said. "It doesn't matter whether they're good ones or not. If we can come up with enough ideas, sooner or later we will find one that will work."

"I would prefer not to die today," Istnofret said. "I think we should go through the gates. Go into the tunnels and find the way back out again. It must still be there. We just missed it somehow."

"The gates might not lead us to the same place again," Renni said.

"We go back into that temple, find Osiris, and make him give my daughter back," Intef said.

"That's not going to get us home," Renni said, very gently. "And if that's the price Samun had to pay, then he won't return the child. I don't think a deal with a god can be broken."

"We haven't even tried," Intef said. "I cannot walk away. I won't leave her in this gods-forsaken place."

His words made me cry again. He would never forgive me. It wasn't only me who had wanted this child. She was the thing he had wanted most in the world too.

"If we could find another god," Behenu said. "Maybe we could strike some kind of deal to get us out of here."

"The only problem with that is they're not exactly walking around all over the place," Renni said.

"The gates," Istnofret said. "If we can get the guardian to speak with us again, maybe they have the power to send us home. Maybe they can summon a god for us. Or something. We just need *someone* to talk to."

"That's the best idea we have had so far," Renni said. "Intef, what do you think?"

"I suppose it is a better plan than killing ourselves and hoping we will wake up in our own world," he said.

"Let's get Samun up then," Renni said. "It is not too far of a walk and it is short enough that we can carry her if we need to."

"I will walk," I said.

Intef stood with his back to us as Renni and Istnofret hauled me to my feet. With one of them on each side to support me, we slowly made our way back to the gates.

We hadn't gone far before I realised what a bad idea it was. But I gritted my teeth and tried to push past my pain and exhaustion. Istnofret and Renni kept me upright. All I had to do was move my feet.

When we finally reached the gates, they lowered me to sit on the grass. My head spun and I would have toppled over if Istnofret hadn't grabbed my shoulders.

"Now what?" she asked.

"It is your plan," Intef said, somewhat sourly.

She gave him a glare. "You're just angry because you couldn't come up with a better plan yourself."

"You think that's why I am angry? You don't think it has anything to do with the fact that she gave away my *daughter*?"

"I am sorry," she said. "That was thoughtless of me."

He continued to glower, including all of us in his anger.

"Intef," I said.

He immediately turned his back.

"Don't speak to me. I cannot bear to hear you right now."

"I am sorry if you hate me, but I did what I needed to."

He spun around to face me.

"It wasn't your decision. She isn't only your daughter. She is mine too. You had no right to do that without discussing it with me."

"You wouldn't have agreed."

"At least you're right about that. I never would have let you turn our daughter over to... to some... I don't even know what it was."

"It was Osiris. And it was the only way. He would have accepted nothing else. The price was set long before we got here."

"The price was too high."

"Please, Intef."

My eyes were swollen and my nose ran, but it seemed I still had enough tears to cry again. Why was I even trying to convince him? He was too angry to hear me, but I didn't seem to be able to stop myself.

"How shall we do this?" Renni asked as if nothing had been said between Intef and I. "Do we call out and hope someone hears us?"

"I think we should knock," Istnofret said. "It is only polite."

He gestured towards the gates. "Go on then."

"Me? Oh no, it shouldn't be me."

"Why not?"

"Well, because... I am not important enough. It should be Samun. Or Intef. Or you. Or-"

"I think it should be you," Renni said. "You are as important as anyone else here."

She looked at him for a long moment, then glanced towards me. I could feel her stare even if I couldn't meet her eyes.

"No, really, it shouldn't be me," she said. "It is not my place."

"Go and knock, Ist." Renni's tone was gentle but firm.

At length she sighed and stepped up to the gates. Her knock boomed out and she stumbled backwards, startled.

"I don't think there's any doubt they heard you," Renni said.

I desperately wanted to lie down on the grass and go to sleep. Let them deal with it. I had done enough. Too much, Intef might say. It was time for someone else to take charge.

The gates opened a little. An eye peered out.

"Yes?" came a husky voice, the same one that sounded neither male nor female.

"We are sorry to bother you again." Istnofret's voice wavered a little, but then she straightened her back and held her head up higher. "I know you must be very busy, but we were hoping you might be able to tell us how to get back to the world of the living."

The gate opened a little wider and a leonine face peered out at us. It looked us over one by one, lingering longest on me. Eventually it looked back at Istnofret.

"What do you want?"

"We need to return to our own world, but we aren't quite sure of the way. We hoped you might help us."

"Why?"

"Why?" Istnofret faltered. "Do you mean why do we want to go back?"

"Why would I help you?"

"Well, because... Because this is not our world. We didn't come here intentionally."

The guardian's gaze went to the box in my hands.

"Then why do you leave with that? Give me the box and I will tell you how to get back to your own world."

"Uh-" Istnofret glanced at me.

"We intend to take the box with us." My voice was thready.

I cleared my throat and tried again. "We have been searching for it for a long time."

"So she lied when she said you didn't come here intentionally?" The guardian's gaze flicked back to Istnofret who looked like she was about to faint.

"No," I said. "Osiris brought us here. He gave me the box. He knows I am leaving with it."

"Osiris is not the guardian of Anubis's gates," the creature said, rather waspishly.

"Surely Anubis would not want to override Osiris's decision?" Had we walked into some territorial fight? Perhaps I shouldn't have mentioned Osiris.

"I do not presume to understand the mind of Anubis," it answered. "My task is to determine who may pass through the Gates of Anubis. And who may not."

"Perhaps you could tell us what we must do to pass through?" Istnofret asked. "Or whether there is another way to return to the world of the living?"

The guardian ignored her and continued to eye me. "The Gates of Anubis are the only way out of this realm. If you wish to return to your own world, you must pass through here."

"And will you grant us passage?" I asked.

"I will," the guardian said.

My hope rose. It was easier than I expected.

"In exchange for the box," it said.

Hope came crashing down.

"We are willing to negotiate," I said. "What else may we offer you?"

"I want only the box and what it contains."

"There must be something else. Perhaps something from the world of the living. We could fetch whatever you want."

"Just the box."

"We have gems. They are very pretty. Perhaps-"

"I want the box."

"Please," I said. "Surely there is something else we can give you. We have travelled such a long way to find this. It has taken us many months. We have lost much along the way. But we serve a higher purpose. We intend to restore peace to Egypt and we need this box to do that. The gods would not have led us here if they didn't support our aim. They intend for us to do this."

The guardian at looked each of us again. Eventually it sighed.

"There is perhaps one other thing I would accept."

"Tell me," I said. "If it is within my power, I will give it to you."

"I will take a soul. A living soul."

I stared at the creature. "I don't understand."

"One of you will stay to be my companion. The others may leave. With the box."

"We cannot do that," I said. "This is no place for a mortal to live."

"That is my final offer. If you choose to accept, you may knock again. Otherwise, do not waste my time."

The head withdrew and the gates closed abruptly with just the slightest clang.

We stared at each other.

"Should I knock again?" Istnofret asked. "Perhaps we can come to some other agreement."

They all looked at me and I noticed for the first time how pale Behenu was.

"You can try," Renni said. "But I don't think it intends to be persuaded."

"We have to do something," Istnofret said. "We cannot stay here. I am tired and hungry and thirsty, and you need to rest."

"We all do," Behenu said, her voice weak.

Renni nodded at Istnofret. "Go ahead and knock. Let's see if we can convince the creature to change its mind."

"Intef, what do you think?" I asked.

He gave me a sour look and turned away from us.

Renni sighed. "Go and knock, Ist. Surely there is something else we can offer."

Istnofret knocked, but this time the knocks didn't boom out like they had before. She knocked again. Still they made no noise. She turned back to us.

"I think the guardian knows we have not decided to take up its offer. It doesn't intend to speak with us again."

I looked down at the box in my hands. Could I give it up now? After everything? After I had traded my daughter for this amulet? After we had lost Setau and Mau and Intef's arm? Was it all for nothing? Intef's voice startled me from my thoughts.

"I will stay," he said.

"No," Istnofret said at the same time as Behenu said, "Intef".

"You cannot do that, man," Renni added.

They both looked at me, beseeching me to change his mind. I looked at Intef, but he still had his back to us.

"You would be stuck here forever," I said. "We don't know what this place would do to a mortal. We don't even know whether you would ever die. You might live forever here."

He finally turned back to us. He didn't look at me, only at the others.

"The guardian has named its price. One of us needs to pay. There is nothing left for me in the mortal world, but you two"

— he nodded at Istnofret and Renni — "you have things to live for." He looked towards Behenu. "You deserve the chance to go home to Syria. And she has a task to complete." He didn't even look at me. "It may as well be me who stays."

I wanted to convince him to change his mind, but I was suddenly so tired I couldn't even speak. I had known I would have to offer the babe to Osiris, but I hadn't realised that in doing so, I would lose not only my daughter, but her father, too. Surely somewhere deep inside of me I had known this would be the outcome. I just hadn't let myself think about it. I wouldn't have had the strength to do it if I knew I would lose both of them. In a way, I had made this decision for him.

Intef eventually met my eyes and whatever he saw there must have told him that I wasn't going to argue.

"I suppose that's settled then," he said.

Renni stepped forward to hug him, followed by Behenu.

"I thought you might say I should stay," she said to him. "After all, I am just a-"

"Don't say it," he said, in a tone that was far gentler than he had used with me. "You're one of us. And you, just as much as any of us, deserve to go home after this is all over."

Istnofret came to haul me to my feet.

"Go to him," she hissed. "Change his mind. You are the only one who can."

"He is doing it because he hates me."

I did allow her to pull me up, though.

"He is doing it because he loves you and he wants to see you complete your task. We will find another way. You have to convince him."

She hugged Intef and he finally turned to me.

"There must be something else we can try," I said.

His face was devoid of emotion and when he spoke, it was

in that voice that told me nothing of his feelings. The one he used to use when he was my captain and had to relay some piece of unpleasant news.

"There is nothing left for me. All I wanted in this world was for you and me to find ourselves a little house. A couple of children, a little garden, maybe a cat. You've taken that dream from me. I have no reason to keep living."

"We can-"

"Don't say it," he said, fiercely. "Don't you dare say we can have another child. Not after what you did."

"Intef." My voice broke and tears ran down my face. "Please don't do this. There will be another way. The gods wouldn't have led us here if they didn't intend for us to get what we needed."

"You got what you needed. You can keep going. As for me, I will stay here."

Before I could say anything further, he approached the gates and knocked. It echoed through the air. The gates swung open and the guardian's head appeared.

"So," it said. "You have decided."

"I will stay with you," he said.

The guardian withdrew its head and the gate opened a little further. Intef walked through and the gates closed behind him.

"No!" I rushed over to the gates and knocked but there was no sound. I slapped my palms against them as hard as I could. "Intef."

"Come back from there." Renni put his arm around my shoulders and pulled me back a few paces. "He has made his choice, Samun. We must let him do what he needs to."

"He cannot stay here." He probably couldn't understand

what I said through my sobs. "He has to come with us. There will be another way."

Istnofret wrapped her arms around me and I cried into her shoulder. Behenu rubbed my back. They were all silent as I sobbed. As my tears finally subsided, the gates opened again. The guardian cleared its throat.

"You wished to know how to return to the land of the living," it said.

I shook my head, but Istnofret spoke quickly before I could say anything.

"We do," she said. "Will you tell us now?"

The guardian nodded and the gates opened wider. Beyond them lay a large pond that seemed to be filled with red water. There was no sign of Intef.

"That is your way back to the land of the living," the guardian said. "Enter it through the Lake of Fire."

"Lake of Fire?" Istnofret asked, her voice faint. "Surely you don't mean…"

"Do you intend to pass through the Gates of Anubis?" the guardian asked. "If so, I suggest you move promptly. I will not wait all day."

"May we know your name?" Renni asked.

"I am Keeper of the Lake," the guardian said. It looked at each of us in turn, then turned to motion towards the lake. "If you intend to go, do it now. Once I close the gates, the price must be paid again if you change your mind."

"Let's go," Renni said.

He and Istnofret took hold of my arms and pulled me with them through the gates. Behenu followed close behind us.

"Wait," I said, before we could go through. "Please, there has been a misunderstanding. Intef needs to come with us."

Keeper of the Lake looked at me coldly. "If you intend to pass through, do it now. Before I close the gates."

"Come on," Istnofret muttered. "We have to go."

They pulled me along with them and my traitorous legs carried me through the gates. We had barely passed through before they swung closed behind us.

"Wait," I called.

I knocked on the gates but there was no sound.

"Intef!"

"He is gone, Samun," Renni said.

"Will you really leave him here?"

"There are rules in this place," he said. "That we didn't know of them before we came here matters not. If we wish to leave, we must follow the rules. Intef made his choice and we must respect that."

"It isn't fair."

Where did all these tears come from? Surely I had cried more today than any other day in my life.

"I don't think anyone has ever accused the gods of being fair," he said. "We have no choice but to accept their rules."

I studied the box through my tears. Had it been worth it? I had the Eye, but it had cost me both Intef and our daughter. But who had really made those decisions? Me? Intef? Or the gods? How much choice did any of us really have if the gods had already determined what was to pass?

"Come on," Istnofret said. "Let's see what this Lake of Fire is all about."

THIRTY-NINE

The closer we got to the lake, the more scorching the air became. My face burnt and sweat trickled down my back.

"Isis, it is hot," Istnofret muttered, wiping her forehead.

"Surely the guardian cannot have meant for us to go into the lake." Renni stopped at its banks. "It will melt the flesh from our bones."

"It is hot enough to melt our bones even," Istnofret said.

"I am not going in there," Behenu said. "I don't care if that's the only way home."

"So what did the guardian mean when it said we needed to pass through the Lake of Fire?" Renni asked.

I stared down into the red waters. I couldn't tell whether they were more fire or water, but the heat and steam coming from them indicated I didn't want to get close enough to find out.

"Maybe we should walk around the lake," Istnofret said. "The answer might be obvious if we look at it from the right direction."

I couldn't restrain my sigh. The lake wasn't that big but walking all the way around it was more than I could manage right now.

"I will go," Renni said, quickly. "Ist, wait here with Samun. Keep your eyes on me and if I disappear, go straight to that spot. It probably means I have inadvertently walked through the door that leads us home."

She clasped his hand briefly and he set off.

"I need to sit down." My legs wobbled fiercely and I would likely fall down soon enough.

Istnofret helped me down onto the grass, then sat beside me. Together we watched Renni's progress around the lake. At one point he paused and reached out as if feeling for something unseen. But he continued on and soon enough he had made it all the way around.

"Anything?" Istnofret asked, even though the answer was clear to all of us.

"I thought I saw something ahead of me at one point," Renni said. "A vague shape. But I think it was just the steam from the lake moving through the air."

"What do we do now?" she asked.

We all looked at the lake.

"There's nothing else here," Renni said. "Even from the far end of the lake, there is nothing to be seen but grass and sky, and the gates behind us."

I pulled a piece of grass from the ground and ran it through my fingers.

"Why does this place even have grass?"

"Now that you mention it, that is odd." Renni crouched down to run his fingers over the ground. "It is so hot that surely grass shouldn't be able to grow here."

"Babylon was hot and it had grass just as lush," Istnofret said.

"But it rained a lot there," Behenu said.

"It was a different kind of heat," Renni said. "This heat feels like it should shrivel the grass. It shouldn't be this thick and lush so close to such a heat source."

"I can almost feel it sucking the moisture from my skin," Istnofret said. "Even in the time we have been here, my hands feel drier."

Renni stared out at the lake.

"I will go first. I suppose there is nothing for it but to dive in."

"Renni, you cannot," Istnofret said. "You will die."

"The guardian said the lake was our way back. What else do you suggest?"

"I think we should wait and think it through properly," she said. "There must be another answer. We just haven't figured it out yet."

"I am hungry, Ist, and I am tired. We all are. I just want to get this over with. I will go into the lake. If it goes badly, I have no doubt you will know it. But if I don't return, it means I have found the path back and you should follow me."

"Renni, no."

"Ist, love, give me a hug and I will see you back in our own world."

He pulled her to her feet and wrapped his arms around her. She leaned against him and banged her fists against his chest.

"You will kill yourself," she said.

"I don't think so. I truly think this is the way. It is a test. We can do nothing but grit our teeth and endure it."

"You say you have no talent, but you underestimate your

determination. If you truly have as little talent as you think, then your will must be stronger than anyone else's."

She kissed him fiercely, then he untangled himself from her and stepped back.

"See you soon," he said.

He rested his hand on Behenu's shoulder and squeezed it gently. He gave me a nod and a half smile, then he turned and walked back to the lake. Istnofret moaned as he stepped up to its edge. He turned back to look at her one more time, then dived in.

I held my breath as I waited, but he didn't surface again. There was no disturbance to suggest he struggled. He was just gone.

"He found the doorway," Behenu said.

"Or he died instantly," Istnofret replied.

"I don't think so," Behenu said. "I think he went through."

"It is a test like he said," I said. "Help me up and let's get this over with."

They hauled me to my feet and in moments we stood on the lake's edge. The heat rising from the waters felt like it wrapped itself around us, smothering us. I barely believed we could survive this, but I had seen Renni disappear into it with my own eyes. I had to trust that the gods wouldn't lead us here to die.

"Together?" I asked.

Istnofret held out her hands to each of us. I clasped one and took a deep breath. With my other hand, I gripped the box containing the Eye.

"On three," Istnofret said. "One. Two. Three."

We jumped.

FORTY

I held my breath as we jumped. The water burned but, strangely, it wasn't nearly as hot as I might have expected.

We fell down into the depths of the lake.

Then I lay on grass, staring up at a blue sky that had just the faintest tendrils of sunset weaving through it.

"Samun?" Renni stood over me, blocking my view. "Are you well?"

I stared up at him. My mouth didn't work. I couldn't move either. I started to panic.

"Easy," he said. "It took me a few moments, too. Just breathe and everything will be fine."

Soon I was able to twitch my fingers. It was only then that I realised I no longer held the box. I managed to turn my head and relief flooded through me when I saw it sitting beside me on the grass, apparently undamaged. On my other side lay Istnofret and Behenu.

Renni helped them up, then returned to me.

"Give me your hands," he said.

I managed to reach up to him and he hauled me up.

"Are we home?" Behenu asked.

My gaze went to the ruins of the palace. The cart and the elderly ox waiting patiently to go home. The lingering sunset, which suggested we hadn't been gone as long as it seemed.

"I think we are," Renni said.

Any joy I might have felt at finding our way back to the realm of the living was tempered by the loss of Intef and our child. I could only pray to Isis that finding the Eye would be worth all we had lost.

"Come on," Renni said. "If you think you can walk, let's get you in the cart and we will head for home. It will be dark before we get back."

My heart was heavy as I sat in the cart with Istnofret beside me while Behenu walked with Renni. I kept my gaze on the cart's floor and tried to hide my tears. Istnofret reached over and squeezed my hand. It seemed I wasn't hiding my tears as well as I thought.

"We could have found another way," I said. "He didn't have to do that."

"Somebody had to stay."

"Would you be so calm if it was Renni?"

"I am sorry."

We didn't speak again until we arrived at the house. It was all in darkness and it was only then I realised I had been hoping that somehow Intef would be here. That he would have lit the lamps and closed the window shutters. Behenu and Istnofret would prepare a hot meal, and we would all sit together on cushions while we ate and discussed our day. And they would laugh at how I cried thinking we had left him behind.

But of course he wasn't here. He and our babe were both

gone. I didn't know whether they were dead or something else. But they were not here.

I pulled off my ruined dress and went straight to bed. The clatter of Behenu preparing a meal couldn't keep me awake. I had neither the heart nor the energy to eat anyway. My sleep was deep and dreamless, borne of utter exhaustion. When I woke it was well past dawn. Somebody had left a plate with some bread, now rather dry, a few figs and a mug of beer. I drank, but the thought of eating made me retch into the empty mug.

"I thought I heard something." Istnofret appeared in the doorway. Her face was wan and shadowed.

"Have you slept?" I asked.

She shrugged and looked away as tears welled in her eyes.

"I tried. I am too…"

"Me too."

"You should eat. You won't regain your strength without food."

"I cannot."

"Behenu is baking fresh bread. I'll bring you a slice as soon as it is ready. At least eat the figs."

I took one from the plate and held it to my lips. Satisfied, Istnofret left and I set the fig back down. She was right. I should eat. I just couldn't do it yet. It seemed wrong to lie in bed and eat breakfast when Intef and our daughter were gone. My hands found their way to my empty belly still swollen from the child. My breasts were engorged with milk. I lay down and tried to go back to sleep.

Sometime later, Istnofret brought fresh bread. She sat beside me and badgered me until I ate a few bites. Then she left and I went back to sleep. The chamber was dark when I woke next. Lamp light shone through the open doorway. My stomach growled.

"Aah, you are out of bed," Renni said when I came stumbling into the other chamber. "I've just heated some water if you want a bath."

My mouth was too dry to speak. I tried to pour myself some beer, but my hands trembled and I dropped the mug. It shattered.

"Let me do that." Renni fetched another mug and poured me a drink. He pressed it into my hands and held it there until he was sure I wouldn't drop it. Istnofret had started to sweep up the shattered mug.

"I am sorry," I said.

"No matter. Renni will take some water into the other chamber for you. Drink your beer and then have a bath. Dinner is almost ready."

It was a sombre meal with just the four of us. Behenu had made a soup with vegetables and young squid. There was fresh bread and more beer. I forced it down, almost gagging as I made myself swallow, but as I ate my head started to clear.

"You haven't eaten much yet." Istnofret shot a worried glance at my bowl which I had pushed away even though it was still half full.

"Maybe later," I said. "It is all I can take for now."

"I suppose we should talk about what to do next," Renni said.

I inhaled sharply. His words hurt although I knew he hadn't intended them to punish me.

"I need to take the Eye back to Egypt. But that is my task. You don't need to come. I know you like it here. Maybe you should stay. We can split the gems between us. You can take Intef's share as well."

"Maybe we should wait a few days before making any decisions," Istnofret said.

My heart sank as I realised she was actually considering staying. Three days passed before Istnofret told me they had decided to come back to Egypt with me.

"Just while you do what you need to," she said. "Then Renni and I intend to come back to Crete, and Behenu will go home to Syria."

"I will never see you again."

"You could come back with us. We could have two little houses, side by side."

I smiled sadly but didn't reply. It was her dream to live by the sea, hers and Renni's. I couldn't impose myself on their future.

We departed for Egypt the following day on a merchant ship. I tried to pretend I wasn't scanning the crowd for my sisters as we waited to depart. Istnofret shot me a sharp look as if she knew what I was doing.

This final sea voyage would take a little over a week if we had favourable winds. I had expected that we women would once again be confined to below decks, but the captain seemed accustomed to taking paying travellers and as long as we stayed out of the way, he didn't much care where we went. Renni didn't offer to help the crew and I supposed he couldn't bear to let Istnofret out of his sight in case something happened to her too.

I grieved as we sailed. For Intef and our babe. For Setau. For Mau. For my shadow, who was once again merely a reflection of myself rather than an independent being. For my sisters, who I had been so close to seeing. I knew I would never find them again. Tey would be sure to take them as far away from Crete as she could. She would never know that Intef was gone. For Sadeh and Charis and Intef's father.

As we approached Egypt, my heart was heavy. This was not the triumphant home coming I had anticipated with the five of us standing together on the deck, ready to use the Eye and expel Ay from the throne.

How different might things have been if I had gone by myself? But then again, would I have had any chance at success on my own? Intef, Istnofret, Renni, Behenu — they had all aided my quest in various ways, some larger, some smaller, but all had been essential. Intef had saved my life in more ways than I could count. Istnofret had been responsible for getting all of us out of the prison in Thebes. Behenu had been a quiet support, often saying little, but always ready to prepare a meal or brew beer. And Renni... well, he undoubtedly saved me at some point, but Istnofret loved him, and that meant almost as much to me as if he had saved my life.

Even now I could feel the pull of the Eye, urging me to take it out of its box. Urging me to use it. I had wrapped the box in a blanket and tucked it into the bottom of Renni's pack. He felt no pull from it himself, so his task was to ensure that I didn't take it from him.

I had to be constantly on guard, for the Eye was ever seeking to twist my thoughts. As fatigued as I still was from the babe's birth and all that had happened afterwards, I had little will to resist it. It reminded me over and over of what it had been like to be queen. It made me crave power and authority. Dominion over my subjects. If I wasn't careful, it drew me down into fantasies of being not just queen, but pharaoh. Maybe even a goddess.

"Samun?"

Istnofret's hand on mine brought me back to awareness of

my surroundings and I realised I had once again succumbed to the siren song of the Eye.

I must not forget that I was no longer queen. That those who travelled with me were not my servants but my friends. I must never forget that Intef gave his life so that I could continue my quest. I must never forget that I once had a son, and also a daughter, and that I loved them fiercely. That it was with my own daughter's life that I paid for the Eye.

If I could keep those thoughts and memories with me, maybe — just maybe — I could resist the Eye long enough to bring down Ay.

My sacrifices would save Egypt.

**

Ankhesenamun's journey continues in
Book 5: Lady of the Two Lands

ALSO BY KYLIE QUILLINAN

The Amarna Age Series

Book One: *Queen of Egypt*

Book Two: *Son of the Hittites*

Book Three: *Eye of Horus*

Book Four: *Gates of Anubis*

Book Five: *Lady of the Two Lands*

Book Six: *Guardian of the Underworld*

Daughter of the Sun: An Amarna Age Novella

Tales of Silver Downs series

Prequel: *Bard*

Book One: *Muse*

Book Two: *Fey*

Book Three: *Druid*

Epilogue: *Swan* (A mailing list exclusive)

Standalone

Speak To Me

See website for more books and newsletter sign up.

ABOUT THE AUTHOR

Kylie writes about women who defy society's expectations. Her novels are for readers who like fantasy with a basis in history or mythology. Her interests include Dr Who, jellyfish and cocktails. She needs to get fit before the zombies come.

Her other interests include canine nutrition, jellyfish and zombies. She blames the disheveled state of her house on her dogs, but she really just hates to clean.

Swan – the epilogue to the Tales of Silver Downs series – is available exclusively to her mailing list subscribers. Sign up at kyliequillinan.com.

Made in the USA
Coppell, TX
08 May 2022

77564021R00187